Schrödinger's Gat

A Novel by Robert Kroese

This is a work of fiction. Any resemblance to actual persons is purely coincidental.

Published by St. Culain Press.

For Josh.

"[T]he present quantum theory … reminds me a little of the system of delusions of an exceedingly intelligent paranoiac, concocted of incoherent elements of thought."
— Albert Einstein, from a letter to D. M. Lipkin, July 5, 1952

"It is often stated that of all the theories proposed in this century, the silliest is quantum theory. In fact, some say that the only thing that quantum theory has going for it is that it is unquestionably correct."
— Michio Kaku

"When I hear about Schrödinger's cat, I reach for my gun."
— Stephen Hawking

Part One: Hamlet of the San Leandro BART Station

Everything happens for a reason. What a horrifying thought. I'd never believed it until the day I tried to kill myself, and frankly I wish I could go on not believing it.

You can probably guess the reasons for my suicide attempt. Tolstoy said that every unhappy family is unhappy in its own way, which I suppose is true, but in my experience suicidal people are all pretty much alike. God knows I've met enough of them. There are probably a million different recipes for suicide, with varying amounts of congenital depression, parental disappointment, personal failure and loneliness, but they all add up to the same lousy cake. That's a metaphor, and a shitty one at that. I use shitty metaphors sometimes because I'm a shitty writer.

Anyway, I'm only starting with the suicide attempt because that seems like the logical place to start. I'm telling you this so that you won't think this is one of those books about an anxiety-ridden writer trying to find Meaning in a cold, unfeeling Universe. Well, maybe it is, partly. But mostly it's about two women. One is the girl of my dreams. The other is a nightmare. And we're three fucking paragraphs in, so I guess I should get started.

OK, so there I am, standing at the San Leandro BART station, waiting for the train to arrive. But as you can probably deduce by my earlier remarks, I'm not planning on being *on* the train; I'm planning on being *under* it. The chief ingredient in my personal recipe for suicide is my father. The standard feelings of inadequacy plus the suspicion that I'm not-so-gradually turning into him. My father blew his head off with a shotgun at fifty-five. I'm only thirty-six at the time of the BART incident, which I figure makes me precocious.

Predictably, I start to have second thoughts about the whole thing. I'm indecisive; I get that from my dad too. Dithering like fucking Hamlet of the San Leandro BART station. Hands in my pockets, I realize I'm clutching the 50p coin my dad gave me when I was ten. At the time he gave it to me I thought it was the coolest thing ever, like some kind of ancient artifact from Atlantis. I'd never been to the UK, so I had no idea there were millions of those coins in circulation. To me it was precious, especially since my dad never paid much attention to me. I thought he had found this fantastic treasure and entrusted it to me. Later I realized he had been cleaning out his pockets after a trip to London. But some of the magic of that coin stuck; even after traveling to the UK in college I could never quite convince myself that there wasn't something special about *my* coin, so I held onto it. I didn't carry it everywhere I went or anything ridiculous like that, but I kept it in my desk and occasionally pulled it out and flipped it over my knuckles when I was thinking about something or grading papers or whatever. Sometimes I would slip it into my pocket without thinking and then find it there later. This was one of those times.

So I think, OK, Hamlet, to be or not to be. You can't seem to make up your own fucking mind, so let's let Fate decide. I flip the coin: heads, I live; tails, I die. It comes up tails.

Oh, but there's something else I should tell you; something I forgot to mention because like I said, I'm a shitty writer. There's this girl watching me. I say girl, but she was probably twenty-five. Pretty brunette wearing a black wool coat and a red hat. It's February, so she's bundled up against the cold. Or what passes for cold in the East Bay anyway. Just standing back by a pillar, watching me out of the corner of her eye. Now I'm a decent looking guy, but there's no reason for a girl like that to fixate on me. And no, I'm not acting all crazy or anything. For all she knows, I'm just waiting for the train like everybody else.

Anyway, it comes up tails, and I'm like, OK, that's it, and I take a step forward. I'm right on the edge of the platform now, and the train is maybe a hundred yards away and coming my way fast. I'm near the beginning of the platform, so it will still be going a good thirty miles an hour by the time it hits me. Fast enough. I'm about to step off when I hear someone shout, "No!"

Somehow I know it's the girl, and I know she's talking to me. It rattles me enough that I forget to take the step and before I know it, the train is passing. Frankly, it pisses me off. Do you know how hard it is to psych yourself up to actually step in front of a moving train?

I turn and see the girl running down the steps, off the platform. At this point, I'm thinking, what the hell? How can you interrupt a suicide attempt and then not follow through with at least some kind of pep talk? Tell me life is worth living or give me a suicide prevention hotline number, something. You can't just yell "No!" and then run off.

So I go after her. Partly I'm mad and partly I'm curious. How the hell did she know what I was going to do? Because she pretty clearly had her eye on me before I made my move. And I suppose some small part of me thought, maybe this girl has the *answer*. Maybe she knows something I don't know. About, you know, life or whatever.

So I'm chasing her down the steps, yelling, "Hey! Stop! I just want to talk to you!" But she won't stop. She's running at top speed down the street now in her black leather boots and I can see she's headed for a cab parked about fifty feet away. I'm faster, and I get there just as she's closing the door. I hold the door open and slide in next to her, slamming the door behind me.

"Embarcadero," she says to the driver. "Get me there in fifteen minutes and I'll give you …" She's going through her purse. "Four hundred eighty dollars." She doesn't even glance my way.

"Embarcadero?" asks the driver, confused. "In the city?" The city in this case being San Francisco.

I'm about to say something but I hold off because I want to see what the guy does. The driver's a good looking young guy, probably Indian or Pakistani. I can see what he's thinking: *there is no way in hell I can make it to Embarcadero in fifteen minutes.* The only way to get there is to cross the Bay Bridge, and at mid-morning just crossing the bridge takes ten minutes – and we're ten miles from the bridge. But he looks at the wad of cash the girl is holding, looks at her face and sees she's dead serious. One more look at the cash convinces him. For $480, he's willing to break not just every state law on the books but the laws of physics as well. He throws the car in gear and slams the pedal down. The car, a ballsy old Crown Vic, lurches forward like a charging rhino, scattering Hyundais and Nissans like hyenas on the prairie. That's another shitty metaphor. Whatever.

I keep wanting to ask this girl who she is, where she's going, how she knew what I was doing back there, why she stopped me … but every time I'm about to open my mouth I find myself biting my lower lip in an effort to keep from screaming. I've had some crazy cab drivers, but this guy – I think his name was Hussein (and don't get offended; I don't think that all Middle-Easterners are named Hussein, but I'm pretty sure I'm remembering correctly that this guy was, so take it up with his fucking parents) – is hopping curbs and cutting off old ladies and nearly running down pedestrians in crosswalks. Whatever public transportation karma this girl had earned by saving my life she more than canceled out by waving a wad of cash under Hussein's nose. I'm not ashamed to admit I was terrified. Well, maybe a little ashamed. But holy shit is this guy driving crazy. And yeah, I get the irony of being scared of a car crash only a few minutes after I'd almost killed myself, thanks.

Soon we are *flying* down Interstate 880. I don't dare look at the speedometer but judging by the way we're passing cars – on the left, on the right, on the shoulder, between lanes – we must be doing a buck twenty at least.

"Slow down!" I finally yell. "You're going to kill us!"

"You got big plans for today?" the girl asks me. Cute. She turns back to the driver. "Don't listen to him. Keep going."

"What's the rush?" I ask her.

She's pulled a phone from her coat. She's brushing her thumb across the screen and frowning. "I've got an appointment at Embarcadero and Beach in thirteen minutes."

"What kind of appointment? What could possibly be this important?"

She doesn't answer.

"Look, if you're going to risk my life getting me there, you can at least tell me …"

"I didn't ask you to come along."

"What did you expect me to do? What was that about, back there?"

A cloud passes over her face. "I'm sorry about that," she said.

I sort of snort-laugh at that. "You're sorry you saved my life? What the fuck kind of thing is that to say?"

"I'm sorry I interfered," she says, finally looking up from her phone. "Not sorry I saved your life."

"What's the fucking difference?" I say.

"You swear a lot," she says offhandedly, looking back at her phone. She's right, I do.

"Look," I say. "I'm trying really hard to be civil. But don't you think you owe me some kind of explanation?"

"Yeah, probably," she says distractedly, with a hint of agitation. "When this is done, OK? After my appointment, I'll tell you anything you want to know. Sound good? I'll buy you coffee. But right now you need to let me concentrate."

"Fine," I say. Truth is, I'm kind of glad we're done talking, because I'm getting nauseous from Hussein's driving. I'm taking deep breaths and trying to keep my eyes fixed on a point in the distance. You'd think you could see mountains from the East Bay, but you can't. Just warehouses and gas stations and shit. My left hand is clutching the door handle and my right hand is braced against the seat in front of me. I'm pretty sure I'm going to puke. I roll the window down and lean my head out. At one point Hussein swerves and I get a bloody lip from the edge of the window, which of course doesn't roll down all the way. We take the Fast Pass lane at the toll gate and get on the bridge. Hussein continues to drive like a fucking maniac. I can't believe we aren't pulled over.

We cross the bridge and exit at Folsom. Miraculously I haven't puked yet. I spare a glance over at the girl, who is looking at her phone and chewing her cheek. Occasionally she glances out the window as if looking for something. I check my own phone: it's 10:35, and I'm guessing we got in the cab around 10:25. Laws of physics be damned, Hussein is going to make it.

He gets us to Embarcadero. "Stop here!" yells the girl, and Hussein slams on the brakes. She shoves the wad of cash through the slot, gets out and starts running. She crosses in front of the car and darts into the street. I follow. We're on Embarcadero just before Beach, a touristy part of town. She's still staring at her phone, barely looking up in time to avoid getting hit. Fortunately the light is red so the cars are slowing to a stop. They honk recreationally as we cross.

And then she just stops. It's a good thing I'm still feeling kind of sick and lagging behind or I'd have run right into her. She's just standing in the middle of the sidewalk, holding up her phone like it's a tricorder gathering data on an alien planet.

"What are you ..." I start.

She shushes me. I follow her eyes and see that she's watching a man and a woman standing on a corner having a conversation. The woman is tall and blond, wearing a fancy designer suit. He's shorter and Hispanic looking, built like a weightlifter. Also wearing a suit, but clearly off the rack. They're an odd couple, but they *are* a couple – or at least an aspiring one. They stand close and look each other in the eye; they talk so quietly that I can only grab a few words.

They seem to be discussing where to go for lunch. The guy wants to go to a Mexican place nearby (again, don't blame me, I'm just the guy telling the story) and the girl keeps motioning toward Pier 39 across the street. He keeps saying the word "tourists," and I empathize. Nobody goes to Pier 39 but tourists. It's crowded and the restaurants are mediocre and overpriced. The couple obviously aren't tourists; I get the impression they're meeting on their lunch break. I hear her say "Maggiano's," which is an Italian joint on the pier. I'd been there once. Not bad, but nothing special.

The guy pulls a coin from his pocket. He says something I don't catch and she rolls her eyes but nods. Coin goes up, comes down on his hand. The guy scowls and the woman laughs. He shrugs and takes her hand. They move to the crosswalk to wait for the light to change.

The girl standing next to me slips her phone back into her coat. She's trembling, and I think she might faint. I try to put my arm around her, but she brushes me off.

"I'm OK," she says, obviously relieved. "It worked. I did it."

"Did what?" I ask. "Do you work on commission for Maggiano's?" Dumb joke, my specialty.

"Come on," she says, and starts off after the couple as the "Walk" signal comes on. "I'll show you."

We tail the couple across the street and down the pier. I'm sort of laughing to myself, because I thought I'd be smeared along train tracks by now and instead I'm taking a nice walk on Pier 39 with a pretty girl. I have no idea who she is or why we're following some random couple down the pier, but still, nice.

She holds her hand up to indicate we're stopping. She's looking at her phone again. I can't see the screen very well, but it looks like a GPS app.

"They're getting away," I say. Maggiano's is about a hundred feet down the pier on the left.

"Can't get any closer. Too dangerous."

Sure, that makes sense.

The couple is about to walk into Maggiano's when the guy stops abruptly, holding the door open. The woman continues into the restaurant, not realizing he isn't following. He seems to be watching something, and I follow his gaze: a man, tall and heavy-set, wearing a trench coat, has just pulled a ski mask over his head.

"Oh, shit," I mumble. There's no skiing on Pier 39.

The man in the trench coat and ski mask is standing in the middle of the pier, surrounded by hundreds of tourists. The Hispanic guy has let the door go and his right hand is in his jacket. He's maybe fifty feet from Ski Mask. I found out later that the Hispanic guy's name was Dave, so that's what I'm going to call him, even though I didn't know that was his name at the time, because I'm sick of calling him Hispanic guy. Whatever.

Ski Mask reaches into his coat and pulls out a sawed-off shotgun. Before anyone can react, he's firing into the crowd, seemingly at random. An elderly man and a teenage girl fall before Dave blindsides Ski Mask, tackling him to the ground. Ski Mask must have fifty pounds on Dave, but Dave doesn't give him a chance to use his weight. He's grinding his left knee into Ski Mask's right hand, making it impossible for him to fire the shotgun or even lift it off the wooden planks that make up the pier. With his right hand, Dave is pistol-whipping the guy. Ski Mask is wriggling around like crazy, so it takes Dave seven or eight tries to subdue him. Finally Ski Mask lies still and Dave pulls off the mask. For some reason I kind of expect to recognize the guy, like at the end of a movie where they pull off the bad guy's mask and it turns out that it was the prosecuting attorney all along. But of course I don't. He's just some random asshole with a shotgun. In any case, I don't think his own mother would recognize him in his present condition: his face is pretty fucked up after what Dave did to it. Good for Dave.

I lean over and finally puke. Moon Over My Hammy from Denny's – what was supposed to be my last meal. It had been trying to get out ever since I got on Hussein's Wild Ride, and the sight of Ski Mask's crumpled-in face pretty much did me in. By the time I straighten up, a crowd has gathered, cutting off my view.

"Let's go," says the brunette.

"Shouldn't we stick around? Those people might need our help." I hear sirens in the distance. "And we're witnesses."

"They don't need us," says the girl authoritatively. "What's going to happen is going to happen." Ordinarily I hate that sort of bullshit platitude, but the way she says it gives me chills, like this whole thing is just a scene in a movie she's already seen. She turns and walks back the way we came. And to be honest, I have no desire to stick around and contemplate my breakfast any more. I go after her. As we reach the start of the pier, a team of paramedics runs past us the other way.

She'd offered me coffee, but we both need something a little stronger by this point. I'm feeling better, having emptied my stomach, but now I'm weak and shaky. She doesn't look much better. She's been on edge since I first saw her at the BART station, and I can see she badly needs to sit down and decompress. We find a bar a couple blocks from the pier. I go to the bathroom to clean up. My bottom lip is swelling up pretty bad, but there isn't much I can do about it. I splash some water on my face, rinse my mouth out and head back into the bar. I flag down the bartender and ask him for some ice for my lip. He gives me a glass full. I see the brunette sitting at a table near the window and I go sit down across from her. Before I can say anything to her, a waitress comes by and asks us what we want. Thankfully, it's now just after noon, so we can order drinks. Gin and tonic for me; whiskey for the girl. She orders a sandwich too. I'm not hungry. That out of the way, I finally get around to asking the girl her name.

"Tali," she says. Nice name. It doesn't seem to come with a last name. Not yet, anyway.

"I'm Paul," I say. "But you must know that."

I see some color return to her face. She's blushing.

"Seriously?" I say, holding an ice cube to my lip with a napkin. "You don't know my name?" For some reason I had thought she must know something about me to have figured out what I was doing at the BART station. My fucking *name*, at least.

"I never know their names," she says. "That's just how it works."

"*Their* names? Who is *they*?" I take a sip of my drink. The alcohol hits the split in my lip and I wince.

She sighs. "It's complicated. And I don't mean, like, Mah-Jongg complicated. I mean quantum physics complicated. Look, Paul, I know I said I'd tell you everything, but trust me, you're better off not knowing. I wish *I* didn't know."

"Better off not knowing?" I ask. "Is this one of those red pill/blue pill situations? Because lady, I've been on the blue pill for a while. Pills, actually. Prozac, Zoloft, Celexa, Lexapro, Cymbalta, Effexor … probably others I can't remember. The blue pill isn't really working out for me, in case you hadn't noticed. What's the worst that could happen? You tell me that I'm actually a brain in a vat in a laboratory on Mars? Because that's a step up from where I'm sitting." I'm exaggerating, of course. Finding out I was a brain in a vat would be pretty devastating. And of course I don't really think she's going to tell me that. But I get the feeling she's trying to play Morpheus to my Neo, so I play along.

She thinks for a moment, taking a sip of her drink. "OK," she says. "But you can't tell anybody. I mean, *no one*. It's for your good as well as mine. Anybody you tell will think you're delusional, and with your history …"

"My history?" I ask, a little irritably. "I thought you didn't even know my name."

"No, you're right," she says. "I'm sorry, I shouldn't have said that. But I do know that you've seriously tried to kill yourself at least once, and you've told me that you've been on just about every antidepressant known to man, so I'm extrapolating. If you start talking about this to the cops or whoever, people are going to look into your medical history. I don't mean this as a threat, but trust me, it's not going to go well for you."

"Why would I tell the cops? Are you involved in something illegal? Did you know that guy was going to start killing people at the pier?"

She shakes her head. "No," she says. Then: "Well, yes, I knew there was a high probability of a mass murder on the pier."

I'm stunned. "What? Why didn't you tell someone? That guy shot at least two people. They could be dead for all we know. You could have prevented that!"

She shakes her head again. "It doesn't work like that."

"Why did you stop me?" I say. "At the BART station."

She bites her lip. "I … interfered."

"That part I know," I say irritably. Her phone rings. "Shit!" she says and grabs the phone from her coat. "I'm sorry!" she says into the phone. "I had to get out of there in a hurry and I forgot to check in. What? No, Pier 39. No, there was a problem with the first crux. No, I just … didn't get there in time. No, I'm fine. I know, I know, I said I'm sorry. I don't know, maybe an hour or so. OK, see you then." She mutters something to herself and slips the phone back into her coat. "Where was I?"

"You interfered."

"Right! I interfered with the coin toss. What did it come up as?"

I'm confused now. "Tails," I say.

"Then it was going to be heads. Before I interfered. You'd have walked away from the platform and gone back to your life."

Some life, I think. I suck at my job, I can't get a novel published, my wife just left me, taking our two kids … Anyway, all the shit you didn't want to hear about earlier.

I pull the 50p coin from my pocket, regarding it. "You *made* it come up tails? That's impossible."

"Technically, I made it more probable that it would come up tails. And then I felt bad about it. That's why I called out. I'm … not very good at this." I realize she's on the verge of tears.

"Hey, it's OK," I say, because I'm fantastic at comforting people. That's why my wife left me. "I'm lousy at my job too." Nice, you just compared her to a suicidally depressed loser. Keep going! Finally I think of something helpful to say. "You stopped that guy on the pier. I don't know how you did it, but you sent that cop down there. If he hadn't been there …."

She smiles weakly, tears in her eyes. "Yeah," she says. "That's true."

Her sandwich arrives, and she pecks at it a little. At this point I'm not sure I even believe her about controlling the coin toss, but she seems to believe it, so it helps. I'm starting to think she's the crazy one. Only one way to find out. "So tell me how it works."

She asks me if I believe in ghosts. I say no, even though I don't really have any feelings on the matter, one way or another. What do ghosts have to do with anything? Another mark in the crazy column for her.

"Some people think that when someone dies violently, they leave some of their life energy behind, and that's what we experience as a ghost. It's a sort of impression, or a shadow of the person left behind after their death."

"Uh huh," I say, trying not to sound skeptical.

"I'm not asking you to believe in ghosts," she says. "I don't, at least not in the typical sense. But it's a helpful way to think about this."

"All right."

"OK, so someone dies violently –"

"Like those people on the pier."

"Well, yes, theoretically," she says. "But let's use a different example, because I don't want to confuse you. You remember that gas main explosion in San Mateo three months ago?"

"Yeah, somebody hit it with a backhoe. Killed a bunch of people."

Eight," she says.

"If you say so."

"So these people die violently –"

"You consider that violence?" I interject. "It was an accident."

"When I say violent, I mean suddenly and unexpected, as a result of external causes. Not somebody dying of a heart attack in his sleep."

"OK."

"So these eight people die suddenly, and they leave behind a sort of shadow of their life force, for lack of a better term. Maybe think of it like those shadows of people burned into the buildings at Hiroshima. Some remnant of their living existence left behind."

"I think I'm following you so far."

"Yeah, so here's where it starts to get complicated," she says. "Let's say this 'life force' actually exists partially outside of time as we understand it. So that the shadow not only goes forward; it also goes *back*."

"You mean back in time."

"Yes. The trauma of the event of death is so strong that it projects both into the future and into the past. So that the person's ghost, if you will, haunts the location of the person's death even before their death actually occurs. This would be one way to explain premonitions of train wrecks and other horrific events. Maybe some people are more sensitive to these impressions, so they can sense the tragedy before it occurs."

"Sounds like bullshit," I say, starting my third drink. "But I'm still following you."

"Anyway, most of this is academic. The thing you need to understand is that it's theoretically possible to know in advance about some tragedies. The more people that are killed, the greater the impression and therefore the easier it is to predict. Impressions fade over time, both forwards and backwards, and with distance. So the easiest tragedies to predict are those that involve a large number of deaths and that are going to happen nearby, in the near future."

I'm pretty buzzed at this point, having downed two G&Ts on an empty stomach. My lip isn't bothering me anymore and I'm starting to notice how attractive Tali really is. Thick, curly dark hair, big brown eyes, tiny little freckled nose. She takes off her coat and I catch a glimpse of some significant cleavage down the V of her blouse. Focus on the nose, I tell myself. I don't really care what she's talking about anymore; I just want to keep her talking. "So you see that something bad is going to happen, and you stop it. Like with me at the BART station."

She grimaces. Adorable. "No, not exactly. I was actually trying to get you to kill yourself."

I'm suddenly stone cold sober. "What?" I ask.

"I mean, that's not why I went there," she says hurriedly. "I was trying to stop this." She's waving her hand behind her, vaguely indicating Pier 39.

"What does me jumping in front of the train have to do with some nutjob shooting people on the pier?"

She shrugs. "Maybe the shooter was on the train. Maybe jumping in front of it would have stopped him."

"He'd just come back another day."

"Not necessarily. Maybe he gets caught with a shotgun on the train. Maybe he loses his nerve."

Yeah, maybe he does, I think. Maybe it was hard enough to get up the nerve the first time. But I say, "Maybe he goes to Jack London Square next time."

"Could be," she says. "I just don't know. Maybe he wasn't even on the train. You're familiar with the butterfly effect?"

"Small random events have huge, unexpected consequences. A butterfly flaps his wings in Moscow and there's a hurricane in the Gulf of Mexico."

"More or less. The point is that in a chaotic system, the end results of an alteration to the system can be difficult to predict. Maybe there's no easily identifiable link between the train and the shooter. But somehow jumping in front of the train stops him, through some unforeseeable chain of events."

"OK," I say. "So you make the coin toss come up tails so that I'll jump in front of the train, but then you have second thoughts and try to stop me. But that means you've failed to stop the shooter at the BART station, so you have to come here. Right?" She's crazy, I think, but it's a sort of crazy that she's obviously put a lot of effort into.

"Right."

"I still don't understand why you didn't just call the police and warn them. Or just call in an anonymous bomb threat and clear out the pier. That would have stopped him, wouldn't it?"

She shakes her head tiredly. "No. I mean, yes, it would have, if it had worked. But it wouldn't have worked. It's a deterministic system. Ananke has accounted for all the variables. Except for true randomness. She can't deal with true randomness." OK, now she's not even making sense anymore.

"Who's Ananke? Your boss?"

She laughs and finishes her drink. "Yeah, something like that. Look, I don't think I have time to explain the rest. I've got to get home."

"Boyfriend?"

She doesn't answer, but the way she purses her lips, I get the feeling there's no boyfriend.

"Where's home?"

"Near Palo Alto. But my car's still at the San Leandro BART station."

I laugh. "Mine too. I guess neither of us was planning on coming to Pier 39. You want to share a cab?"

She agrees. We pay the bill (OK, she pays it but I do offer) and get a cab.

"So who's Ananke?" I ask, once she's instructed the driver to take us back to the BART station. This guy's a sleepy Eastern European type who's in no hurry. Good.

"She's an ancient Greek goddess, the personification of necessity or compulsion. In a sense, she's the boss of all of us."

"You talked about her like she's a real person."

"Yeah, that's how personification works. Use another word if you like. Call it God or the Universe. Or Destiny or Karma. I prefer to use Ananke, because it has fewer built-in connotations. Also, I like to think of her as a she, because she's a real crafty bitch sometimes. Ananke basically runs the show."

"The show," I repeat dimly.

"The universe. The space-time continuum. Pretty much everything."

"So Ananke is God."

She grimaces at the word. "Not in the sense you're thinking. She has no grand plan, she doesn't create, and she doesn't care about ethics or morality. She just makes things happen. She's necessity, compulsion, destiny. The laws of nature. Everything that must happen happens because of Ananke."

"This sounds a little like Deism. God sets the universe in motion, and then it just runs based on its own internal logic, like a watch." My liberal arts education at work, ladies and gentlemen.

She nods. "Sort of," she says. "But the Deists believed in a distant, uninvolved God. Ananke isn't distant at all. In fact, she'll get right in your face if she has to, to make sure that she gets her way. Like I said, she's a bitch. But she has a weakness, a blind spot."

"True randomness," I say, remembering her words.

"Exactly."

"Like a coin toss."

She sighs and looks out the window. We're getting back on the bridge. "See, this is where it gets really complicated. Do you know anything about quantum physics?"

"Does Schrödinger's Cat count?"

"Yes," she says. "Actually, Schrödinger's Cat is a good starting place. You know the scenario?"

"There's a cat in a box. You don't know if the cat is alive or dead until you open it. So as far as you know, it's both. Or neither."

"Sort of," she says. "But it's not 'as far as you know.' The cat really is objectively both alive and dead at the same time. It's called quantum indeterminacy."

"OK, maybe I need a refresher on Schrödinger's Cat." (Look, I'm pretty sure I did understand this stuff at one point, but I'm a high school English teacher and aspiring crime writer. I don't have a lot of time to keep my knowledge of quantum physics fresh. If you're some kind of physics buff, feel free to skip the next few paragraphs. Come to think of it, if you're one of those people who hears "quantum indeterminacy" and your brain starts to hurt, you may want to skip this part too. It's not absolutely vital that you understand this stuff.)

SKIP THIS PART

I'm doing my best to reconstruct Tali's explanation, with the help of Wikipedia. I've had some time to think about this since the conversation occurred, and I think I have a pretty good handle on it, but again, I'm no expert, so don't come bitching to me if I get this slightly wrong and you end up with a dead cat in a box.

Earlier I mentioned Deism. Thomas Jefferson and some of the other Founders were Deists; it was big in the Eighteenth century. Deism is the belief that God created the universe with the laws of physics embedded into it and then basically checked out. Nobody really knows what the Deist God does with His time; maybe he plays Parcheesi with Vishnu. What He *doesn't* do is involve himself in the day-to-day operations of the universe. That's because the universe He created runs of its own accord, like clockwork. The Deist God is basically a watchmaker. Maybe eventually the watch runs down and the universe ends. Who knows?

Deism isn't very popular these days, and I've got a couple of semi-educated guesses why. First, why bother to believe in God at all if He isn't going to *do* anything? The Deist God is what a scientist might call "an unnecessary hypothesis." Why shove God in there at the beginning of the universe when you could just as easily say "And then the universe started, nobody knows how or why"? Throwing God in there doesn't really do anything but complicate matters unnecessarily.

But I think the main reason Deism fell out of favor is that it doesn't offer a very compelling model of the universe. When Isaac Newton was tossing out universal laws governing all of reality left and right, it really must have seemed like people were finally getting a handle on how all the gears of the watch worked. It was like he had described the winding mechanism and how different sized gears caused the hands to turn at different speeds, and how potential energy was stored in the spring, and all that was necessary was to figure out how all these parts worked together. Except he couldn't. And neither could anybody else, for the next 200 years. The watch worked just fine, and Newton and others had done a bang-up job describing the workings of the watch's various parts, but *no one could figure out how the parts worked together to actually make the watch function*. Eventually the whole idea of the universe as a ticking watch fell by the wayside, and with it the idea of the uninvolved Watchmaker.

And it wasn't just that they couldn't figure out how the parts worked together; it was starting to seem like the different parts of the watch actually followed completely different sets of rules. One set of rules is what is known as "classical physics." This is basically the physics that you learn in high school. $F = ma$ and all that. If you're designing cars for General Motors, classical physics is probably the only kind of physics you'll ever need.

Then Einstein came along and introduced the theory of special relativity, which overturned the concept of motion from Newton's day by positing that all motion is relative. Einstein showed that space and time were not two separate things but rather two aspects of a single thing called spacetime. The rate at which time passed was shown to be dependent on velocity: time slowed down as one's velocity increased.

Finally, folks like Werner Heisenberg, Max Planck and Neils Bohr came up with the idea of quantum mechanics, which says that at a subatomic level the universe operates on a completely different set of rules from classical physics. The rules are so different down there, in fact, that they are almost inconceivable. You may be familiar with the Heisenberg Uncertainty Principle, which I learned in high school as "It's impossible to know both the speed and location of a particle at the same time, because by observing the particle you change at least one of those properties." That's weird enough, but it's nowhere near as weird as what quantum mechanics actually says, which is that *until the location of the particle is observed, it has no definite location*. The particle (say an electron whizzing around the nucleus of a hydrogen atom) can only be thought of as having a *range of probable locations*. And I don't just mean that you don't know where the electron is, like it's the Ace of Spades in a deck of cards. I mean that the electron *has no location until you observe it*. It simply isn't anywhere. Or it's everywhere within the range of probable locations at the same time. Or both, depending on how you think about it.

Even Einstein, who was pretty open-minded about such things (and no slouch at physics), balked at some of the implications of quantum mechanics. Einstein seems to have been wrong, though. Quantum theory flawlessly describes the operations of the universe at a subatomic level. The problem is that although quantum theory is theoretically universal, when you try to apply the rules of quantum theory at scales significantly above the subatomic, seemingly impossible things start to happen. The most famous example is Schrödinger's Cat. In Erwin Schrödinger's legendary thought experiment, a cat is penned up in a steel chamber, along with a Geiger counter and a small amount of radioactive substance. Over the course of an hour, there is a fifty percent chance of an atom decaying, causing the Geiger counter to click. If the Geiger counter clicks, a mechanism connected to it releases a hammer that shatters a small flask of hydrocyanic acid, killing the cat. If an atom decays, the cat dies. If it doesn't, the cat lives. There is a fifty/fifty chance of either happening in an hour. So is the cat alive or dead at the end of the hour? Both, says quantum theory. At least until you look in the box. As soon as you observe the cat's state, the probability function collapses into one possibility or the other. But before you observe it, it's both alive and dead the same time. That's quantum indeterminacy. As Schrödinger states, "[A]n indeterminacy originally restricted to the atomic domain becomes transformed into macroscopic indeterminacy, which can be then resolved by direct observation." In other words, the experiment amplifies the scope of the quantum weirdness so that we can experience it on a macro level.

The funny thing is that Schrödinger's cat has become sort of the poster boy for the weirdness of quantum theory, but that isn't how Schrödinger intended it at all. He was trying to point out that quantum theory, if taken literally, is absurd. He was trying to show that quantum theory couldn't possibly be right (or at least it couldn't be the whole story), because the idea of having a cat that's both dead and alive is ridiculous. But quantum theory has proven so reliable that physicists have basically just accepted that a cat can be both dead and alive simultaneously. I get the impression from Tali that most physicists these days try not to think about it too much.

OK, START READING AGAIN HERE

"So what does any of that have to do with coin tosses?" I ask. "Are you saying that when the coin is in the air, it's both heads and tails until it lands and you observe it as one or the other? Just like Schrödinger's cat is both alive and dead until you open the box?"

She shakes her head. "Coin tosses are mostly deterministic, like everything else. "The result of the coin toss is determined almost entirely by forces known to classical physics. How hard you flip the coin, the angle and orientation of the coin at its starting point, atmospheric conditions, et cetera."

"Mostly deterministic. Not completely deterministic."

"Right. Nothing is completely deterministic, because underlying everything is a state of quantum indeterminacy. At the subatomic level, the universe is random, within certain limits. But the range of the randomness is so small that you're not aware of it on a macro level. It is possible, though, to channel and amplify quantum phenomena, like we do with lasers and superconductors."

"Still not seeing the connection with coin tosses."

"Sorry," she says, realizing she's gotten off track. "My point is that it is possible to duplicate quantum indeterminacy – true randomness – on a macro level. Like with Schrödinger's cat. Some physicists believe there's no reason you couldn't actually carry out Schrödinger's thought experiment and have an actual cat that is both dead and alive. Well, there's one reason, I suppose."

"The ASPCA?"

She laughs. "That too. But I was thinking of the fact that the cat would have to be cooled to near absolute zero."

"Ah. That would sort of defeat the purpose, wouldn't it?"

She laughs again. "Yeah, the cat would be pretty definitely dead. And unable to inhale poison gas, in any case. What I'm trying to say is that there are ways of making coin tosses truly random. You just have to have a sort of quantum phenomenon amplifier – something that translates a random subatomic action into a physical push at the macro level."

"And you have such an amplifier."

She smiles coyly. "Right here," she says. But she isn't talking about the amplifier. She's telling the cab driver that we've reached her car. We're on the street that the BART station is on. My car is in the lot up ahead.

"I'll pay," I say, before she can get out her wallet. "Please. It's the least I can do."

"OK," she says, opening the door. Her car is a blue Lexus with a parking ticket on the windshield.

"If this is your idea of explaining everything …" I start.

"I know, I know," she says apologetically. "How about dinner on Wednesday? I've got to get home."

It's hard to overstate how much better this day is going than I had expected. For me, anyway. Not so much those people on the pier.

"Sure!" I say, a little too eagerly. Down, boy. "Where at?"

"You know Garibaldi's in Fremont?"

"I can find it."

"Six o'clock?"

"Works for me."

"See you then, Paul."

"See you."

"Oh, and Paul? I'm looking forward to seeing you. So don't do anything that would significantly decrease the odds of you making it."

I smile and she shuts the door. I have the driver take me to my car.

Part Two: Particles and Waves

I get in my little blue Ford Focus and drive home. Home is a dingy one-bedroom apartment a couple miles from the BART station with an air mattress on the floor. Deb got the house. I'm not sure how that happened. *She* left *me*. Why don't I get the house? The kids, right. She gets the kids, the kids stay in the house, I get to sleep on the floor next to a stack of cardboard boxes. Fuck.

I arrest this train of thought and go back to thinking about Tali, trying to prolong the high I felt while talking with her in the cab. On some level I'm aware that it's a little morbid to be so thrilled about meeting Tali, considering the circumstances of our meeting. The adrenaline and endorphins and hormones and whatever else are all mixed up in my brain; it's hard to say exactly what I'm feeling and why. Above all I feel *alive*, which is something I haven't felt for some time. Am I simply infatuated with Tali, or is the intensity of my feelings related to the excitement of the day? Maybe, I think, this is just what it's like to be around Tali. However she did what she did, this clearly wasn't the first time. I wonder how often she does that sort of thing. Is it some kind of job? Does she get up in the morning and check her phone to see what tragedy she needs to prevent that day? Does she do this on her own or does she work for someone? I realize that I actually know very little about her. I don't even know her last name.

What does it feel like to hold people's lives in your hands? To know that you're actually helping people, making a real difference in the world? When I was a kid, I dreamed about being a cop or a firefighter, somebody who saved lives, somebody who made a difference, but at some point I decided I wasn't cut out for that sort of life. I took the road less traveled, decided to be a novelist, and that has made all the difference: I'm a divorced high school English teacher living in a shitty apartment in San Leandro. Not that there's anything wrong with being a teacher, but I'm not one of those teachers who gets thanked during a former student's Nobel Prize acceptance speech. I'm the teacher whose classes are filled with kids who drew the short stick when scheduling their electives. I fell into teaching because I figured I could tolerate it for a few years while I worked on getting my novel published. That was fourteen years and three novels ago. I've pretty much given up on making any kind of difference in the world.

The idea of "making a difference" goes both ways, of course. That psycho with the shotgun on the pier thought he was making a difference too. That's the easy way. When you've given up on trying to accomplish anything positive, you can always cause mayhem. Tough luck for that asshole that Tali was there to stop him.

On some level I can understand that sort of thinking, the desperation to have some kind of effect on the world, even if it's just destruction. Instant fame, or infamy, and these days what's the difference? As low as I've gotten, at least I had the decency to try to check out without taking anyone with me. My legacy would have been making a few hundred commuters late for work one day. And hey, at least they'd have had an interesting story to tell their co-workers. But Tali foiled that plan too.

I pour myself a drink, boot up my laptop and open my latest abortive attempt at a novel. I guess I'm thinking that maybe the rush from the day's excitement will translate into inspiration, or at least motivation, but it doesn't work out that way. In fact, instead of my mood helping me to write, the inertia of the unfinished novel seems to be oozing out of the screen into my body, threatening to quash whatever is left of my buzz.

The novel isn't bad. None of them are bad. They just aren't good. I'm not aiming for Dickens, mind you. I write genre stuff, mysteries mainly. The trick in writing a novel, I've learned, is to find the proper balance of order and chaos. You've got to let things get a little bit out of hand to keep the reader's interest, but you can't get too crazy or you'll never wrap things up satisfactorily. You have to allow your characters some freedom so they seem real, but you also have to find a way to somehow guide them inexorably to their doom (or happily ever after, if that's your sort of thing. It's not mine.) The problem is that I work so hard to tie up everything nicely that the characters become cardboard cutouts. They're not real people; they're just puppets of doom. Or I let them do whatever they want and the whole plot falls apart. I can't ever seem to get the balance right. Anyway, you don't care about this shit.

I have another drink and go to bed. Bed being an air mattress on the floor.

The next morning I awaken to the sound of my phone ringing. The school again. I put it on silent and go back to sleep. I've already got five missed calls from them since I didn't show up yesterday. I didn't bother to call in sick; I figured I'd let that fat ass of a vice principal earn his pay by scrambling to find a replacement or, God forbid, fill in for me himself. That was my nod to the cause of mayhem, I guess. I am become death, irritant of public school bureaucrats.

The buzzing of the phone on the box where I had set it wakes me up again an hour later. So much for "silent." The phone's display reads *Mom*. I sigh and answer it.

"Paul?" says my mom's voice. "Aren't you at school?"

Flashes of playing hooky in junior high. "Took the day off," I reply. "Why are you calling if you didn't think I would answer?"

"I was just going to leave you a message. Don't you already get a lot of days off? Do you have extra vacation days?"

"I just needed some time to unpack," I say.

"Why don't you unpack on Saturday? You can't just take days off whenever you want, you know."

"I know, Mom." *Because I'm thirty-six fucking years old.* "What do you need?"

"What do I *need*?"

"I'm sorry, Mom. How are you." It's supposed to be a question, but I don't quite manage the little lilt in my voice.

"I'm fine, Paul. I was hoping you could come over and help me with something. I was thinking this Saturday, but since you're not doing anything …"

"I just told you I was unpacking."

"Well, how much can you have to unpack?"

"What do you mean? It's everything. Everything I own, except the furniture."

"Is that a good idea?"

"I don't … what do you mean is it a good idea?"

"To move everything, I mean. That woman is going to think you're never coming back."

"Her name is Deb, Mom. And I'm not coming back. We're splitting up. She made that pretty clear."

"Well, she can't just do that. Don't you have any say in the matter?"

"What do you want me to do, Mom? I can't force her to stay with me."

"A marriage is a two person arrangement, Paul. One person can't just end it. You need to make sure she understands that."

"OK, Mom." It's easier just to go along than to argue when she gets like this.

"And why do you have to move out if she's the one with the problem?"

"The kids are staying with her."

"Pfft," she says. This is the noise my mother makes when the conversation has veered toward a subject she doesn't want to talk about. My mother has no interest in my kids. I'm not sure if this is because she doesn't like Deb or because having grandchildren makes her feel old. Probably a little of each.

"So what did you need my help with, Mom?"

"Oh, it's just this thing for your father, this award. They need some pictures of him for the presentation, and I thought you could help me go through the photo albums and pick some out."

"Oh. Yeah, I can come over after lunch."

"You aren't too busy with your packing?"

"I can make some time. See you in a little while, Mom."

"Goodbye, Paul."

I get dressed and get in the car, stopping at Taco Bell on the way over. When I get to my mom's house in Pleasanton, she's got photo albums spread out all over the kitchen table.

My father is receiving a posthumous award from some literary society. I hadn't heard of the group, but I guess they're sort of a big deal. Ever since my father killed himself, my mother has dedicated herself to being the conservator of his memory. They fought like feral cats when he was alive, but the day he shot himself it was like a switch got flipped in her head. Suddenly he became a saint and she would brook no mention of any of his faults, of which there were many. I wouldn't be surprised if she'd lobbied this group for the award. Not that he didn't deserve it; by all accounts my father was a genius. His first novel, *A Dying Breed*, won just about every award except the Pulitzer. His second novel, *Retribution*, won that too. His third novel was, according to most critics, bloated and derivative, but by then his reputation was firmly established. Rather than risk slipping further on his fourth, he shot himself between the eyes. Nobody says it in so many words, but I get the impression that his suicide actually helped secure his reputation as a genius. It would certainly explain the comparisons to Hemingway, which obviously didn't arise from similarities in their prose. Clarity and directness weren't Dad's strong suits; frankly I think he used cryptic language to camouflage the fact that he didn't really have much to say. But then, he's the one with all the awards, so what the hell do I know? I'm comforted by the fact that if there is a heaven, Hemingway is probably up there beating the shit out of my dad right now.

I spend two hours going through the albums. It's almost comical how many photos there are of my dad and my older brother, Seth. I suppose that's typical; everybody takes more pictures of their first kid, but my parents' obvious obsession with Seth is almost creepy. If Seth's future biographers ever want to know the exact date Seth was potty-trained, they'll be in luck. And it's pretty much inevitable that somebody is going to want to write that biography; Seth is only two years older than me and he's already known around the world as the inventor of a form of cochlear implant that "learns" from its environment, providing better quality sound to its recipient based on feedback over time. Currently he's working on a device that is supposed to repair damage to the auditory nerve, providing almost normal levels of hearing to individuals who are effectively deaf. Seth is a pompous asshole, but there are kids who can hear because of him. In ten years I'll probably be going through these same albums looking for pictures of him to use when he's awarded the Nobel Prize in medicine. Hopefully posthumously. I kid.

My mother vetoes all my choices of photos, which is par for the course. I try not to take it personally; I like to think that she puts me through these exercises because she likes spending time with me rather than because she wants to rub my nose in my father's and brother's successes. I try to make pleasant conversation, but not many appropriate topics are available. I have no interest in hearing more of my mother's opinions on my marital situation, and like I said, she has no interest in my kids. My job bores both of us, and in any case I'm on the verge of getting fired. I'm tempted to announce that I almost stepped in front of a train yesterday, but I can't see that going well either. I can almost hear my mom's disapproving response: "How do you *almost* step in front of a train?"

So I make the mistake of bringing up my latest attempt at a novel instead. I should know by now that this is a mistake, but I keep thinking that someday my mother is going to come around. The problem is that my mother views all novels as attempts to replicate my father's work. That's not an exaggeration; she once told me that F. Scott Fitzgerald should have read *A Dying Breed* before he wrote *The Great Gatsby*. She seemed to be dead serious, despite the fact that my father hadn't been born when *The Great Gatsby* was published. My mother only reads "literary" fiction, and by "reads" I mean she skims the first few chapters, decides the author is no Edward Bayes and then puts the book on her shelf with all the other great literary works she's never actually read. My mother spends most of her time watching soap operas. Once, in a misguided attempt to bridge the gap between us, I mentioned that a writer who had worked on one of her favorite soaps two years earlier had just won an Edgar Award for his latest mystery novel. Her response: "That wasn't a very good season."

So her response to my statement that I might try to finish the novel I'd been working on is predictable. She says, "Is all this writing distracting you from your job?" If, by the way, I had made a comment about my job, she would have said something along the lines of "How long are you going to keep teaching at that school?" She disapproves of my job but also disapproves of the idea of me neglecting my job. Just like she disapproves of both my marriage to

Deb and my divorcing Deb. Not that I particularly care about her opinion, but you see how it's difficult to sustain a conversation with the woman. I don't really want to get into a discussion of my job situation, so I ask her if she's heard any news about Seth's latest endeavor. This sends her into a seemingly endless explanation of clinical trials and the FDA approval process. After twenty minutes, I beg off, telling her I need to get back to unpacking.

I drive home and unpack a few boxes, thinking that it will make the apartment feel more like home. It doesn't. It makes it feel more like a failed imitation of home. I didn't even particularly like the house that Deb and I lived in, but at least it felt like home. This place feels like a box with a bunch of my shit in it.

I take a break and have a drink. I find myself staring at an unlabeled box, trying to remember what's in inside. Not a dead cat, I hope.

I remember reading a book about quantum physics a few years back and thinking how much more interesting it was than the physics I learned in high school. In high school you learn almost entirely "classical physics," which is all about exciting stuff like how fast a rock will fall or what will happen if it hits another rock. It's more "useful" than quantum physics, I suppose (although why the average person needs to know how fast a rock will fall is beyond me), but quantum physics is so much more fascinating, because it relates to philosophical issues like free will and the underlying nature of reality. Tali got into a little of this yesterday; I figure I'll spend a few hours doing research online so that I'll sound reasonably intelligent when we continue our discussion tomorrow night. I start by reading a little about the history of classical physics and how it differs from quantum physics.

Probably the most important thing to know about classical physics is that it's completely deterministic: every event has to have a cause. Strictly speaking, that means there's no such thing as free will. You may *feel* like you're making free choices, but in a deterministic world, every choice you make is necessarily determined by something that has gone before. So it may feel like I chose to go to my mother's house and be subjected to her canonization of my brother and father, but in fact my actions were predetermined from the beginning of time. I couldn't decide to refuse to go to my mother's house any more than a rock could refuse to fall at nine point eight meters per second squared. Looking at life from this perspective, it seems pretty pointless.

Of course it isn't the job of physicists to find meaning in human existence, but still, it's a little rough to have to come out and say, "We've got this theory that explains everything, and oh, by the way, it means that life is pointless." Classical physics got around this problem by essentially ignoring it, taking its cue from Rene Descartes, who divided nature into a mental part and a physical part. The mental part contains our thoughts, ideas and sensations, whereas the physical part is defined as those aspects of nature that can be described by assigning mathematical properties to space-time points. This is the classic Cartesian notion of *dualism*.

Isaac Newton built on Descartes' notion and the observations of Galileo, Kepler, and Brahe to create the foundation of classical physics. Later thinkers like LaPlace refined Newton's ideas, but the framework built on his ideas is still referred to as "Newtonian." According to the Newtonian framework, the entire physical universe, from the largest objects to the smallest ones, is bound by the principle of physical determinism, which is the notion that a complete description of the values of all physically described variables at any one time fully determines the values of the physically described variables at any later time. In other words, if you knew the location and trajectory of every particle in the universe, you could (theoretically) predict the entire future of the universe and reconstruct the entire past.

But Descartes and Newton were careful to say that these principles applied only to the *physical* part of the universe; not the mental part. Since the workings of the human mind were far beyond the understanding of science at the time of Newton (and still are, for the most part), this was a sensible way to divide things up. As a bonus, leaving mental reality out of classical physics allowed them to preserve the notion of free will: because minds are not part of the physical universe, they don't necessarily have to follow the laws of physics. I get the impression from my research that physicists have historically been ambivalent about this limitation of their realm: on one hand, they were relieved not to have to deal with nebulous ideas like human freedom, but on the other hand, they resented the fact that there were areas of reality that science couldn't penetrate. They reacted by marginalizing the mental (and spiritual) parts of reality as much as possible. Religion and spiritualism were derided; there was little tolerance for the idea that there were avenues to truth outside of empirical observation. The Wikipedia entry on Newton notes that the father of classical physics didn't seem to have a problem with the existence of an unobservable reality: Newton was a mystic who wrote more on biblical hermeneutics and the occult than he did on science or mathematics.

Anyway, the point is that although classical physics seems at first glance to be hostile to the notion of free will, it has a built-in escape hatch: classical physics has little to say about minds, so minds aren't constrained by the ironclad process of cause and effect. Still, as the sciences of neurology and psychology advanced, it became clear that a lot of human behavior could be explained in terms of cause and effect: as a matter of brain chemistry or, more broadly, biological determinism or conditioning. The physical sciences were gradually encroaching on the territory of the mind, and although there was little danger of the idea of free will disappearing completely, more and more constraints were being put on it. Darwin rocked traditional morality and ethics with the idea that human beings could best be understood not as creatures created in the image of God but as animals who had – purely by chance – developed traits that allowed them to survive. The idea that all of human behavior was completely explicable in physical terms gave rise to the school of thought known as behaviorism, of which B.F. Skinner was the major proponent.

So it was probably a bit of a relief to religious folks and others concerned about free will when Heisenberg and friends came along and said, "Hey, you know how we were trying to figure out deterministic principles to explain the entire physical world? Yeah, that's not going to work." For one thing, it turns out that at a subatomic level, events can happen without a cause. This is kind of a freaky notion, if you think about it: the whole universe is made up of subatomic particles, and these subatomic particles can apparently do things without any reason. And if the universe is made up of particles that can do things for no reason, what's to keep the whole universe from suddenly disappearing or, say, turning into a giant purple chicken? An article I find online provides this answer:

> Fortunately there are still a lot of limitations on these particles. They can act randomly within certain strict parameters, but they can't just do whatever they want. A particle can't just disappear out of existence, for example, because that would violate the principle of the conservation of matter and energy. What a particle can do, though, is appear first in one spot and then in another, for no apparent reason – and without passing through the space between these two locations. This is known as a "quantum jump" or "quantum leap." The scale on which a particle can do this is so incredibly small, of course, that you would have no way of knowing that it's happening without an extremely powerful microscope.

Even weirder is that, as I mentioned earlier, until you observe the particle at one location or another, it actually exists in *multiple places at once*. It has no "definite location"; it can only be said to have a certain probability of being found at one of several locations. Another article explains it by describing what is called a "double slit experiment." (If you're willing to trust me that objects can have no definite location, feel free to skip this part.)

> In the experiment, a beam of light illuminates a plate pierced by two parallel slits. Initially, one of the slits is covered, so light can only pass through the top slit. The light passing through the slit is observed on a screen behind the plate.
>
> If light consisted strictly of particles, and these particles were fired in a straight line through a slit and allowed to strike a screen on the other side, we would expect to see a pattern corresponding to the size and shape of the slit. However, when this "single-slit experiment" is actually performed, the pattern on the screen is a diffraction pattern in which the light is spread out. Despite this fuzzy behavior, however, the light is always found to be absorbed by the screen as though it were composed of discrete particles or photons. So the light appears to act like a wave, spread over an area, and like a particle occupying a specific point in space.

Now the cover is removed, so light can penetrate both slits. If light consisted strictly of particles, the expected pattern on the screen would simply be the sum of the two single-slit patterns. In actuality, however, the pattern changes to one with a series of light and dark bands. We can only explain this by looking at the light as if it were made up of waves: a wave is emitted from each slit, and when the two waves come into contact, they sometimes cancel each other out and sometimes amplify each other, producing what is known as an interference pattern.

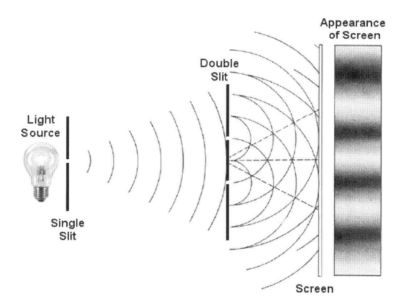

Recall, though, that each photon hits the screen as a single, discrete particle, not as a spread-out wave. How is it possible for discrete particles to produce an interference pattern? One explanation is that part of the photon travels through each slit, and afterward the two parts come together as a single particle before hitting the screen. Why they should do this is unclear, but it would explain the disparate observations.

To determine whether this is the case, the experimenter decides to observe the photons as they travel through the plate. To her surprise, the experimenter finds that a photon always travels through one slit or the other – never both. Not only that, but when the photons are observed, the interference pattern goes away. Simply observing the photons as discrete particles causes them to act like discrete particles. If the experimenter does not observe the photons as they travel through the plate, however, the light reverts to acting like waves.

The critical point here is that the behavior of light is *affected by the way in which the experimenter chooses to observe it*. The observer can decide whether or not to put detectors into the interfering path. That way, by deciding whether or not to determine the path through the two-slit experiment, she can decide which property can become reality. If she chooses not to put the detectors there, then the interference pattern will become reality; if she does put the detectors there, then the beam path will become reality.

The author makes it clear that this strangeness doesn't arise simply from the detection equipment somehow interfering with the particles, causing them to behave differently. It's not the detector that causes the light to act weirdly, it's the observation. If you set out to demonstrate that light is made up of particles, you will find that it is made up of particles (and not waves); if you set out to demonstrate that light is made up of waves, you will find that it is made up of waves (and not particles). The fact is that logically, light can't be both waves and particles, and it isn't. It's one or the other, and which one it turns out to be depends on which experiment you decide to perform. You, as the observer, determine the answer by deciding which question to ask.

While pondering this, I fall asleep on my air mattress.

I feel a little better the next morning. The school has finally stopped calling; maybe they've gotten the hint. I do some more brushing up on quantum jumps and Planck's Constant and then force myself to write a few more pages of my novel. It's mostly crap, but I tell myself I'll fix it on the rewrite. At five o'clock I quit for the day, shower, shave, and put on the least wrinkled clothes I have. Time to meet Tali. I feel giddy, like a high school kid picking up his date for the prom. It's been a long time since I've met a pretty girl for dinner.

Part Three: Indeterminacy

There's only one Garibaldi's in Fremont. I've checked three times now. It's six forty p.m. and Tali's not here. I've been stood up.

That's my first thought, anyway. And my third, fifth, seventh, etc. In between bouts of self-pity, I consider the possibility that something has happened to her. Like what? Murder, rape, kidnapping. Or the more prosaic possibilities: she got in a car wreck, she came down with the flu. She couldn't call me because she doesn't have my number. Or even my last name. Nor do I have hers. Still, she knew where I'd be; she could have called the restaurant. She hasn't.

I describe her to the waiter on the off-chance he might remember her. Presumably she's been to this place before, and she's a pretty girl; hell, I'd remember her. No luck, though. Having filled up on Heineken and bread, I leave a twenty on the table and walk out.

I sit in my car in the parking lot and feel like crying. Self-pity is like an old pair of slippers to me these days. But as comfortable as it is, something doesn't feel right. She had been worried about me not showing up, worried that I'd re-enact my performance at the BART station. *I'm looking forward to seeing you*, she'd said. You'd have to be one cold bitch to say something like that to someone who had tried to off himself two hours earlier and then flake. I don't think she's that person.

On the other hand, I barely know her. It's not lost on me that Tali's sudden entrance into my life and subsequent mysterious disappearance are like something out of a mystery novel. As I mentioned, on days that I'm not occupied with scribbling in red ink over incoherent high school composition essays, I fancy myself a thriller writer, and the *femme fatale* is an archetype of the genre. Really, the archetype predates the genre: the *femme fatale* goes back to Delilah, Salome, and the Sirens who tried to lure Odysseus to his doom. Tali is a textbook case: beautiful, clever, mysterious, and involved in a legally and morally dubious enterprise over which she seems to have little control. All she lacked – before she met me – was a struggling and disillusioned man whom she can lure into committing some crime of passion. Jesus, did she see me coming or what?

But Tali is a person, not an archetype. Yes, she was somehow involved in the shooting at the pier, but her involvement was benign, wasn't it? That's what she led me to believe, anyway. She could have been lying. Or this whole quantum coin-flipping thing could be some sort of paranoid delusion. I'd have fallen for anything she told me, even if it was … actually, I can't think of anything more absurd than what she actually *did* tell me. If she was nuts, she was also a genius to come up with something like that. And she did somehow know about the shooting in advance, unless that was just an amazing coincidence – or she knew the shooter. But I just couldn't make myself believe it. She had saved my life, and I owed her the benefit of the doubt, at least. On the other hand, if she was to be believed, my life wasn't actually in danger until she came along. OK, so I may be a complete sucker, but for now I'm going to take her story at face value. She's not a homicidal maniac, and she didn't deliberately stand me up.

Back to the other possibilities: murder, kidnapping, rape, accident, severe illness. I have no reason to suspect any of them in particular, but if half of what she told me is true, then there's some reason to believe she has enemies. Could she really know about tragedies before they happen and stop them? I have to admit, as crazy as she sounded, it sure looked like it yesterday. Lots of people would like to get their hands on that sort of technology. The FBI and plenty of foreign governments, for starters. I have no idea who

Tali works for, or if she works for anybody. I'd been so dazzled by her talk of quantum indeterminacy – OK, and her adorable nose – that I'd failed to get any concrete information from her. Who the hell is she? I have no idea. Dumbshit.

All right, back to what I do know: I'd seen her get into her Lexus, and she'd said she was going home. Where is home? Somewhere near Palo Alto, she'd said. Not particularly helpful. I pull out my phone and search the traffic sites for information about a recent accident in the area involving a Lexus. Nothing.

What if someone had been waiting near her car? Or *in* her car? I realize that I'd never actually seen her pull out. For all I knew, her car might still be parked at the San Leandro BART station. I drive there. It's almost seven now, and I'm going against the traffic, so it only takes me about half an hour. Her car isn't there. I go home to my depressing box of an apartment.

Had she told me anything else useful? Something that would give me a clue regarding her identity or where she lived? I don't think so. Our whole conversation had been abstract, except for her mention of the San Mateo gas explosion. She said she lived "near Palo Alto," but then so do half a million other people. And she hadn't mentioned anyone by name, unless you count what's-her-name, Ananke. Despite having read hundreds of mystery and detective stories, I find myself completely devoid of any investigative inklings on the matter.

Eventually I resort to the primary investigative tool of any modern day Mike Hammer: the Internet. I Google "Ananke" and come up with nothing particularly helpful: A Wikipedia entry, a software company by that name and several mythology websites. I browse a few of the sites but nothing catches my eye. I try "Ananke Tali" and come up with nothing. Same for "Tali Palo Alto." Next I try "Ananke Schrodinger's Cat." The first result is an Amazon page for a book called *Fate and Consciousness* by a Dr. Arlin Heller, PhD. Interesting. I buy the book, download it and start reading. Within a minute, I'm convinced that Tali either read this book or helped write it. A lot of it I don't follow, but her description of Ananke is there in black and white:

Some readers will bristle at my choice to personify this deterministic force. I'm afraid, though, there's simply no better solution. Any description of the force is necessarily going to be metaphorical, because it is something of which we have no direct experience. Even the word force is a metaphor rife with unfortunate connotations. Ananke isn't a force like gravity or electromagnetism any more than she's a Greek maiden looking down on us from Mount Olympus. I used to think of her as such a force myself and I found that doing so caused me to constantly underestimate her.

There are elements of Ananke that can be described with axioms and equations, but she's far too complex to be completely described in this manner. In some ways, studying Ananke is more like studying psychology, sociology or economics than studying physics. Ananke lives in a world of tendencies and probabilities. She lives in the world of physics and mathematics too, but then so do all of us, and I doubt any purely physical or mathematical description would suffice to describe you, dear reader, any more than it would me.

In any case, personification shouldn't frighten us. Just this morning, a colleague was telling me her car "didn't want to start," and I chose not to take it upon myself to explain to her that her car was an inanimate object and had no "wants" to speak of. Similarly, I've heard people talking about information "wanting to be free," or of rain "trying to get in" to someone's apartment. In none of these cases did I suspect the speaker's grasp on reality was failing, and I would ask that you allow me the same benefit of the doubt. I realize that Ananke is not a person, but I assure you that she is much more than a "force" or a "medium" or a "tendency."

With that out of the way: Ananke wants to control the universe, and her desire to do so is a trillion times more potent than your car's desire not to start or the rain's desire to get into your apartment. Ananke is, above all, the sheer brute force of determinism, but it's a mistake to think of her as naïve or uncalculating. Ananke knows exactly what's going to happen before it happens, and she has already anticipated any attempt you might make to keep it from happening. Ananke can be fooled neither by unfathomably complex plans nor by spur-of-the-moment decisions. She can be taken in neither by supercomputers that can calculate every possible outcome of a situation nor by the toss of a coin. She has already stymied any possible tactic you can dream up to trick her. Ananke is, for all practical purposes, unstoppable.

That last part gives me chills. Is that what Tali meant when she said she couldn't stop the shooter at the pier? That it would do no good to call the police because fate had already accounted for the possibility that she would try? I make myself a drink and Google the author. Turns out Dr. Arlin Heller was a theoretical physics professor at Stanford up until about a year ago. His Wikipedia entry says that he's fifty-eight, which seems young to retire. Don't those guys usually hang around forever once they have tenure? Heller's got several books in print and has had dozens of papers published. There are YouTube videos of a lot of his lectures, some of them with tens of thousands of views. He seems like the kind of guy the university would want to keep around if they could. *Fate and Consciousness* is his last book, and the reviews I find of it range from tepid to scalding. One calls it "a regrettable departure into pseudoscience by one of the great minds of our day." Ouch.

As far as I can tell, Stanford was the end of the line for Heller, professionally. There's no indication he's dead, but after his tenure at Stanford he just disappeared. No more books, lectures, papers or YouTube videos. Did he retire in disgrace after *Fate and Consciousness*? You'd think a man of his stature would be allowed a regrettable departure or two.

The bio in the back of *Fate and Consciousness* says that he lives – or lived – in the Palo Alto foothills. I find an address for A. Heller in Portola Valley, which would seem to qualify. No phone number though. I wonder what his connection to Tali is. Is she his daughter? One of his students? I decide to pay Heller a visit in the morning. I stay up late drinking and reading Heller's book. It's a long, rambling book with digressions into mythology, theology, philosophy, history, mathematics and of course physics. I get the feeling that he's circumambulating something, like he's on the verge of making some definitive point and then he retreats back into the abstract. I have to skip most of the math and a lot of the physics, because it's (sometimes literally) Greek to me. The thesis of the book seems to be that the universe is deterministic – that we are trapped in an inescapable cycle of cause and effect. Free will is possible for sentient beings, but it's by no means assured. It's something that we have to fight for, against the almost irresistible pull of fate (You can probably skip this excerpt if abstract philosophical discussions bore you):

> The idea of inexorable fate is a very old one, cropping up in cultures all over the world. The classic example is Oedipus, who was cursed to marry his own mother. As is typical in such stories, foreknowledge is not an effective prophylactic; Oedipus travels to the ends of the earth to avoid his fate, and in so doing brings about the very prophecy he has been attempting to thwart. In Greek mythology, inevitability is represented by the three Moirai (also known as the Fates), who have their analog in the Germanic Norns. In Islam, fate is represented by the force of kismet and in Hinduism and Buddhism as karma. The Calvinist tenet of predestination is another manifestation of this idea.
>
> In many of these traditions there is a counterpoising force of chance or luck, such as the Greek goddess Tyche and her Roman counterpart Fortuna. Most of the major religions, however, allow little room for chance. Islam denies the possibility of randomness, asserting that there is only the will of Allah. Calvinist theology has no place for free will, let alone random action. And karma, at least of the Hindu or Buddhist variety, depends on a deterministic universe, where everything that happens does so because of something else that has already happened.
>
> The Jainist idea of karma is completely different from the idea of karma as it is used in Hinduism and Buddhism, as well as the colloquial use of the term in western society. Jainism sees karma as an invisible, material substance which adheres to the soul (jiva), weighing it down and determining the conditions of the next reincarnation. Karma is the link which ties the soul to the body, and the cause of bondage and sorrow. Every action that a person performs, good or evil, opens up channels of the senses (sight, hearing, touch, taste and smell), through which karma filters in and adheres to the jiva.
>
> In Jainism, karma is not a benign (or even morally neutral) force that rewards the good and punishes the wicked, but rather a sort of sticky, nasty muck that we are forced to wade through and which constantly weighs us down. As in Hinduism, karma is deterministic, as it comprises the whole realm of cause and effect. But Jainist karma isn't part of some grand scheme put in place by the gods to keep the universe on track; it's all the garbage that we run into that keeps us from realizing our potential. Jainism doesn't

posit the goal of human existence as somehow submitting to one's place in the deterministic schema but rather struggling against the schema itself. The first step in this struggle is, of course, to see that one is mired in the muck.

I find the Jainist notion of karma compelling because it comports with my own intuitions regarding the material world (informed by a thirty year study of both classical and quantum mechanics). It seems to me that we live in an almost completely deterministic universe. I don't see how one can come to any other conclusion. We understand the laws by which the physical universe works (and one mustn't take the qualifier *physical* as a hedge; by physical I mean the entire universe of which we can have any knowledge; if there is some other non-physical universe out there somewhere that we can know nothing about, it is, if you'll pardon the expression, immaterial), and we can predict the outcome of actions (above a subatomic level) with near-certainty, assuming we have access to all the relevant variables beforehand. This knowledge extends to the workings of the human brain, which is largely (if not entirely) a deterministic machine.

Free will in such a universe is necessarily a fleeting thing, almost impossible to acquire. Some will argue that what matters is not actual free will but rather the perception of free will – in other words, what difference does it make if all my actions are predetermined, as long as I *feel* free? This is, in my mind, an absurd and somewhat chilling question. If there is such a thing as real freedom, wouldn't you prefer it over its counterfeit? The only universe in which it makes sense to be satisfied with counterfeit freedom is a universe where true freedom doesn't exist – that is, a completely deterministic universe. In a universe where freedom is possible, settling for its counterfeit is tantamount to lying down in the muck.

That's the last thing I remember reading before falling asleep on the air mattress with my Kindle in one hand and a drink in the other.

The next day, a little after noon, I drive across the Dumbarton Bridge to Portola Valley and locate the address I had found for A. Heller. It's a scenic, hilly area where the houses are a mix of old ranches that have been around since this was a farming area and newer McMansions occupied by software company executives. The address I have for A. Heller is one of the former. It has a long blacktop driveway that's barred by a swinging metal gate, which is chained shut and padlocked. I park on the narrow apron of asphalt before the gate and get out. There's a post with an ancient intercom box on it; I press the button for giggles, but nothing happens, as far as I can tell.

I take off my jacket, throw it on the passenger's seat of my car and lock the door. It's chilly up here, but I don't want whoever lives here to suspect I'm hiding a gun in my jacket. I squeeze between the two sections of the gate, stepping over the chain, and walk up the driveway toward the house, hands hanging visibly at my sides. I'm willing to bet that most of the people living in these houses have guns, and I don't want to give someone an excuse to shoot first and ask questions later.

When I'm about fifty feet away, the front door opens and a man steps out. He's short, stocky, with thin white hair, looks to be in his late fifties or early sixties. I'm not positive, but I think he's the guy from the YouTube videos. He doesn't have a gun, as far as I can tell. I'm a little disappointed because I've always wanted to use the line "Easy, old-timer."

"Can I help you?" the man asks. That's a little disappointing too.

"Are you Dr. Arlin Heller?" I ask.

"Who the hell wants to know?" That's more like it.

"My name is Paul Bayes," I say. "I'm a friend of Tali's."

He frowns, but not a *who-the-hell-is-Tali?* frown. More like a *this-schmuck-isn't-good-enough-for-Tali* frown. I might be projecting.

"How do you know Tali?"

"I, uh, actually only met her two days ago. At the BART station in San Leandro. It's complicated. I was supposed to meet her for dinner yesterday and she never showed up."

This time I'm sure I'm not projecting. He's giving me the same look that the waiter at Garibaldi's did last night.

"Look," I say, "I know how it sounds, but I swear I'm not some kind of stalker. I'm just worried about her. If you tell me Tali's OK, I'll leave right now."

He regards me for a while, finally says, "Tali never came home on Monday. Last I heard from her was around one o'clock in the afternoon. Said she'd be home in an hour."

"I was there," I say. "When she called you. She said she got distracted, forgot to call you. She apologized and said she'd be home in about an hour. We were at a bar near the pier. Where … it happened." I had to assume he knew what Tali was doing at the pier. The person she had talked to on the phone was clearly in on it.

"Did she leave right after that?"

"Pretty much," I say. "We took a cab together back to San Leandro. I saw her get into her car. That's the last I saw of her. We had made plans to meet and Garibaldi's in Fremont at six the next day, but she never showed."

"She gave you this address?"

I shake my head. "I did a little research online and found you. To be honest, sir, I don't even know Tali's last name. Is she your daughter?"

He laughs. "Do you have some ID on you?"

I approach and show him my driver's license and my California state teacher ID.

"So you're not with Peregrine?"

"Who?"

"The insurance company."

"No, sir."

He regards me for a moment. "OK, come on in, Paul."

He's cordial after that. We sit in the living room and he gets me a cup of coffee. Turns out that Tali was a graduate student of his at Stanford and is now sort of a live-in assistant. He's clearly agitated about her disappearance, but trying not to show it. He seems to be avoiding the subject of what exactly Tali was doing on Monday and his own involvement in it. I mention that I've been reading his book.

"Which one?" he asks. "*Gauge Theory of Elementary Particle Physics?*"

I shake my head. "*Fate and Consciousness.*"

He chuckles to himself. "I know, that's the only one normal people read. It outsells the others a hundred to one. And my colleagues *hate* it."

"Yeah, I read some of the reviews. One of them called it 'pseudoscience.'"

"To some people, anything that isn't science is pseudoscience. Especially if it's written by a scientist. I could write a book of poetry for children and some idiot reviewer would call it pseudoscience. That book wasn't written for scientists. I'd already written three of those, and if I had wanted to write another, I would have."

"But there's a difference between popularizing a subject and bowdlerizing it," I say. "It seems like a lot of the reviews were making the point that you were jumping to conclusions. It almost seemed to me like you were deliberately leaving things out."

He smiles at me. "So tell me, Paul Bayes, what were you doing at the San Leandro BART station?"

Ouch. OK, we're changing subjects, I guess. At least maybe I'll get him to explain what he and Tali are up to, besides writing nutty books. "I was flipping a coin," I say evenly. I figure he knows that much. I wonder what else he knows.

"And Tali interfered," he says.

"She ... tried to," I say. Tried and succeeded, actually. Then she un-interfered, leaving things more or less as they would have been. Except that instead of going home, I went to Pier 39 with Tali.

"Now who's leaving things out?" Heller says, taking a sip of his coffee.

I decide to level with him. "I'll tell you everything you want to know, Dr. Heller," I say. "But Tali interfered with my life ... made a choice for me that should have been mine. To make amends, she promised to explain everything. Why she interfered, what she was trying to accomplish, how she knew about all this stuff in advance. She explained some of it that day, and she was going to tell me the rest last night, but she disappeared. If you're willing to make good on Tali's promise, I will tell you everything that happened the day she disappeared."

He seems skeptical. He probably figures it isn't an even trade, and he's probably right. Time to apply a little leverage.

"I suppose I could just go to the police," I say. "Let them dig into what Tali was doing and see if they come up with anything."

He regards me carefully for several moments. "Do you have a scientific background, Paul?" he finally asks.

"Does Mrs. Philips' honors chemistry class count?"

He doesn't crack a smile.

"I'm a high school English teacher," I say.

"Did Tali impress on you the importance of not discussing this with anyone?"

"Yes, she did," I say. "I'm not going to say anything, Dr. Heller. My only concern is Tali."

Another long pause. Then he nods. "All right. Tell me what happened the day Tali disappeared and I'll tell you about my work."

I proceed to tell him the whole story, just the way I told you. Well, I leave out the part about looking down her shirt. A guy's got to keep some things to himself.

"Did she seem worried?" he asks. "Or frightened?"

"Frightened?" I reply. "No. Did she have something to be frightened about?"

"No, no," he says, a bit too quickly. "If I tell you about my work – our work – you have to promise not to say anything about it to anyone."

"We've been through this, doc," I say, getting a little irritated. "My lips are sealed."

He nods and beckons to me to follow him. He leads me to a workshop that has set up in an old barn just behind the house. The barn's exterior is made of redwood planks, most of which appear to be several decades old. One section of the barn has been recently repaired, though; the planks in this area still have some of the reddish hue of fresh redwood.

The barn doesn't look like much on the outside, but it's a high-tech shop on the inside, with lathes, grinders, drill presses, welding equipment, soldering irons, and a lot of other stuff I don't recognize. There are big tanks labeled Helium, Argon, and Nitrogen. In one corner of the shop is a neatly organized desk that I somehow immediately know is Tali's.

Heller directs me to a workbench littered with electrical components: circuit boards, silicon wafers, batteries, capacitors, transistors, spools of wire and lots of other doodads and thingamajigs. He hands me one of the doodads. It's a black box that's about the size and shape of my first cell phone, back in 1999. It even has a little rubber-coated antenna sticking out of the top.

"What's this?" I ask.

"Psionic field detector," he says. "I make them myself. I've got close to 300 of them up and running all over the Bay Area. I have Tali stick them on the backs of stop signs or on telephone posts, or wherever they won't be noticed. They can run on battery for about a week, but the ones in the field have small solar panels connected to them to keep them charged. Every once in a while somebody will find one and take it down, but there's enough redundancy that we always have pretty good coverage."

"Coverage of what exactly?"

"Psionic field disruptions."

I'm inspecting the doodad. It doesn't look like much. "Does that qualify as science or is that some of the pseudoscience stuff?"

He shrugs. "It's a bit out on the fringe. You ever watch any of those ghost hunter shows?"

Here we go again with the ghosts. "I've seen a couple."

"They use EMF detectors to detect electromagnetic disturbances that are supposed to be evidence of supernatural activity. It's mostly bullshit, though, because ghosts don't leave much of a trace in the electromagnetic spectrum."

"You're saying there's such a thing as ghosts."

"Sure, in a sense. Conscious beings leave traces of themselves in their environment that are detectable even after the person is dead."

"And before the person is dead."

"Ah, you *have* been talking to Tali," he says, smiling. "Yes, I was getting to that. OK, what's the simplest way to explain this? Have you heard of quantum computing?"

I shake my head. "Tali and I talked a little about quantum mechanics. Schrödinger's Cat and all that. And I've done a little reading since then."

"So you know about quantum indeterminacy? The idea that it's possible for matter to be smeared across an area probabilistically?"

I sort of shrug-nod.

"Are you familiar with Moore's Law?"

"The one about computing speed doubling every year?"

"Eighteen months. Gordon Moore's original formulation was that the number of transistors that can fit on a circuit board doubles every eighteen months, give or take. It's the rare example of a law outside of the hard sciences that appears to be deterministic. Nobody knows why it happens, exactly, but for some reason just enough breakthroughs in miniaturization occur in the computer industry every eighteen months that computing power doubles. But recently we've reached the limits of miniaturization. We've literally made circuits that are as small as they can possibly be made: only one atom across. This has prompted a lot of people to predict the end of Moore's Law. But these limits apply to the current paradigm of computer design, and may not hold true for different sorts of computers. One direction that industry might go in the future is quantum computing."

"Which means what, exactly?"

"You know how quantum mechanics allows a particle to be in two different places at the same time? Well, imagine a computer that can try out two different solutions to a mathematical problem simultaneously, by being in two different states at the same time. And if you can have a computer that's in two states simultaneously, there's no reason it couldn't be in four, or eight, or a thousand. You could theoretically increase a computer's power infinitely simply by putting it into a state of quantum indeterminacy."

"And how do you do that?"

"Well, you have to put it in a state of complete isolation from the rest of the universe, so that it can't be observed or interacted with in any way. That's easy enough to do with a few atoms, if you've got the right equipment, but assembling those atoms into something like a computing machine and getting them to do any actual computing before they decohere – that is, before they drop out of a state of indeterminacy – is, well, problematic."

"I can imagine," I say. I can't, of course. I'm starting to think he's making this up as he goes along.

"There are people experimenting with quantum computers right now, but there are some problems with the idea that may be intractable. I suspect that the solution – if there is a solution – will be to create a sort of an interface module that connects a classical computer with a quantum computer. You'd have to sever the connection while the quantum computer is working, of course, or it wouldn't be properly isolated. But when the quantum computer finds a solution, it could re-establish contact with the classical computer and Bob's your uncle."

My head hurts. For all Heller's initial reluctance to talk, he seems downright eager to spill everything now. It's like he's been holding it in for years and he's overcome with relief at his chance to finally talk to somebody about it. But I don't want to know the history of quantum physics; I just want to know where Tali is. I interject, "What does any of this have to do with what Tali and you are doing?"

"Excellent question," he answers without even a momentary pause. "You know what the most powerful computer in the world is? The human brain. It's lousy at low-level deterministic stuff, but the human brain is capable of making decisions in a matter of seconds that would tie up a super-computer for hours. And yet the human brain is a biochemical system that seems at first glance to run much more slowly than the typical silicon-based computer. How is this possible? Well, clearly the human brain is a qualitatively different sort of computer. One theory is that the human brain is a quantum computer, and therefore able to be in multiple quantum states simultaneously. The quantum brain is assigned problems to solve by the classical component of the brain. When the quantum brain comes up with a solution (or solutions, as the case may be), it reports back to the classical brain. You see, the human brain has somehow evolved to take advantage of quantum indeterminacy in order to work faster than would normally be possible."

"I still don't …"

"Almost there," he says. "So the question is, what happens to this other part of your brain, the quantum part, when you die? Well, presumably it dies as well – falls apart, ceases to be an ordered system, in compliance with the second law of thermodynamics. But we know already that the quantum brain has to be able to work independently, because in its calculating state, it's completely isolated from the rest of the universe. So what happens if your brain in this dimension is destroyed so suddenly that it's unable to 'power down' the quantum part of your brain? What if, in fact, your brain sends out a last-minute 'distress signal' to the quantum brain, desperately trying to solve some sort of existential threat it is facing? Every available bit of energy is sent from your brain in this dimension to the quantum brain, in an attempt to solve the problem – but then the connection is permanently severed. What then?"

I think I see where he's going. "The quantum brain continues to exist for a while, still trying to work out that last problem."

"Exactly! So what the psionic field detector does is to detect the disturbances in the psionic field made by quantum brains in that condition."

"I don't recall learning about psionic fields in my high school physics class," I reply.

"That's because most physicists don't acknowledge their existence. A number of studies have been done indicating that the human brain can remotely influence physical objects. We refer to the medium of this influence as the psionic field."

"You're talking about telekinesis."

"Yes, but on a very, very small scale. We're talking about a person being able to slightly alter the expected statistical behavior of a sampling of subatomic particles, not being able to bend a spoon. The point is that the effect, although tiny, is real and detectable. It also occurs largely at the unconscious level. That's part of the reason it's so difficult to detect. Your conscious brain works almost entirely at the classical, not the quantum, level. Have you ever had the experience of spending hours trying to work out a particularly difficult problem only to have the answer pop into your head later, when you weren't even consciously thinking about it?"

"So you're saying that if I want to bend a spoon, I should give the job to my unconscious."

"You're better off doing it with your fingers," says Heller. "Your unconscious is unlikely to cooperate because it probably has better things to do. Anyway, that's the problem with studies of psychokinesis, or telekinesis as it's popularly known. They start by telling the subject, 'Do X with your mind.' So the subject tries to do X, but their subconscious is thinking about the shoes they're going to buy with the money they got for doing the study. The psionic field detectors work the other way around. They look for disturbances in the statistical distribution of events on a quantum level and then try to locate the mind associated with the disturbance. The disturbances are faint, though, and there's a lot of noise, so at this point we can only detect a pattern when several quantum brains in close proximity experience what we call a 'catastrophic neural shutdown' nearly simultaneously."

"Like if there's a mass shooting on Pier 39."

"Precisely."

"I still don't understand how you can detect these disturbances before the event happens."

"Ah," he says, nodding. "That has to do with probabilistic futures. You see, there isn't just one future; there's an infinite range of possible futures, some more probable than others. All of these futures 'exist,' in a sense, but some are much more probable than others. The disturbances from the quantum brains extend a ways into spacetime, both forward and backward. The more probable the outcome, the stronger the impression is. So a violent death that is very likely to happen leaves a stronger impression than a less likely one. The overall strength of the impression is a function of how many people are involved, how probable the event is, and its proximity to the detector in spacetime."

"And by 'detector,' you mean this doodad," I say, indicating the doodad.

"Yes. They're WiFi enabled, so all the data they gather can be uploaded to a central server. That box right over there." He points at an ordinary looking tower computer.

I can't help but laugh.

"I know," he says, grinning. "Being a mad scientist ain't what it used to be."

"So how much advance notice do you get? Tali almost got us killed driving from San Leandro to Embarcadero, but I wasn't sure if that was because she didn't get much notice or because she missed her first appointment ... oh, shit."

I pull my phone from my pocket. It's almost four p.m. I promised Deb I'd pick up the kids from soccer practice. I wasn't that concerned about it when I thought I was going to be dead by now; figured that she'd make alternate arrangements. Death has its drawbacks, but it's a pretty good excuse for missing appointments.

"I've got to go," I say, "or my probable near future is going to get very unpleasant. Have you got a pen and paper?"

He directs me to a notepad on the workbench. I scribble on it. "That's my cell number. Please call me if you hear from Tali." He nods. He doesn't offer me a number and I don't press him. "I still have some questions for you. Is it all right if I come back tomorrow? Say around two p.m.?"

"I'll be here," he says. He seems almost happy to hear that I intend to come back.

"Thanks for your hospitality, Dr. Heller. I'll see myself out." I shake his hand and leave, running back to my car. There's no way I'm making it to San Leandro by four fifteen, but with a little luck I might be only fifteen minutes or so late.

Luck is not on my side today. I'm half an hour late, and the kids are pissed. They get in the car and slam the doors. Neither of them will talk to me. Just as well. I never know what to say to them. Meet my kids, ladies and gentlemen. Martin, ten and Sylvia, eight. They get A's and B's in school, have never been arrested, and are above average at *Call of Duty* on XBox.

I drop the kids off and head home. I force myself to do some more unpacking. If I'm going to live for a while yet, I might as well be reasonably comfortable. What would Tali think if she saw this mess?

Another wave of self-pity. Tali probably doesn't give two shits about me. I just hope Heller remembers to call me when he hears from her. *If* he hears from her. Tali could be dead for all I know. I smile ruefully as I think of Tali in a box, alive and dead at the same time. I suppose she could remain that way, if Heller never calls. Or if he calls and I don't answer. (I know, it doesn't work like that. It's a fucking metaphor, relax.) Anyway, I'm not sure I trust him, which is the main reason I asked to come back tomorrow. I mean, I want to hear the rest of his story too, but mostly I want to see if Tali shows up.

I wash the dishes in the sink and do a little straightening up and then go back to reading Heller's book. I have nothing else to occupy my time, and maybe understanding Heller's work will help me figure out what happened with Tali. The book isn't all gooey quasi-mystical stuff; much of it is devoted to a rather lucid explanation of the weirdness of quantum phenomena – the same weirdness demonstrated by the "double slit experiment." Heller further illustrates this weirdness with something he calls a "Box-Pairs Experiment." The experiment has some similarities to a shell game, where the player has to try to guess which shell a pea is hidden under. The difference is that with the shell game, observation only *reveals* the location of the object. With the Box-Pairs Experiment, observation actually *determines* the location of the object. If you're willing to trust me on that, you can skip this excerpt:

> In a shell game, the pea has an equal chance of being under each shell. But this probability is purely epistemic. The pea has an actual location under one of the shells, so its location cannot be fully described in terms of probability. Observation doesn't *change* the pea's location; it only *reveals* its location.
>
> In our experiment, we will put equal parts of the waviness of a single atom in each of two boxes, so that the atom has equal probability of being in either box. But our experiment differs from the shell game in that there is no "actual atom" in a particular box. The wavefunction split between the two boxes is the complete description of the physical situation. And in our experiment observation *does* change the physical reality. Here's how it works:
>
> You have two boxes, called Box A and Box B, which are specially designed to trap and hold individual atoms. There is no way to tell whether one of these boxes holds an atom without opening the box. You arrange a semi-transparent mirror in front of these boxes as indicated in the diagram. This mirror is designed so that if an atom hits it, there's a fifty percent chance that the atom will bounce off the mirror and get trapped in Box A and a fifty percent chance that the atom will go straight through and get trapped in Box B. You have a gun pointed at the mirror. The gun has the capability of firing a single atom at a time.

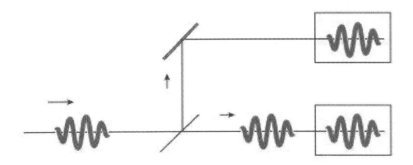

You pull the trigger on the gun, trapping the atom. The question is: where is the atom? Common sense would tell you that it's either in Box A or Box B. But common sense doesn't apply to quantum mechanics. The fact is, until you open one of the boxes, *the atom is in both boxes simultaneously*. It isn't split in two, with half of it being in Box A and half of it in Box B; it's both entirely in Box A and entirely in Box B.

Here's how we know this to be the case: let's suppose that we have a large number of box pairs that have been prepared as described in the previous paragraph. We position a box pair in front of a screen on which an impacting atom would stick. We open a narrow slit in each box at the same time. An atom hits the screen. If we repeat this action with many identically positioned box pairs, we will find that atoms cluster in some areas of the screen and not others, demonstrating an interference pattern. Further, if we change the spacing of the box pairs, we will find that the regions where the atoms cluster together are spaced differently: the larger the spacing between the boxes of a pair, the smaller the spacing between the places where atoms hit. What does this mean?

Well, let's take the "common sense" explanation, which would tell us that for each box pair, the atom was either in Box A or Box B, and that when we opened the slits, the atom left that box and struck the screen. But if this is the case, why would the location of the *other* box determine the region on the screen where the atom was "allowed" to strike? How can we explain the location of an *empty box* affecting the location of the particle? We can't. The "common sense" explanation leads us to an absurd conclusion. So we are left with the conclusion that the atom was somehow in both box A and box B simultaneously. More precisely, the probability of the atom being emitted from one box or the other was "smeared" across both boxes, so that until the atom hit the screen, it would be meaningless to say which box it was in.

But now, instead of opening the slits at the same time, let's open the slit in one of the boxes and then later open the slit in another box. What we will find in this case is that the atom will either come out of the first box or the second box, but not both. And if we actually look in the boxes one at a time, we will find the atom in one box or the other. If we look in Box A, we will either find the atom or not find it. You will never find *half* an atom. If we find the atom in Box A, then the atom is entirely in Box A and not in Box B. If we don't find the atom in Box A, then we will find the atom in Box B.

I should note that this is not a hypothetical scenario. Experiments conceptually identical to this "box pair experiment" have actually been carried out, producing the results that I have described here. Thus through experimentation, we have been able to show that an atom is in one box or another. But we have also shown, *under identical circumstances*, that an atom was in both boxes.

To understand the import of this statement, imagine Galileo dropping objects of different mass from the Tower of Pisa and finding that gravity acted differently depending on how he chose to *look* at it. Imagine that he could first do an experiment conclusively proving that the two objects hit the ground at the same time, and then immediately thereafter do another experiment proving that the heavier object struck the ground first. Imagine further that no matter how hard he tried to find a single authoritative law of gravitation, it eluded him, and he lived out his days never knowing whether all objects fall at the same rate or not – believing, in fact, that they must sometimes fall at the same rate and sometimes must not, and that the way the objects behaved seemed to be completely arbitrary. Imagine Galileo's peers and successors, the most brilliant minds on earth, devoting their lives to understanding why gravity acted in this way and none of them being able to explain it. Imagine, finally, decades after Galileo's death, that science had concluded it was impossible for anyone to understand why gravity acted in this capricious manner and that the best solution was to just accept the fact and stop trying to explain it.

If that had happened, there would have been no scientific revolution. The idea of using experimentation to test hypotheses would have been dismissed as the quaint conceit of an eccentric. Newton would never have published his *Principia*, a cornerstone of modern science. Einstein would never have discovered general relativity. If any sort of technological progress occurred over the next 400 years, it wouldn't have been based on a scientific method designed to get at basic laws underlying the universe, but rather a sort of technical trickery based on an arbitrary collection of randomly acquired facts about the material world. What passed for science would really be alchemy, an inexact but occasionally useful body of hermetic knowledge passed down from one generation to the next. Theoretical science would be even more divorced from empirical reality, becoming indistinguishable from mysticism.

To a large extent, we can see this very thing happening in theoretical physics today. By 1981, the field of physics had experienced two hundred years of dramatic growth. Successive discoveries deepened our understanding of nature, because in each case theory and experiment worked in tandem. New ideas were tested and confirmed and new experimental discoveries were explained in terms of theory. Then, in the early 1980s, progress ground to a halt. The last major, empirically verifiable discoveries in physics occurred prior to 1982. Since that time, we have seen a proliferation of theories in the absence of empirical evidence. The most fundamental of the sciences now flirts openly with mysticism.

I remember reading that Neils Bohr once remarked that if you aren't shocked by quantum theory, you haven't understood it. I'm not sure I understand it, but I'm definitely a little weirded out by it. How can a particle be both entirely in Box A and in Box B? And how can looking in one of the boxes cause the particle to choose to be in one box or the other? What he is saying is that by looking, you are forcing the atom to "choose" to be either in Box A or Box B. In other words, *your observation seems to cause the atom to be in one place or the other.*

And if that isn't weird enough, Heller then goes on to explain something called a "delayed-choice experiment," which seems to indicate that observing which path a particle took can retroactively alter its behavior. That is, let's say you do a double slit experiment but don't observe the results. Since the experiment is unobserved, all of the light going through the slits will act as waves rather than particles. But if you store information about which slit a photon went through and later look at that information, *you will create a history of the photon having gone one slot or the other.* If you observe the results of the experiment after looking at the information, you will see that the photon went through the correct slot. If, however, you destroy the information without looking at it and then look at the results of the experiment, you will see that the photon went through both slots. Heller says that no matter how many times you perform the experiment, the results of the experiment will always correlate with your later decision to either look at or destroy the information about the photon's path. Again, if you're willing to set aside the complete absurdity of that statement and just go with it, you can skip the next few paragraphs:

> This means that on a subatomic scale, cause and effect can apparently go backwards. That's the only possible explanation if we accept that our choice of observation caused the photon's behavior. If we deny the possibility of causation moving backwards through time, we are left with an even more troubling possibility: that the behavior of the photon determined our choice of observation. In that case, free will is an illusion: our apparent choice was in fact constrained by the behavior of the photon. (Another possibility is that both our choice and the photon's behavior were caused by some other factor outside of our control, which also negates the possibility of free will.)
>
> One could argue that these experiments are "special cases," and that we might therefore still have free will in other cases, but it's hard to see how this could be. If the subjective perception of free will can be demonstrated to be an illusion in one case, what reason do we have to think that free will exists in other cases? Further, to say that the observation of quantum phenomena is a "special case" has the matter backwards. We expect principles deduced from observing the subatomic level to apply universally. Quantum physics is the general case; classical physics is the special case. We know for a fact that classical physics is *wrong*. Classical physics is only a useful approximation. The sensible conclusion, it seems to me, is that our perception of free will is a similar sort of approximation, a useful concept that nevertheless fails to conform to reality at a basic level.
>
> This is not some esoteric problem purely of academic interest. All of science is based on experimentation, which is to say performing an experiment and then observing the results. If how we observe the results can retroactively affect the experiment, then we have a very fundamental problem in the scientific method. It may be reassuring to think that the problem occurs only at the quantum level, but how can we know? That's simply the only arena in which we've observed the problem, and it's the reliability of observation that is in question here. It's fine to say that we will perform multiple experiments and gauge how observation affects the experiment, but all this does is kick the problem up a level. By

observing how observation affects an experiment, we are essentially conducting another experiment, a "meta-experiment," if you like. How can we know that the way we are observing the results of this meta-experiment isn't affecting the outcome?

Let's suppose that we perform a double slit experiment a hundred times, each time observing which path a particular photon takes. Every time, the photon acts as a particle, traveling through either one slit or the other. Now let's suppose that we perform another double slit experiment a hundred times, without observing which slit the photon travels through. Every time, the photon acts as a wave, seeming to travel through both slits. Thus our hypothesis is confirmed: if we observe a photon, it will act as a particle, but if we do not observe a photon, it will act as a wave. But how do we know that the confirmation of this hypothesis isn't the consequence of the way we set up our meta-experiment? How do we know, in fact, that the 200 double slit experiments would act the way they did if we weren't observing the meta-experiment? We don't. Not only that, but we have some pretty solid evidence, based on our knowledge of the way light behaves, that our observations cause reality to act differently than it would if we weren't observing.

If, on the other hand, we refuse to admit the possibility of reverse-chronological causation, how can we explain the exact correlation between our choice of experiment and the behavior of the photons? As I see it, there are two possibilities. The first is that rather than our observation causing the photon's behavior, the photon's behavior is constraining our choice of which experiment to perform. The second is that both the photon's behavior and our choice of which experiment to perform are both determined by some other, unknown phenomenon. In either case, our choice of which experiment to perform is not free but is instead determined by some force outside our control. If that's the case, then we have an even bigger problem.

Science is based on the possibility of the experimenter making free choices. We assume, for example, that we could freely choose to perform either an interference experiment or a which-path experiment. If, however, light is objectively two completely different things at different times and it (or something else) arbitrarily prevents us from performing certain experiments by somehow controlling our choice of which experiment to perform, then we live in a conspiratorial universe that actively resists certain types of scientific endeavors.

Both the reverse-causation hypothesis and the conspiratorial universe hypothesis are counterintuitive and highly troubling. Further, it is clear that we can no longer accede to the fiction that the universe can be neatly divided into the "physical" and the "mental." Either our observations contribute to the creation of reality or our seemingly free choices are in fact completely constrained by that reality.

My personal intuition is that these two possibilities are complementary, and that they both obtain to some extent. Thus the duality of mind and matter is replaced with the duality of volition versus determinism. This comports with the Jainist idea that human beings are constantly struggling against the weight of karma. And yet, if we take this notion to its logical conclusion, a strange inversion takes place: to conceive of a force that is capable of anticipating and thwarting my efforts to understand the universe, I cannot help but to imagine an intelligent, volitional being or beings guiding that force. This idea is implicit in the idea of a "conspiratorial universe." If the universe is conspiratorial, then what is conspiring against me? A purely passive, mechanistic force cannot conspire, cannot anticipate nor intentionally thwart my intended actions. Only something that is a mirror of my own intentions – a sort of anti-intention – could do this.

The situation is reminiscent of the ancient Chinese concept of Yin-Yang. Yin is cold, dark, and passive and Yang is hot, bright, and energetic, and the two swirl around each other, one becoming the other. Western science since Descartes has insisted on a false dichotomy, with science (Yang) studying the natural world (Yin) from outside. It was assumed that the natural world was essentially passive and mechanical – that it had no intelligence or intentions, and therefore it would sit still for us to contemplate it safely from within the objective realm of science. As our knowledge of Yin expanded, however, we came up against the border between Yin and Yang and realized to our surprise that while Yang pushes on Yin, Yin is pushing back. Further, it's not always clear who is pushing whom. Does the existence of a photon cause us to observe it, or does our observation cause the photon to exist? I don't believe there's any definite answer, because as with Yin-Yang, the border is a continuum.

In addition, the further we go into the heart of Yin, the more it seems like Yang; and the further we go into the heart of Yang, the more it seems like Yin. This fact is represented in the Yin-Yang symbol as a white dot in the black swirl and a black dot in the white swirl: each aspect contains the seed of the other and literally turns into its opposite. Pure volition in the absence of determinism becomes a sort of determinism, and pure determinism in the absence of volition becomes a sort of volition. So I may think of myself as a volitional being struggling against determinism, but the only way determinism can successfully thwart my intentions is by anticipating my intentions and replacing them with its own. Passive becomes active; dark becomes light; Yin becomes Yang.

It is a mistake, though, to think of the intentional Yang as somehow being pitted against the deterministic Yin. The activity of Yang cannot be understood except in relation to the passivity of Yin. What we call "reality" is really the interplay of these two elements, the line between dark and white. And yet, if we look closely, we see that there is no line, only the beginning of one thing and the end of another. Until the 20th century, science had been content to take the existence of the line as a given, but quantum mechanics has forced us to look at the border between two, between passive and active, being and becoming, physical and mental. The closer we look, however, the clearer it is that there is no line to be seen. There is no reality except the interplay of these two elements.

I can't tell if this part is really deep or if it's more pseudoscientific nonsense.

Part Four: Ananke

I return to Heller's house the next day. He's sitting in front of a monitor in the workshop, half in a trance. He barely looks up when I walk in. I stand there awkwardly for a few moments while he works. I notice an obituary for a "Dr. Emil Jelinek" tacked to the wall. Apparently Jelinek was a colleague of Heller's at Stanford who died in some kind of accident a little less than two years ago. That's as far as I've read when Heller speaks.

"Gotta keep an eye on that one," he says.

I walk up next to him. Most of the monitor screen is taken up by what I eventually realize is a map of the Bay Area. Superimposed on the map are a dozen or so red dots with a series of numbers next to them. He taps a dot in Hayward, just across the bridge from here. The dot appears a little larger than the others.

"Is something going to happen there?" I ask.

"Maybe. The intensity of the measured disturbance is a function of several variables. Probability of occurrence, proximity of the event to the detector, number of catastrophic neural shutdowns ..."

"You mean the number of people who will die."

"Yes."

"So all you have is a single number to go by? And all of those factors feed into that number?"

"Correct. We call it the psionic disruption coefficient, or PDC."

"Any word from Tali?"

He turns away from the monitor, shaking his head.

"Has she ever disappeared like this before?"

"No. She's very conscientious about such things. I think she ... that is, I suspect she might be gone for good."

That sounds ominous, but I don't press him on it. He seems pretty upset. I'm trying to make out the numbers on the map behind him. "So this PDC number ... you say that a bunch of variables factor into it, but you don't have access to those variables. All you see is the output of the function, right?"

"That's right."

"So," I say, trying to make sense of this, "does that mean that an event that has a one hundred percent chance of killing five people looks the same as an event with a fifty percent chance of killing ten people?"

Heller seems glad to be off the subject of Tali's disappearance. "The function is more complicated than that, but that's the idea. Below a threshold of about five people dying for certain, though, there's usually too much noise to separate out a probable event from random psionic behavior. Although you have to take into account proximity to a detector, as well. One time we got a very strong reading that turned out to be a man being shot directly underneath a street sign to which Tali had affixed a detector. We thought it was a fluke, because usually disruption events register on at least two detectors. That's how we can get some idea of the scope or probability of an event, as well as pinpointing its location."

"How far can you know in advance about an event?"

Heller sighs. "If an event occurs, you will see the PDC increase gradually as you approach the spacetime coordinates of an event, until it eventually spikes dramatically upward a few seconds before the event actually occurs. When the event occurs, the PDC will reach one and then begin to gradually fall off. If an event does not occur, you will usually see the PDC increase gradually and then gradually fall off a few minutes before the non-event, and then continue to fall off afterward at around the same rate. We filter out disturbances with a PDC below point one eight, because so many of them are non-events. Just noise. So, to answer your question, anywhere from eight hours to a few seconds. The ones where we only get a few seconds' notice are events where only a few people died, or where they died outside the range of the detectors, or there wasn't sufficient trauma to create a catastrophic neural shutdown in all the victims. As I say, there are a lot of variables. Theoretically, if there were a massive event affecting hundreds or thousands of people in the Bay Area, I could know about it a day or more in advance."

"So how big is that event in Hayward?"

"We call it a 'case,'" says Heller. "Until it happens, it's only a probable event. If it happens, it's an event. If it doesn't happen, it's a non-event. Until we know which it is, we refer to it as a case. Right now this case is registering on three receptors, at point one nine, point two four and point two eight. That puts it in this area." He taps the screen with his finger.

"Do you know when it will happen? I mean, if it happens?"

"Three thirty-five p.m. today, give or take a minute."

"How likely is it to happen?"

"It's either very likely that a relatively small event will occur, or somewhat unlikely that a relatively large event will occur there, or somewhere in between." He grins. "It's not an exact science. I'll keep an eye on it, and if the PDC spikes ..."

"What?"

"Well, ordinarily Tali would go to the crux ..."

"What do you mean, crux? Tali used that word the other day and I didn't know what she was talking about."

"Oh," says Heller. "That's the neatest part of this. The cruxes are the only reason we're able to sometimes prevent these events from happening. You see, there are often pivotal events that either allow an event to happen or prevent it from happening."

"Like the couple tossing a coin at the pier to decide where to go for lunch," I say. "Heads, they go to a Mexican restaurant, tails they head down the pier. Tali made the coin come up tails, so they went down the pier, and as a result, the guy stops the killer on the pier."

"Exactly. That was actually an interesting case, because there were two cruxes. That hardly ever happens. Of course, at the first one she failed to ..." He trails off, remembering that Tali nearly sent me to my death by screwing with my coin toss.

"Are the cruxes always coin tosses?" I ask.

"Yes," he says. "Well, they don't have to be. But coin tosses are the easiest to pinpoint, because they're binary, and the two possible results often lead to two very distinct futures."

"Is this more of that probabilistic future stuff? There are two possible futures; heads, the universe takes one path, tails, it takes the other?"

"Sort of. The fact is that coin tosses aren't really random; they're pseudorandom. Whether the coin lands on heads or tails is primarily determined by ..."

"The starting location of the coin, how hard you toss it, air pressure ... yeah, Tali went over this."

"OK, so the important thing to understand is that although coin tosses are *almost* completely deterministic, there is just enough objective randomness that a coin toss can create a non-zero probability of an alternate future occurring. This non-zero probability shows up in our data as a seemingly arbitrary drop in the PDC. When these drops first started to show up in our data, we thought it was some sort of noise that we hadn't accounted for. They didn't always show up, but when they did, they were persistent, and they almost always centered on spacetime coordinates near the case site. What we eventually realized was that for many events, there was a related event that the main event was dependent on – an event that had to happen before the main event could occur. Tali investigated some of these pre-events and found that at the specified spacetime coordinates, someone was invariably tossing a coin. Coin tosses seem to have a very distinct probability signature that shows up in our data."

"So if the coin comes up heads, the event happens, and if it comes up tails, it doesn't happen."

"Right. Of course it's completely arbitrary; the event may be dependent on the coin coming up heads or on it coming up tails. And whichever it is will occur with a probability exceeding ninety-nine percent, because as I say, coin tosses are almost completely deterministic."

"Um, OK."

"You don't have to understand all the details. The important thing to understand is that we know, because of the drop in the PDC, that the coin toss has to come up a particular way in order for the event to happen. If we don't tamper with the outcome, the coin will almost certainly come up with the result that allows the event to occur. But if we tamper, we have roughly a fifty percent chance of preventing the event from occurring."

"What if someone stops the coin toss from happening?"

"Most likely they would fail. But if they succeeded in preventing the coin toss, then they would probably cause the crux to collapse to the most likely future."

"Meaning that the event would occur as if the coin toss had happened."

"Yes."

"But then your data was wrong. Your data indicated a coin toss that never happens. Or happened, whatever."

He shrugs. "Sometimes there are errors with interpreting data. If you prevent a coin toss that seemed to be required for the event to occur and the event occurs even though the coin toss didn't happen, then we were wrong about the data. Maybe it was the *possibility* of a coin toss that produced the alternate future. Or maybe it was just noise in the data that looked like a coin toss. Like I said, this isn't an exact science."

This sounds kind of like bullshit to me, but maybe I just don't understand it. "I still don't really get why you can't interfere with the event itself. Like, why couldn't Tali have called in a bomb threat at the pier? The police would have shown up and cleared the area. There's no way that guy could have gotten away with shooting a bunch of people."

"The simplest explanation I can offer you is that Ananke would have anticipated that action and prevented it from interfering with her plans."

"And the complicated explanation?"

"The universe is a deterministic system. Any action that Tali took would have been a result of other variables in the system. The ultimate outcome of the event at the pier was dependent on the full set of all variables in the system, which includes Tali's actions. If Tali had tried to prevent the shooting, her efforts would have been factored in by Ana … that is, by the system. You can't change the output of a deterministic system by being a cog in the system."

"You mean that if Tali had tried to prevent the shooting, it would have ended up happening in a different way. And maybe her actions would somehow bring about the shooting. For that matter, it wouldn't have to be a shooting, would it? Maybe something she does sets in motion a chain of events that starts a grease fire in the kitchen of Maggiano's, and it's the fire that kills all those people." I think I'm finally starting to understand this stuff.

"That's one way of looking at it," he says. "Thinking in counterfactuals will drive you crazy, though."

"Counterfactuals?"

"Hypotheticals. What-if scenarios. Ultimately, asking 'what if Tali had acted differently at the pier?' is a meaningless question. Tali is part of a deterministic system. She *couldn't* have acted differently. You might as well ask 'what if Martians beamed the shooter into space a second before he pulled the gun.' They didn't, because it's impossible."

"You're saying there's no such thing as free will."

He sighs again. "You know those posters that appear at first glance to be a sort of abstract painting? But then, if you unfocus your eyes a little and sit there for a minute, it turns into a picture of Marilyn Monroe? That's what free will is like. If you look at it too closely, it disappears."

Free will is like Marilyn Monroe. Got it. "So if you can't interfere with the event itself, how can you interfere with the coin toss? Isn't that part of the same deterministic system?"

"Excellent question," he says. "Yes. The coin toss itself is part of the system. The reason we can interfere with the result has to do with *how* we interfere." He goes to a drawer in the workbench and pulls out a rectangular metal box a little larger than the receptor doodad he showed me earlier. He hands it to me. The thing is featureless except for a little clear plastic panel that hides a recessed button. Next to the button is a glowing green LED light. I press on the panel and it slides open.

"Don't push that!" Heller shouts, suddenly panicked. "You'll wipe out all my data!"

I slide the panel back. "OK, OK. What is it, some kind of electromagnetic pulse weapon?"

"Not a weapon, but it does generate an EMP. In any case, wiping out magnetic media is a side effect. The purpose of the device is to disrupt the central nervous system."

"But it's not a weapon," I say dryly.

"The effect on a human being is minimal. You probably wouldn't even feel it. But it will disrupt your central nervous system slightly for about a millisecond. Just long enough to slow down your motor response a little for a few seconds afterward. So that if you were to, say, toss a coin during that period, the result might be different than if you hadn't been hit by the randomizer."

I'm looking over the device. It sure doesn't look like much. "So Tali had one of these on her. That's how she manipulated the coin toss."

"Yes," says Heller.

Something is still bugging me. "Isn't this thing, the randomizer, part of the deterministic system too? How is using this device any different than trying to stop the event by calling the police?"

He smiles, as if anticipating the question. "Very good. You're exactly right. The magic of the randomizer isn't in the electromagnetic pulse it sends out, but in the way it determines whether to send the pulse. You see, inside the box is a small amount of a radioactive isotope. Don't worry, it isn't dangerous. The isotope emits a particle about once every two seconds, and there's a component that detects the particles as they are emitted. The device has a counter that is always set to either one or zero. If, during a given second, a particle is detected, then the device sets the counter to one. If it doesn't detect a particle, the counter is set to zero. The randomizer will only emit a pulse if the trigger is pushed while the counter is at one. If it's at zero, the randomizer will do nothing."

I'm now thoroughly confused. "So it doesn't work half the time?"

"The probability isn't actually fifty/fifty, for reasons that are difficult to explain, but for our purposes, let's say that it doesn't emit a pulse half the time. That isn't the same as it not working half the time. Although it's also true that the interference doesn't work half the time. It's very complicated."

Yes, it is. Heller proceeds to explain it, but it doesn't really penetrate. I'm going to do my best to reconstruct his explanation from my memory, later reading in his book, and other research (mostly Wikipedia). Again, you can skip this part if you don't really give a shit how the randomizer works.

SKIP THIS PART

Essentially the randomizer works a lot like a real-life Schrödinger's cat. In Schrödinger's thought experiment, the cat is either alive or dead because of something that happens at the subatomic scale. Since there is a fifty percent chance of a particle being emitted over a certain time frame, the cat has a fifty percent chance of being alive and a fifty percent chance of being dead. The essence of the experiment is the transference of quantum indeterminacy from the subatomic level to a macro level. And along with this indeterminacy comes true randomness: it is impossible to predict whether a particle will be emitted, and therefore the cat's status is non-deterministic, which is to say that it's objectively random.

In fact, I found at least one company online that sells devices similar to Heller's randomizer (without the electromagnetic pulse part, of course). You can buy a device that will plug into a USB port on your computer that will generate truly random numbers based on quantum phenomena. There are other services that use atmospheric noise to generate random numbers, but although these numbers are random for all practical purposes, they are not *truly* random. Numbers produced from atmospheric noise are produced by the same deterministic system that Heller is trying to get around. Of course, unless you're a quantum physicist doing some really wacky things (like Heller), there's absolutely no reason you'd need true randomness. If atmospheric noise isn't random enough for you, you're either a genius or a nut. Possibly both.

Anyway, the point is that because of its reliance on quantum phenomena, the behavior of Heller's randomizer is truly random. There's a fifty percent chance that when you push the button, the device will generate an electromagnetic pulse, and no one, not even Ananke, can predict whether a pulse will be generated. Now let's say that a particular event will only happen if a certain coin toss comes up heads. Tali shows up at the location of the coin toss and pushes the button, thereby injecting randomness into the situation. If a pulse is emitted, the coin will come up tails. If a pulse is not emitted, the coin will come up heads. Ananke has no way of knowing which will happen.

The obvious question is: "Why not make the pulse fire every time you push the button? Don't you have a better chance of interfering with Ananke's intentions if you do your best to interfere with the coin toss every time?" Paradoxically, the answer is no. This is because Ananke will attempt to anticipate any action you take to thwart her, and if you interfere with the coin toss every time, she will simply invert the required result. It will turn out that instead of heads being required to bring about the event, tails was required – and by altering the result, you have just brought about the event you were trying to prevent. If you act in a predictable, deterministic fashion, you're on Ananke's turf. She'll win every time. Heller uses this illustration in his book:

> Think of a boxer, Dan, who is much better at striking with his right arm than his left. Dan is facing a skilled opponent named Tim, who knows that Dan's right is his best weapon. Tim will anticipate that Dan will try to use his right arm at every opportunity and constantly block every attack. As a result of Tim's blocking, Dan often resorts to using his weaker arm because Tim isn't expecting it. Of course, Tim will quickly catch on to what Dan is doing and begin to block Tim's left as well. What you end up with is an endless feedback loop where Tim is attempting to anticipate Dan's actions and Dan is attempting to anticipate Tim's reactions. If Dan is skilled enough, he may occasionally land a punch despite Tim's blocking, not because he always attacks with his stronger arm but because Tim is unable to predict what Dan will do.

The point is that, paradoxically, in order to exert one's will against Ananke, one must cede some power to her. Only by failing to interfere half of the time do you have any chance of preventing her from realizing her intentions. I think this gets back to Heller's Yin-Yang comments in his book. Pure volition becomes pure determinism: if you try to exert your own will against Ananke one hundred percent of the time, you will fail one hundred percent of the time. It's a counterintuitive concept, but it makes perfect sense in a perverse sort of way.

Now Heller's strange statement starts to make sense as well:

It doesn't emit a pulse half the time. That isn't the same as it not working half the time. Although it's also true that the interference doesn't work half the time.

What he means is that half of the time Ananke is unable to anticipate the result of the coin toss. She guesses wrong half the time because she has no way of knowing whether a pulse will occur. And it's important to understand that what causes this uncertainty is not the pulse itself, but the *possibility that a pulse will occur*. It's like the boxer example: sometimes Dan strikes with his right and sometimes with his left. What allows him to occasionally get through Tim's defenses is not his overpowering right arm; it's the *uncertainty* of whether he will strike with his left or his right. Similarly, what allowed Tali to occasionally thwart Ananke's intentions was the uncertainty of whether she would interfere with the coin toss or not. Heller tells me that Tali has been successful in preventing the event roughly fifty percent of the time whether or not the pulse occurred. In other words, half of the time that Tali interfered, she did so by *not interfering*. To distinguish these two sorts of interference, Heller uses the word "tamper" to describe the introduction of quantum randomness into a situation, and he uses the word "interfere" to describe physically altering the coin toss result. So you can tamper by randomly interfering or not interfering. In the cases where Tali tampered but didn't interfere, what Tali essentially did is fool Ananke into thinking that she *would* interfere, which caused Ananke to reverse the required coin toss result. So just as Ananke could cause Tali to bring about the very event she was trying to prevent, *Tali could do the same thing to Ananke.* And that brings us back to free will, determinism, Yin-Yang, and all that. Which is the cause and which is the effect? Who is pushing whom?

And then there's Heller's statement that the probability of a pulse being emitted isn't actually fifty/fifty. He explained this too, but I'm still not sure I understand it. I think the problem is that even when the pulse is emitted, it doesn't invert the result of the coin toss one hundred percent of the time: either the effect on the central nervous system isn't enough to change the result, or it's so great that it causes the number of rotations of the coin to change by an even number, so the result is the same as it would have been if there had been no interference. So the odds of a pulse occurring have to be jacked up a bit above fifty percent to even the odds of the interference altering the result. Something like that, anyway.

OK, START READING AGAIN HERE

"So," I ask him, "you've injected randomness into the coin toss, but the toss itself was going to happen either way, right? That means it's part of the deterministic system. And if that's true, why doesn't Ananke just stop the toss from happening in the first place?"

"Ananke isn't omnipotent. There are limits to what she can do. Every event is dependent on every other event, and some of those events are predictable – that is, predictable to *us*. And that gives us some power. How hard she fights to make a particular event occur is a function of how badly she wants that event to occur, and she clearly cares more about some events than others. She allows us to prevent some minor events so that she can focus on the ones she really cares about."

He turns back to the computer and hits refresh. "Hmm," he says. "Hayward's mean PDC is up to two point nine. And it's got a crux at three twenty-six, right at the epicenter."

The clock on the wall says two forty. That means the crux is in forty-six minutes. Hayward is a good half hour from here. "Is two point nine high?"

"If Tali were here, she'd want to head to the crux location, just in case."

"So are you going to go?"

He shakes his head. "I don't tamper. Not anymore."

"Why not? If that event happens, people are going to die. You could save them."

"I wish it were that simple," he says wearily. "I used to think Tali and I were doing some good, but these days … I just don't know. Trying to alter the future, it messes with your head. She fails half the time, you know. Tali, I mean. More than half the time, because sometimes she doesn't get to the crux point in time. And when she does get there and successfully interferes, and the event occurs anyway – well, in a very real sense she was the *cause* of the event. It wouldn't have happened if she hadn't interfered."

"But she couldn't know that. And overall, the effect of her interference is positive, isn't it?"

"I think that's another question you can't look too closely at. Think of it this way. As you said, although Ananke can't know the result of the toss, she does know that a toss is going to occur – and if you intend to interfere with the toss, she knows that too. And that means she knows that there's a fifty percent chance that you will prevent the event from occurring. The effect of all this is that your attempt to prevent the event is factored into the probability of the event. In other words, an event that you intend to prevent is inherently less likely than an event that you don't intend to prevent, and that decreased probability will show up as a lower PDC. This is another reason that only large-scale events are detectable through the system: in order for the PDC to be high enough to detect, the scale of the event has to be something like twice as great in order to compensate for the decreased probability. Another way to look at it is that by preventing some events from happening, you're forcing Ananke to make the events that do occur to be worse than they otherwise would be. By saving some, you're dooming others to die."

"That's some pretty abstract reasoning. I mean, I think I see what you're getting at, that somehow, no matter what you do, the scales come out even. But it seems to me that if you just look at the situation itself, it's pretty clear that Tali is helping people. She certainly saved a lot of lives at the pier."

"Sure, that time it worked out OK, at least on a surface level. But most of the time it doesn't. Most of the time Tali goes out, she comes back in tears."

"Why did she start tampering in the first place? Tali must have understood everything you're telling me, right? She must have known that she wasn't doing any real good."

Heller shakes his head. "I didn't say that. I honestly don't know whether the net result is positive or not. Like I said, I used to think Tali was doing some good. Now I realize the question may be impossible to answer, at least coming at it rationally. It's like a Zen *koan*: if you concentrate hard enough on it, you'll find yourself thinking about nothing. Or maybe like a Rorschach test: the value of tampering is what you bring to it. In any case, Tali couldn't help it. It's not in her nature to stand by and let bad things happen. It's worn on her, though. I'm not sure she could do it much longer. In fact, it's occurred to me that maybe she left because the whole thing became too much for her. Frankly, I don't know how she did it as long as she did. Have you ever known someone who deals with death every day?"

"I had a friend who was a paramedic for a while."

He smiles. "How long?"

I get his point. It takes a special kind of person to deal with that shit day after day. Most people don't last very long. And you have to have some reason to do it — some abstract notion that you're helping people, because if you focus on the here-and-now, it will bury you. But if what Heller is saying is true, then Tali couldn't take refuge in abstracts either. So why did she do it? Why did she put herself through that kind of suffering, not to mention putting herself in harm's way? Maybe she was just incapable of doing nothing.

"So you're not going to do anything about Hayward?"

"That's correct," he says.

"What if I do it?"

He frowns at me. "Why do you want to get mixed up in this stuff? You'll regret it."

"I can't just sit here and wait for whatever is going to happen. I have to do something." I think I mean it, but part of me is thinking that when Tali does return, she's going to have a more positive opinion of me if I've filled in for her while she's gone. I feel the need to prove myself to her, show her I'm not just some depressed loser. God, I'm an ass.

He regards me for a moment, then shrugs. "What kind of phone do you have?"

"Android," I say, pulling my phone from my pocket. "Why?"

"Too bad. Tali and I use iPhones. I don't have a Tyche app for Android."

The way conversations with Heller veer between the metaphysical and mundane gives me vertigo. "Tyche app?"

"Tyche is the Greek goddess of good fortune. Our weapon against Ananke, if you will. It's our name for the whole system we have set up to monitor the psionic fields. You see, all the data from the psionic field detectors is uploaded to that machine." He points to the computer. "The data then has to be interpreted and displayed in a useful way. There are several ways to look at the data, but the most intuitive way to see active cases unfolding is on a map. I wrote the original application that displays this map with the cases and cruxes marked on it. When Tali first started interfering with the cruxes we would have to be in contact by phone, so I could give her real-time data as the numbers changed. Eventually she adapted the application for her iPhone. You don't really need it, though. I can call you if there are any major changes in the PDCs. All you really need is that."

He means the randomizer, which I'm still holding. "How do I …"

"Nothing to it. The randomizer's range is about thirty feet. You can keep it in your pocket to avoid attention. The pulse is directional, meaning that it will emit in a conical shape from the front of the device. As long as it's pointed in roughly the right direction, you can't miss. Just keep your phone out of its path, or you'll wipe its memory."

"So I just get within thirty feet of the tosser …" I break into laughter.

"We use the word *target*," says Heller.

Recovering, I continue, "I get within thirty feet of the target and press the button. That's it?"

"That's all there is to it. The randomizer will either emit a pulse or not. And make sure you are within range before you hit the button. You'll only get one shot."

"Because it only has one charge?"

"No. I mean, that's part of it. But the randomizer is programmed to work only once every ten minutes. That prevents you from skewing the odds by tampering more than once."

"How do I know if it worked?"

"A lot of people don't die."

"No, I mean, how do I know if the device emitted a pulse?"

"What difference does it make? It isn't the pulse that changes the outcome of the case; it's the possibility of a pulse. Asking whether a pulse was emitted is like asking what color a bullet is. It makes no difference to the outcome. But to answer your question, the button will go dark if a pulse is released, indicating the battery is dead. If the light turns red, the charge hasn't been expended, but you'll have to wait ten minutes before the device will work again."

I shelve my philosophical objections for now. "OK, anything else I need to know?"

"Just get in and out as fast as you can. The crux is right in the middle of the case location, which means that if the event occurs, it's going to happen right around the location of the coin toss. You've got nine minutes between the crux and the event. Don't stick around to see if the tampering worked. It doesn't matter. Just get out."

"Tali knew immediately that her tampering at the pier worked."

"She was looking at the Tyche app," he says. "The PDC of the event will drop to near zero if the tampering works."

"So you'll know immediately after the toss?"

"Yes."

"Send me a text. Yes if it worked, no if it didn't."

"Why? You can't …"

"Just do it. Please."

He shrugs and goes back to the keyboard and taps a few keys. A printer on the workbench spits out two pages. "Here," he says, handing me the sheets. The top one is a map of downtown Hayward; the second one is blow-up of the center of the map. "The crux is here," he says, tapping a dot in the center of the blow-up. The time is approximate, but it will become more definite as the crux approaches. I'll give you a call two minutes before the crux with an exact time. The pulse only lasts for about three seconds, so you've got to be exact."

"Got it," I say, and head for the door.

"Good luck," says Heller, smiling coldly. "Whatever that means."

I run to my car and drive as fast as I dare to Hayward. The area of the crux is an old four-story apartment building in a marginal area of town. I park on the street a hundred yards or so away and make my way to the building. The crux location appears to be inside. Luckily there's an old woman entering the building just ahead of me with a bag of groceries. I run up and hold the door for her. She smiles and says thank you. Her hair is a weird shade of auburn that doesn't match either her complexion or her roots, which are gray. Her eyebrows have been drawn on with a pencil that matches the unnatural hair color. Creepy.

I smile back and then follow her into the building. She walks up the stairs and I keep going down the hall. It's 3:20, which gives me six minutes to reach the crux. As I get farther down the hall, I realize that the crux is inside one of the apartments, probably the one on the back left, 114. Heller said the range of the randomizer is about thirty feet, and presumably it will go through walls without any trouble, so I could probably just point the thing at the door to 114 and press the button. I loiter in the hall, waiting for Heller to call.

There's a noise from upstairs, sounds like an argument. A man and a woman. I can't make out the words, but the tone doesn't sound violent; just typical couple stuff. I don't hear anything going on in 114. What if it's empty? Should I knock? I look at the map again. The resolution isn't fine enough to be absolutely certain that 114 is the right apartment; the crux might be in 113. Or … shit.

The map is two-dimensional. The building has four floors and I have no way of knowing which floor the crux is on. God damn it. Now what? I climb the stairs to the second floor. The noise is coming from inside 214. I scamper up to the third floor and pause briefly at 314. Nothing. I continue to the fourth floor. There are noises coming from down the hall, but I don't hear anything from 414. My phone says 3:23. Come on, Heller. Call me.

I run back down to the second floor, figuring that 214 is my best bet, since there are definitely people inside. And if it ends up being 114 or 314, I can probably still get there in time. I'm shaking and sweaty; I'm not used to this much exercise. As I lean against the wall across from 214, my phone rings.

"Heller!" I whisper. "What floor is it? I can't tell …"

"I know, I'm working on it."

"Working on it? Jesus, I've got less than two minutes."

"The data is still a little fuzzy. I'm pretty sure it's the first or second floor, probably the last apartment on the right." That means 114 or 214. But which one?

"Should I just point the randomizer between floors and hope for the best?"

"Hold on."

Shit. The waiting is killing me. I run back down to the first floor and bang on the door to 114. "Hello!" I shout. "Is anybody in there?" I wait a few seconds. No reply. I bang again. "Anything yet, Heller?" I stop to take a breath. "We're cutting it pretty close here."

"Still can't pinpoint it. The probable crux area is about twenty feet in diameter, right between the first and second floor. You're just going to have to make your best guess."

Now gasping for air and drenched with sweat, I run back up to the second floor. My phone says 3:25. "Do you have an exact time yet?" I wheeze.

"Three twenty-six and fifteen seconds, accurate to within five seconds. I'll have a better number shortly."

"OK." I pull the randomizer from my jacket and point it at the door to 214. I notice the arguing has stopped. Then the door opens.

"Who the fuck are you?" says the tall black man who has just opened the door. "What the fuck is that?"

"I'm … checking the wiring," I say, thinking quickly. "The management company sent me." I wipe sweat from my brow with the back of my left hand, which is still holding my phone. I'm trying not to breathe heavily.

"About fucking time," says the guy. Over his shoulder he shouts, "Tina, the guy is here about the wiring." He motions for me to come in. I step into the apartment. It's messy and small and it smells like mildew and weed.

"Oh, thank God," says a heavyset woman as she emerges from the kitchen. She's lighter skinned than he, and looks to be about eight months pregnant. "You all right?"

I nod, feeling a little light-headed from lack of oxygen. My fingers are tingling.

"You want to start with the disposal or the bathroom outlet?" she says.

For a moment the question makes no sense to me. Then I remember I'm supposed to be the maintenance guy. Disposal or bathroom outlet, I think. This must be the choice, the crux that determines whether the event happens or not. An electrical problem in the bathroom could start a fire. So I should probably check out the outlet. But what if it's my investigation of the outlet that causes the fire? It's hard to see how a garbage disposal could kill twenty people. On the other hand, maybe the electrical fire happens in the bathroom because I'm in the kitchen looking at the disposal. The safest course of action would be to get everybody out of the building. But how?

"Three twenty-six and twelve seconds," says a small voice. Heller is still on the phone. "You've got twenty seconds."

"Got it," I say into the phone and hang up, dropping it into my pocket.

Don't try to outwit Ananke, I find myself thinking. She's smarter than you. "Flip a coin," I say.

"What?" says the man.

"To decide which one I should look at first. Flip a coin. Here." I produce a dime from my pocket and hold it out for the man.

He doesn't take it. "Why don't you just start in the kitchen?" he says. Nobody uses that outlet but Tina anyways. We need the disposal."

"Asshole," says Tina. "I could electrify myself with that outlet."

"I'll get to them both," I lie. "You just need to pick which one I do first. Please."

"Fuck that," says the guy. "Do the disposal." Unbelievable. Why is he making such an issue out of this?

"I'll flip," says Tina, taking the coin. Thank God. "Heads, he does the bathroom first, tails the disposal."

The man shrugs.

Tina places the dime carefully on her thumb. I'm so carried away by the drama that I almost forget to push the button, but I do it, just half a second before her thumb twitches, sending the coin into the air. It arcs, spinning in the air, and comes down on her right palm. She smacks her palm against the back of her right hand and then pulls it away.

"Heads," she says, grinning at the man.

The man glowers at her. "Fuck that," he says. "Do the disposal."

Shit, I think. *Now* what? I don't know what the rules are for this kind of situation. I check my phone. No text from Heller yet.

"I, um, think you have to honor the coin toss," I say.

"Honor the coin toss?" says the man to me. "Shit, man, you for real?"

"We *agreed*, Anton," says Tina angrily. "We agreed that if it was heads, he was gonna look at the bathroom outlet first."

"I pay the rent," says Anton. "And I say that he looks at the disposal first."

"You're a fucking asshole," says Tina.

I find myself laughing. I can't help it.

"The fuck you laughing at?" growls Anton. Tina doesn't seem very happy at my outburst either.

I shake my head, trying to get a grip on myself. I can't explain why I'm laughing. I think it's because for a moment I saw things the way Ananke sees them: Tina and Anton are fighting not because they were *choosing* to fight, but because that's who they *are*. Anton was never going to let Tina win the coin toss, because he is, as Tina so eloquently put it, a *fucking asshole*. They probably have some variation of this same fight a hundred times a day, each of them playing their assigned parts perfectly.

But if Tina couldn't win the coin toss, that meant that the outcome would be the same whether I interfered or not – unless I insisted, despite Anton's demand, on investigating the outlet instead. I almost break into laughter again at the thought. I don't know anything about electrical outlets; I don't even have any tools. Which is good, because if I started messing around with wiring, I'd probably "electrify" myself, as Tina would say.

My phone chirps. Text message from Heller: *NO*.

Shit. That means my tampering didn't work. People are going to die. The light has gone out on the randomizer, which means that a pulse was released. So I had failed to change the outcome. No, that wasn't true; I had succeeded in changing the outcome, and people were going to die as a result. I don't feel like laughing anymore.

"We need to get out of the building," I manage to say.

"What the fuck are you talking about?" says Anton.

"Electrical problem," I stammer. "This device … the light went out, so something is … there's some kind of problem with the wiring."

"Get the fuck out of here," says Anton. I don't think he means it figuratively.

Tina is casting worried looks at me. "Maybe we should …" she starts.

"He can't know about no wiring problem from that box. This is bullshit. I don't think he even a real handyman." Anton is walking toward me now, his shoulders thrown back. I've got a few pounds on him, but he's taller and more muscular. I don't think I could take him in a fight.

"You're right," I say. "I'm not a handyman. But you have to trust me. Something bad is going to happen in this building in …" I look at my phone. " …six minutes. Please, just come outside for a few minutes. If nothing happens, you can beat the shit out of me, all right? But let's just go outside first."

I back away to the door and put my hand on the handle. Then I smell it. Something burning. "What is that?" I ask.

Anton starts, "The fuck are you –"

"Shit!" cries Tina. "The stove!" She runs to the kitchen door and pushes it open. Black smoke pours out. "Anton!" she screams. "Help!"

Anton's eyes go wide and he turns to look at me.

"Where's the fire extinguisher?" says Tina.

"We ain't got no fire extinguisher," says Anton.

Of course not, I think. You don't even have a working smoke alarm in the kitchen.

"Well, find one!" Tina shrieks.

"There's no time," I say, trying to remain calm. "Just get out of the building." I open the door and step outside, spying a fire alarm down at the end of the hall. I run to it and pull the lever. Nothing happens. There are sprinklers above but they don't come on. Somebody's been paying off the fire marshal. I call 911 on my cell phone, tell the operator there's a fire and give her the address. I hang up.

The door to the apartment is still open and I can hear Anton and Tina still bickering inside. They'll probably die that way, bickering till their last breath. I scamper back up the stairs to the fourth floor and start pounding on doors, yelling "Fire!" as loudly as I can. A few doors open behind me, people trying to figure out if this is some kind of prank. I don't stick around to explain. When I'm done banging on doors on the fourth floor, I leap down the stairs to the third floor and do the same thing there. By now I'm wheezing and hoarse; I can barely yell loud enough to be heard through the apartment doors. In the stairwell to the second floor, I can smell smoke. The air in the hallway is hazy, and I have trouble breathing. I have to crawl the distance of the second floor on my hands and knees. I'm too hoarse to yell anymore; if I try to speak I break into a coughing fit. All I can do is pound on doors and hope for the best. Hardly any doors open. I hope it's because the residents are all at work. Finally I make it to the first floor. The smoke isn't as bad here. I still can't yell, but I manage to stagger down the hall, knocking on all the doors. I stumble out of the apartment building and into the street. Looking up, I see flames pouring out of several windows on the second floor. I hear sirens in the distance. Standing along the sidewalk are a few dozen people, some of them barefoot, staring up at the burgeoning inferno. Tina and Anton are among them, but they don't notice me; they're still fighting. I don't see the old woman with the drawn-on eyebrows anywhere.

Part Five: Ghosts of the Past

Heller opens the door to the shop before I can even knock. He hands me a glass of scotch and empties the bottle into another glass. I down half of mine in a single swallow and slump onto the couch.

"Sorry about that," he says. "It would have been nice to have a success for your first run."

"I thought you didn't care," I say numbly.

He frowns. "Of course I care. I don't think there's any point in trying to change the outcome, but that doesn't mean I don't *care* about the outcome. And for your sake, it would have been nice if you could have had a success."

"You mean the illusion of success."

He shrugs. "Whether it's an illusion may depend on your point of view. Tali believes she's making a difference."

"But you don't."

He smiles grimly. "I believe in Tali."

I grunt noncommittally.

"In a sense," he says, "maybe you did succeed."

"How's that?"

"You remember what I said about probabilistic futures?"

"Yeah," I say, trying to remember. "Lots of futures exist, but some are more probable than others. But only one of them ends up actually happening."

"That's correct," he says, "except for the last part. We only *experience* one timeline, but that doesn't mean that only one of them is real. To put it more precisely, when you say that something 'happened,' you're saying that an event occurred that you experienced in some way. That is to say, it occurred on your timeline, in your history. But if there are alternate futures, then who's to say that for people on those alternate timelines, completely different events haven't happened?"

"Sure," I say. "Maybe every time somebody flips a coin another universe splits off from this one, so that there are an infinite number of universes out there, and everything that could possibly happen does happen. So what? What does that have to do with the people who died in that apartment fire in *this* universe? Shall I go round up the families of all those people and tell them, 'Hey, it's OK, your son or daughter or sister or cousin is still alive in another universe?'"

"It's an abstract, philosophical kind of consolation, I'll admit," he says. "But if you're going to be tampering with events, that's how you have to look at things. After all, when you went to Hayward you knew that there was a fifty percent chance you would fail. And what that means is that you imagined two possible outcomes, one in which you were successful and one in which you weren't. What I am suggesting is that nothing has changed in that equation. Those two outcomes still exist, but we happen to be experiencing the unsuccessful outcome. The fact that we ended up on one particular path doesn't make the other any less real. In fact, what we call *probability* is, I think, just a description of the proximity of alternate universes."

"Proximity of alternate universes," I repeat numbly. The words mean nothing to me.

He nods. "As I said, I believe that what shows up in the Tyche data are the impressions made by catastrophic quantum brain shutdowns in alternate futures. That is, alternate universes branching off from our own. The more probable the event, the stronger the impression. But what is meant by 'probable' in this case? I tend to think that there are an infinite number of universes splitting off from our own at any given instant, and that some of these universes are closer to being parallel than others. It's these nearly parallel universes that we describe as being more 'probable.' In reality, they are all equally probable, because they all exist. But for any given universe, some other universes are closer to being parallel than others, and it's the futures in these universes that make the strongest impressions. Probability, then, is really just an expression of the relative proximity of alternate universes."

"You got any more of this?" I ask, holding up my empty glass.

"In the house," he says. "I'll get it." He leaves the shop, closing the door behind him.

I really do need another drink at this point, but mostly I just want to get rid of Heller for a few minutes. When he's gone, I jump up and head to Tali's desk. I've got to figure out what's going on with her. Maybe she left some clue about why she disappeared or what she's up to. The desk is immaculately organized, so I don't have a lot of hope I'll find anything. Papers are neatly stacked in trays, and a cursory glance reveals nothing but bills and other mundane paperwork. A business card with a falcon logo on it catches my eye. On it is embossed:

> Peter Girell
> Claims Investigator
> Peregrine Insurance

There's an email address and phone number at the bottom of the card. I'm trying to figure out why my attention is drawn to the card when I remember what Heller said when I first met him. He had asked me if I was with "Peregrine." I pocket the card on a whim and keep looking.

Drawers contain the expected: stapler, paperclips, hairbrush, lip gloss, et cetera. Not much to go on. There's a laptop on the desk but I don't bother to turn it on. No time, and in any case I'm sure it's password-protected. Next to the computer is a five by seven photo in a frame: Tali and another woman. Once I look at her, I find it hard to look away. Tali is pretty; beautiful even, in a way. But this other woman – she's, well, *striking* is the word, I guess. She's taller than Tali, with straighter, darker hair. Her features are strong and sharp, her eyes defiant. She's smiling, but there's a sadness in those eyes that I feel like something being twisted in my chest.

I force myself to look away, casting about for something else to focus on. But there really isn't anything to look at. Tali's desk tells me nothing about her other than that she's a neat freak. Above the desk hangs her diploma from Stanford, magna cum laude, of course. Next to it is a framed letter with a signature scribbled on the bottom: Murray Gell-Mann. I recognize the name from Heller's book. Gell-Mann was a pioneer in quantum physics; he's the guy who came up with the word *quark*. The letter seems to be a reply to a letter that Tali sent. It's dated April twenty-ninth, 2001. Tali would have been just a little girl at the time; evidently Gell-Mann was a hero of hers. The letter is short but encouraging; it must have meant a lot to Tali to get a letter like that.

I notice a variation in color in the backing behind the letter. I remove it from the wall and open the frame. Behind the letter is an envelope with a thirty-four cent stamp in the corner. On the opposite corner is Murray Gell-Mann's address at the University of New Mexico. In the center of the envelope is scrawled Tali's address in San Francisco. Out the window, I see Heller approaching the workshop. I slip the envelope into my jacket and put the frame back on the wall. Heller opens the door bearing another bottle of whiskey.

"Who is this?" I ask, pretending to be transfixed on the picture. "With Tali?"

"Her sister, Beth."

"She's …" I start, but can't think of how to finish the sentence.

"I know."

"Have you met her?"

He shakes his head.

"Are they close?"

"She's … Tali doesn't talk about her personal life much."

He pours me another drink. I decide I'm done after this one. Heller is a pleasant enough guy, but I still don't trust him and I don't really want to get too chummy. Not until I know more about what's going on with Tali. For all I know, he was behind her disappearance.

"I should go," I say, standing up. "Thanks for the drink. Give me a call if you hear anything from Tali." I could ask him to let me know about any more cases that come up, but I don't.

"Of course," he says.

I walk to my car and drive north on 101 toward San Francisco. After stopping for dinner at a taco place in San Mateo, I continue into the city, toward the address on the envelope. It's in the Pacific Heights area, not far from the Embarcadero. I park at a free meter and walk a couple blocks to the address. By now it's starting to get dark. I walk up the steps and knock on the door.

A small woman with thick, wavy gray hair opens the door. She looks like she's in her mid-fifties. Her resemblance to Tali is unmistakable. She's got the same build, the same little nose. But there's something not quite right about her, and it's not just her age. She's got a sort of exhausted look, like a hunted animal. "Yes?" she says.

"Hello, ma'am," I say awkwardly. "Are you Tali Stern's mother?"

"Are you with Peregrine?" she asks. "I already told that other man I don't know where she is."

Again with the questions about Peregrine. Are they somehow involved in Tali's disappearance?

"No, ma'am," I say. "I'm a friend of Tali's," I say. "She was supposed to meet me for dinner the other night, but she never showed up, and I just wanted to make sure she's OK."

"Tali gave you this address?"

"Who is it?" I hear a man's voice bark from behind her.

"Friend of Tali's," she says over her shoulder. I catch a glimpse of an older man sitting alone in an easy chair.

"I … found this address on some paperwork on her desk. I didn't know where else to look."

"Tali's not here," she says.

"Have you heard from her? In the past few days?"

"Is it the girls?" says the man's voice. "When are the girls coming home?"

"No, honey," the woman says over her shoulder. "It's not the girls. Read your book, OK?"

"I haven't heard from Tali in a long time," says the woman. "I'm sure you have a better idea where she is than I do." She starts to retreat back inside.

"What about Beth?" I ask.

She looks at me as if I've got spiders crawling out of my eyes.

"When are the girls coming home?" says the man again.

She bites her lip. "You should leave now," she says.

"I'm sorry, ma'am. Did something happen to Beth? I don't –"

"You're a friend of Tali's, huh? And she didn't tell you?"

"She didn't say much about Beth," I say. "I just found out she had a sister."

She regards me suspiciously for a moment. "Beth is in the hospital. Please leave."

"Sarah, when are the girls coming home?"

"I'm sorry," I say. "Was there an accident? Please, Mrs. Stern, I'm just …"

"You need to leave now. My husband needs me."

"Sarah!" The voice is angry now.

"Could you tell me which hospital?"

"Mount Zion," she says, and slams the door.

Through the door I hear, "Was that the girls? When are the girls coming home?"

I start walking back to my car, checking the map on my phone. Mount Zion is only a few blocks away. I put another quarter in the meter and head toward the hospital. I don't know what I'm expecting to find there, but I have this suspicion that everything that's happening is somehow connected. Tali is doing what she's doing because of who she *is*. I feel like I have a rough intuitive sense of Tali's personality, but that same intuition is telling me that I'm missing something. And whatever it is, it has to do with her sister, Beth.

It occurs to me that I'm thinking like Ananke, trying to puzzle out Tali as if she were the sum of all the causal factors that brought her into being – thinking that if I only knew more about her, I could figure out why she disappeared, why she was in Alameda, and where she is now. But people don't work like that, reacting mechanically to stimuli. Do they? I'm beginning to wonder. Did Tali choose to stand me up or were her actions the result of phenomena completely out of her control? Neither option is particularly reassuring.

I get to the hospital and ask to see a patient named Beth Stern. Surprisingly, the receptionist doesn't give my any trouble. She just points down a hall and gives me a room number. I head that direction.

The door to the room is open a crack and a man's voice is emanating quietly from inside. I can't make out what he's saying. I push the door open farther and see an elderly, bearded man wearing a yarmulke sitting in a chair, bent over the bed. He appears to be reading to her, but the words are foreign to me. I assume it's Yiddish or Hebrew.

When he finishes, he turns and smiles at me, beckoning for me to come in. I approach the bed and see the woman that was in the picture with Tali. She looks much the same, but more peaceful. She seems to be in a deep sleep.

"I'm Rabbi Freedman," says the man, standing to shake my hand. "You are a friend of Beth's?"

"I … know her sister, Tali," I say. "My name is Paul Bayes."

"Ah, Tali," says the rabbi, nodding.

"You know Tali?" I ask.

"Sure," he says. "I've known them both for years. Tali's a sweet girl."

"Have you heard from her recently? In the past few days?"

He shakes his head. "No, no. But Tali never had much use for me." He shrugs as if to say *what are you gonna do?* "Why? Has something happened to Tali?"

"I'm not sure," I say. "Nobody has heard from her for a few days."

"So you came here to look for her?"

"Honestly, I'm not sure why I'm here. Looking for clues, I guess."

He nods, seeming to understand. "They are close," he says. "Tali, she makes other people's burdens her own."

This guy knows Tali all right. "If you don't mind my asking," I say, "what happened to Beth? What's wrong with her?"

"Overdose," he says. "Xanax. She had a prescription, of course, for anxiety. She's been in a coma for six months now. I come once a week to read to her and pray."

"Oh," I say. I don't have to ask if it was accidental. I know enough about Xanax to have a rough idea how many you'd have to take to slip into a coma. After a moment, I say, "Is there anything that can be done?"

"Sure," he says, smiling. "I'm doing it."

He reads another psalm to her and then we sit quietly for a while. Finally, I say, "What made her do it?"

He sighs, shakes his head. He doesn't speak for a long time. Then he says, "You know what's wonderful about children?" he says. "They don't understand the distinction between what's *in here* —" he thumps his chest — "and what's *out there*. They just *are*, you understand? A child is only aware of right now, the continuous interplay of the ego and sensory phenomena. They have no sense of how big the universe is or how small they are in comparison. A young child feels like she's the center of the universe, and in some ways she's right.

"Eventually, of course, children grow up, and a big part of growing up is building a sort of mental wall between what's in here – me, myself – and the outside world. It's tragic, in way, because dreams and imagination are often casualties. Dreams span the two worlds, you see, the *in here* and the *out there*. We tell children to use their imaginations, to hold onto their dreams, but what we really mean is that if they're going to have dreams, they should reel them back behind the wall. Because if you've got breaches in the wall where your dreams can get out, then stuff from outside the wall can come in through those breaches too. So there's the real world and there's imaginary stuff, and you want to make sure you know which is which, because otherwise you're going to get taken advantage of. And I say it's tragic, but really there's no way around it; the world is no place for people who can't tell the real from the imaginary. There are bad people out there who will use the breaches in your wall to get to you.

"The absolute worst thing that can happen to a child, though, is for one of those people to come along while the child is happily constructing her wall and say, 'Your wall is in the wrong place. Here, let me help you.' Essentially what this person is doing is defining new boundaries of reality. Not only that, but he's actually redefining *who she is* in relation to the rest of the world. And usually what he does is to build her wall in such a way as to specifically let in the sorts of people the wall is meant to keep out. Eventually she realizes that her wall is all wrong, but by then it's too late to do much about it. She withdraws as far as she can inside the wall, but it doesn't really help, because this horrible mess of a wall is still there." He stops for a moment and looks into my eyes. "Do you understand, Paul?"

I nod dumbly. "Are you ... that is, should you be telling me all this?"

"I'm not revealing anything that was said in confidence, if that's what you're wondering," he replies. "And I don't have any solid evidence of what happened. But I've seen and heard enough to know."

A queasy sensation has taken hold in my gut. Puzzle pieces are falling into place. I understand the sadness on Beth's face in that picture and I understand the hunted look in the eyes of her mother. That helpless old man in the chair hadn't always been so helpless.

Now I also understand Tali's need to do something, *anything* to make things right, even if she's doing the wrong thing half the time. How long was Tali aware of what was going on with her sister? How long did she have to sit there and do nothing, because there was nothing she could do? I reflect that Tali started tampering with events shortly after Beth's suicide attempt. Tali probably just couldn't take it anymore, sitting at Beth's side, once again unable to take any meaningful action to help her sister. She had to do something, even if it was wrong.

"Did Tali ..." I start. "That is, was she ..."

"I don't think so," says Rabbi Freedman. "Tali won't open up to me, of course, but I've dealt with enough of this sort of thing that I can usually see the signs. In my opinion, Beth was the only one of the two who was ..." He trails off. After a moment, he adds, "That isn't to say Tali hasn't suffered greatly. Being a witness to great evil and being unable to do anything about it ... it's a heavy burden."

"I should go," I say, getting uneasily to my feet.

"I was just about to leave myself. Would you care to get a drink with me, Paul?"

"Um," I reply, a little disconcerted by the thought of going out for drinks with a rabbi. "Sure, I suppose."

We leave the hospital and the rabbi takes me to my car. I follow him to a local bar. On the way over, the openings to a lot of bad jokes pop into my head, but I do my best to ignore them. I meet him at the entrance and we go in and find a table. "So, Paul," says the rabbi when we've gotten our drinks, "what's bothering you?"

Jeez, is it that obvious? I shrug. "I'm worried about Tali."

"You barely know Tali."

"She … had an effect on me," I say. "I suppose you could say I'm smitten."

"Or infatuated," says the rabbi.

"'Smitten' makes me sound less creepy."

He laughs. "You're not a creep. I've known a lot of creeps, and you're not one."

"That's good to know. Maybe a schmuck, then."

"Maybe," he says, smiling. "I can't blame you for being smitten by Tali, though. She's quite something. Has she really gone missing?"

"Seems like it. She was supposed to meet me for dinner on Wednesday but never showed. Her boss, Dr. Heller, hasn't seen her since Monday. I stopped by her parents' house, but …"

The rabbi shakes his head. "The mother, Sarah, she's a not a bad woman, but she's weak-willed. The opposite of Tali, in many ways. She takes the path of least resistance. And the father …"

"Yeah," I say. "He's one of the creeps."

"To put it mildly," says the rabbi. "He's got dementia, Alzheimer's. The *Paskudnyak*. He forgets, thinks his daughters are still little girls. He doesn't remember any of it. There's a Yiddish curse, *Zol er krenken un gedenken*. Let him suffer and remember. But his slate is washed clean, and he's not even dead yet! I could kill him, you know? But vengeance belongs to the Lord. Anyway, you were telling me about Tali."

"Not much else to tell," I say. "Nobody seems to know where she is. I've been stood up before, but I just didn't get the impression …"

He shakes his head. "If Tali said she would meet you, she planned to meet you. That girl, I don't think she'd tell a lie to save her life."

"That's pretty much the impression I got," I say.

"So what's bothering you?" he asks.

I'm confused. "I just told you, Tali is missing. I'm worried about her."

"Tali is a smart girl. She knows how to avoid being a victim. I suspect that whatever trouble she's in – if she is in trouble – is of her own making. And you can't save her from that."

"Maybe," I say. After a moment, I add, "She saved me from mine."

"Really?" he says. "How did she do that?"

"It's hard to explain," I say, haltingly. "I was considering suicide. Tali talked me out of it."

He smiles. "That's Tali," he says. "She doesn't tolerate quitters. Why did you want to kill yourself?"

"Do I need a reason? I don't mean to be glib, Rabbi, but if you're going to insist on being reasonable, why not ask me what reason I have to live? It goes both ways, right? If I need a reason to kill myself, don't I need to have a reason to go on living?"

"Life is its own reason," he says. "All living creatures want to live. They can't help it. Only human beings can employ reason, and only human beings commit suicide. That's because reason, if left unchecked, can cause a person to doubt his purpose. The universe is just as absurd for a snail as it is for a human being; the difference is that the snail doesn't care."

"But when you say life is its own reason, what you're really saying is that life just *is*. That it just goes on *without* a reason."

"What I'm saying is that meaning is not reducible to axioms."

"So the answer is not to think too much?"

"The answer is to subjugate reason to a higher purpose. Do you know the story of Abraham sacrificing his son, Isaac?"

"Sure," I say. "God commands Abraham to kill his son, but at the last minute God changes His mind and provides a ram for him to sacrifice instead."

"We cannot know the mind of God," says the rabbi. "So we cannot say whether He 'changed his mind.' But we know that God commanded Abraham to sacrifice Isaac, and that Abraham apparently intended to do as God commanded. Once Abraham had demonstrated his willingness to obey, God relented. Scholars disagree on the meaning of the text, but the most common interpretation is that God was testing Abraham. So, we should ask, what is the nature of this test? In short, I would argue that it is a matter of forcing Abraham to choose faith over reason. Abraham was a good man, and a reasonable man; he knew that murdering his son was wrong. There was no way for him to rationalize the act in his mind. It simply was not reasonable. But Abraham believed, despite the obvious irrationality of the act, that somehow things would work out for the best. He had enough faith to overcome his reasonable objections."

"Thus setting the precedent for religious fanatics and suicide bombers all over the world," I say.

"The existence of counterfeits doesn't disprove the existence of the genuine article," says the rabbi, unfazed. "Plenty of schizophrenics claim to hear God speaking to them, but hearing God talking to you doesn't necessarily mean you're a schizophrenic. Nor does it mean you're an unstable religious fanatic. It could simply mean, as with Abraham or Moses, that God is talking to you."

"But the outcome is the same, right? Whether Abraham was schizophrenic or a prophet, he heard a voice telling him to kill his son. Frankly, I'd prefer to think he was crazy. The alternative is that God is evil. Or insane. Sorry, I don't mean any offense. I just …"

"No need to apologize. But you're mistaken. The outcome was not the same. If Abraham had been crazy, the voice in his head wouldn't have told him to stop. Isaac would have died."

"So Abraham is only an attempted murderer. And God isn't evil; he's just a sadist. Or indecisive."

"Or perhaps He was merely trying to communicate something very important to Abraham. That even when human reason fails, God will provide a way."

I shrug. "Seems like a pretty cruel way to make a point."

"Human sacrifice was common among the tribes in that area at the time. The remarkable thing about the story, the reason that it is still told today, is that God relented in His demand. The story contrasts the true God with other gods by showing that He is a God of love."

"He's got a funny way of showing it."

"It got Abraham's attention," says the rabbi. "If it makes you feel better, some scholars think that Abraham knew that God would change his mind at the last minute."

"So, what? Abraham was calling God's bluff?"

"Exactly. We usually think of God testing Abraham, but what if Abraham was also testing God? Can you imagine the chutzpah? Abraham goes up the mountain thinking, 'Sure, the Almighty God told me to kill my son, but He'll back down, just watch.' Unbelievable! But even so, it took an incredible amount of faith on Abraham's part. He was so confident in God's goodness that he knew God wouldn't allow him to kill Isaac. So in a sense you could say that Abraham's behavior was rational, but it was only rational if he accepted the premise that God was good. The belief in the goodness of God came first; reasoning based on that belief came second. If Abraham had only reason and not faith, he could never have passed the test."

"And everyone would have lived happily ever after."

"Sure," says the rabbi with a smile. "The way you were living happily ever after before you met Tali."

"Fine," I say, finishing my drink. "Kick a guy when he's down. I should probably get home." I throw some money on the table and get up.

"I'm not trying to convince you of anything, Paul. But I can tell you're a very smart, very analytical person. You remind me of Tali in some ways. And just like Tali, you're in danger of outsmarting yourself."

"It was nice talking to you, rabbi," I say. "Goodnight."

"Goodnight, Paul. Get some rest."

I walk out of the bar and trudge to my car. The stars twinkle mutely overhead. Some days I wish the voice of God would speak to me, but it never does. That's not my particular brand of crazy. All I hear is an old man's voice repeating: *When are the girls going to come home?*

I should go home, but I really don't feel like being alone right now. I want to be with my kids, to hear them playing in the next room, like they used to back before my life went to hell. I know it's not going to be like it was, but I drive to the house anyway. I'm willing to accept a pale copy of the way things used to be. I'm willing to put up with Deb's abuse and the kids' resentment, just to see them, to make sure they're OK.

I ring the doorbell and brace myself for Deb's onslaught. But Sylvia answers the door. "Hey, Dad," she says, acknowledging my presence without betraying any emotion. Indifference is the best I get from her these days. She turns around and starts to walk away, probably back to the TV show whose laugh track emanates from the living room.

"Sylvia," I say, standing uncertainly on the stoop. I know her well enough to understand that her response is calculated, a deliberate attempt to put me off guard. The door is open, she's saying. Why don't you come in? Oh, that's right, this isn't your house anymore.

"Is Mom home?" I ask.

"She's upstairs."

"Could you get her?" I ask, trying not to let my frustration show. The same rules apply to estranged spouses as to vampires: you can't come in unless you're invited.

Sylvia dawdles a moment, shrugs, and then yells upstairs. "Mom! Dad's here!" Then she disappears into the living room. A couple minutes later Deb comes downstairs. She's wearing a bathrobe and her hair is wet.

"What is it, Paul?"

"Hi, Deb. Sorry to stop by without calling; I just really wanted to see the kids. May I come in?"

"This isn't really a good time, Paul. You can't just show up like this."

"I know, I know. I just had a really bad … several really bad days, in fact."

"The school's been calling here. You haven't been showing up for work."

"I quit," I say.

"You should tell them that."

"I think they've figured it out. Please, Deb. I won't stay long."

She hesitates for a moment. "Five minutes, Paul. I mean it." She goes back upstairs.

I step inside. From the foyer I can see into the living room, where Martin and Sylvia are enthralled in one of those horrible Disney sitcoms where everybody overacts and the laugh track is deafening. "Hey, guys," I say. No response. I wait a moment. "Hey, guys," I say louder. Still nothing. I find myself getting angry. It's not their fault, I tell myself. They don't understand what I need, and it isn't their job to give it to me. They're just kids.

"Martin, could you pause the show a minute?" I say. I've got to speak loudly to be heard over the caterwauling of the show, and it comes out as a near-yell. Martin shows no sign of having heard me. I walk over to him, take the remote out of his hand, hit the pause button, and set the remote back down on the arm of couch. Neither of them looks up.

"Hey, guys," I say for the third time, irritation creeping into my voice. "Could you look at me a second?"

Neither of them looks. I see Martin reaching for the remote, but I grab it before he can get to it. I hurl it against the wall; batteries go flying. That gets their attention. They're both staring at me now, with fear in their eyes. Great.

I hear Deb coming down the stairs. "What was that?" she says, coming into the living room.

"I'm sorry," I say, hurriedly going to fetch the remote.

"Dad threw it against the wall," says Martin.

"It scared me, Mommy," says Sylvia, leaping into her mother's arms.

Jesus Christ, somebody give this kid an Oscar. I'm down on my hands and knees, trying to find the damn batteries. One has rolled under the couch.

"I think your time is up," says Deb acidly.

"I'm sorry," I say again. "I just … Goddamn it. Sylvie, can you reach under the couch and get the battery? My arm is too big."

"Paul."

"Martin," I say, "can you get it?"

Martin doesn't move.

"It's OK," I say. "I'll just move the couch. Can you get up for a sec, Martin?"

Martin looks up at his mom, but he doesn't get up.

"Paul, we'll get it. Just go, please."

I throw my shoulder into the couch, shoving it back a foot or so. Martin nearly tumbles onto the floor. I grab the battery, snap it into place and slide the cover on. I toss it to Martin. "There! Now you can watch your fucking retard show!"

Trembling with fury, I get to my feet. I leave, slamming the door behind me. I get into my car, drive down the street a quarter mile or so and pull over. I don't want to have a breakdown in front of the house, but I know I'm in no condition to drive. I slam my fists repeatedly against the steering wheel, letting loose a minute-long string of profanity.

Why am I so angry? I acted like a complete asshole in there. I want to go back and apologize, but I know I'll just make things worse. What the hell is my problem? I take a few deep breaths, put the car back in gear, and head for my apartment.

Once back home, I make myself a drink and sit down. Occasionally I think that I drink too much, but more often I'm convinced that I don't drink enough. I honestly think I might be better off if I put more effort into short-circuiting my critical thinking abilities on a regular basis. I spend way too much time second-guessing myself and reflecting on my own shortcomings. You'd think that being hyper-aware of your own failings would lead to being a better person, but it never seems to work out that way. I'm self-conscious without being self-aware.

I can see exactly where I went wrong. Hell, I could see where I was *going* to go wrong before I even showed up at the house. And that's exactly the problem: I knew that going to see the kids was a bad idea but I did it anyway. And then, when I was proved correct, I got mad about it. Why? Because I knew it was a bad idea, but I did it anyway. I'm mad at myself for doing something that I knew I was going to be mad at myself about.

It's Heller's fault, I think. Him and that damn book. He's got me looking for the hand of Ananke wherever I go. And the more you look for it, the more you see it, and the angrier you get that she won't just leave you alone. And then the anger blinds you to any other options you might have, and you end up making exactly the mistakes Ananke knew you would make. And that just makes you angrier.

There was a band that was popular when I was in college called Rage Against the Machine. But that's not right, I realize now. You can't rage against the machine; rage is *part* of the machine. If you're going to have any chance of extricating yourself from the machine's gears, you've got to act calmly and deliberately, with a clear head.

On the other hand, if Heller is right, then acting rationally is no help either: Ananke can anticipate rational behavior as easily as irrational. Maybe, I think, the only option is to get stinking drunk. I pour myself another and think about what Rabbi Freedman said about subjugating reason to a higher power. The true God is a God of love, he said. So you have to put reason aside and start with love, and then everything presumably starts to make sense. But how can you put reason aside? How can you force yourself to stop looking for reasons, even for a moment? It's all well and good to say, 'start with love and go from there,' but why pick *love* of all things? Why not hatred or blind religious devotion or Cthulhu or the Flying Spaghetti Monster? Once you put reason aside, you've opened yourself up to all sorts of superstition and nonsense. The kind of shit that makes people fly airplanes into buildings. I mean, suicide bombers aren't irrational people; they're perfectly capable of making rational decisions on a day-to-day basis. What sets them apart from normal people is that one little gap in their ability to reason, that moment where they set reason aside and said, "Oh, Allah wants me to blow myself up to glorify Him? Makes sense to me!" And I still don't see the difference between God telling Abraham to kill Isaac and God telling a man to strap explosives to his body and walk into a crowded marketplace in Baghdad. If you've got to actually kill someone to find out whether you've been listening to the wrong god, then the true God really needs a better way of vetting his prophets.

My thoughts drift back to what Rabbi Freedman said at the hospital. He talked about how children live in the moment; how they don't have a good sense for the difference between the subjective and the objective, what he called the *in here* and the *out there*. Maybe that's why we get drunk, I think: It blurs that line, tears down that wall for a few hours. There's no longer any observer and observed, no Yang and Yin, just raw consciousness, the here and now. Three drinks later, and that's gone too.

The next morning I awake with a word in my head: Peregrine. I don't know how they are involved in what's going on with Tali, but I'm convinced they are somehow involved. Heller mentioned Peregrine the first time I saw him, and apparently someone from Peregrine went looking for Tali at her parents' house shortly before she disappeared. If I was going to figure out what happened to Tali, Peregrine was a good place to start.

I find the business card that I had pilfered from Tali's desk and call the number. A man answers.

"Peter Girell," he says.

"Hello, Mr. Girell," I start awkwardly. "My name is Paul Bayes. I'm calling you because I'm a friend of Tali Stern."

"Yes?" he says.

"Do you know Tali?"

"I've met her, yes. What's this about?"

"Well, Tali is missing. Nobody's seen her for a few days. I found your business card on her desk, and I thought you might be able to shed some light on her disappearance."

"I see," he replies. For a moment, neither of us speaks. I take it from his reply that he knows something, but isn't overly eager to talk about it.

"If you have some time free today," I say, "I'd be happy to meet you at your office. Are you at the Peregrine building in the city?"

"I don't work at Peregrine anymore," he says curtly.

"Oh," I say. "I'm sorry. Well, if there's—"

"Are you a cop?" he asks.

"No," I reply. "Just a friend of Tali's."

He's quiet for another moment. Then: "I'll meet you at the Starbucks on Huntington, in San Bruno, at eleven o'clock. Does that work for you?"

"I'll see you at eleven," I reply.

"I'll be wearing a green jacket," he says. "Don't be late."

It's already after ten, and San Bruno is a good forty-five minutes away, so I get in my car and start driving. Traffic is unusually light and I get to the Starbucks ten minutes early. I order a coffee and wait for Girell to show up. At three minutes to eleven, a stout, balding man in his mid-thirties wearing a green windbreaker walks in. I wave to him and he sits down across from me. His jacket reads *Ray's Auto Body*.

"You're Paul?" he says.

I nod. "Thanks for meeting me, Mr. Girell."

"You said Tali Stern is missing?"

"Well, not officially," I say. "I don't think a missing persons report has been filed or anything. But nobody has seen her for a few days, and I'm starting to get a little worried."

"And you're what, her boyfriend?" He's looking at my left hand. I wonder if he can see the pale band where my wedding ring used to be.

"Just a friend," I say.

He regards me for a moment. The same look I got from Heller, trying to figure out if I'm some kind of nutcase stalker. He seems to decide I'm not. "What makes you think I would know something?"

"Nothing, really," I admit. "I found your business card on Tali's desk. Also, Tali's mother said someone from Peregrine had come looking for her. It seemed a little strange to me."

He nods. "It is strange."

"So it wasn't you, then?"

"Me?" He says. "No, I told you, I don't work for Peregrine anymore. The bastards fired me."

"Fired you? Why?"

He pauses, then says, "Look, I don't know if this has anything to do with Tali, but I'll tell you what happened to me."

"OK," I say.

"Hang on, I need some coffee."

He gets his coffee and comes back to tell his story.

"Do you know Dr. Heller?" he asks.

"I've met him, yes."

"And you know the sort of stuff he's working on?"

"More or less."

"OK, so a little over a year ago," he says, "a very strange accident occurred in Dr. Heller's shop. An electrical fire. Destroyed most of Heller's shop. Peregrine held the policy, and I was sent to investigate the claim. My job was to determine whether Heller's activities in the shop nullified his policy. Peregrine is rather strict about such things; the policy we had underwritten for Heller specified that the shop was to be used primarily for theoretical pursuits. Using a welder or soldering iron on site wouldn't void the policy, but any large scale industrial activity or inherently dangerous experiments would. What Heller was doing was right on the line, so I had to conduct several extensive interviews with Heller. Frankly, I couldn't make heads or tails out of what he was saying. Quantum probability mumbo-jumbo."

"I know the feeling," I say.

"What made the accident even more suspicious was that Heller's partner had died there six months earlier. Another physicist, some kind of Eastern European name."

"Emil Jelinek," I said, remembering the obituary on Heller's wall. "He was killed in Heller's shop?"

"Yeah. Some kind of accident involving a valve breaking off a tank of pressurized gas, supposedly. The police investigated but they couldn't find any evidence of foul play. Still, it seemed fishy that this fire happened just six months after that accident.

Anyway, I interviewed Heller a bunch of times and after each interview I left more confused than when I started. I don't know if Heller's work really is that complicated, or if he was just screwing with me. He seemed to be enjoying himself. I eventually gave up and escalated the matter to my boss, a guy named David Carlyle. Carlyle went out to see Heller. I don't know what Heller told him exactly, but Carlyle ended up denying the claim. I thought the matter was settled. But then three weeks later Carlyle calls me into his office and says he's got some documents he needs Heller to sign. The documents basically said that Peregrine would be canceling his policy based on the fact that we believed, as a result of our investigation, that his work was a fraud. I should have known right then that something was off."

"What do you mean?"

"Well, first of all, like I said, I couldn't even make any sense of what Heller was saying. I'm sure Carlyle is smarter than me, but it's not like he's some kind of quantum physics guru. How the hell did he determine that Heller's work was a 'fraud' after meeting with him one time? He's not qualified to make that kind of assessment. And what does Peregrine care if Heller's a fraud? They've insured everybody from strip clubs to palm readers. They'd be out of business pretty damn quick if they insisted on doing an ethical review on every client."

"Maybe they wanted to cancel the policy for some other reason," I suggest.

"That's the thing," he says. "There are plenty of good reasons to cancel a policy. Usually they do it because they've decided they aren't making enough money on the policy to justify the risk. It's not like it's a big secret. Hell, they don't even need to *give* a reason. They can just send a letter saying, 'We've decided to drop you, tough luck.' I've never once been sent out to a client with paperwork explaining why the company is canceling their policy. I asked Carlyle what was so special about this case, but he wouldn't tell me. He made it pretty clear that if I wanted to keep working at Peregrine, I'd shut up and deliver the papers. So that's what I did."

"How did Heller take it?" I ask.

"You've met Heller," he says. "How do you think he took it?"

"Not well."

"That's an understatement. He chased me off his property. He was *furious*. I thought he was going to have a coronary. And if you ask me, that's exactly what Carlyle had in mind."

"You think he was trying to kill Heller with paperwork?"

"Not kill him. Piss him off."

"Why?"

"That's the real question, isn't it? I never found the answer. A week later I was fired. Carlyle denied knowing anything about the paperwork, said I had 'gone rogue.' Like I just couldn't resist the urge to drive out to a client with some bogus paperwork I had written up. It was total bullshit. Carlyle just wanted to get rid of me, and I don't even know why. I heard a few weeks later that Heller was suing them, but I never heard who won the suit. Like I said, I don't know if any of this has anything to do with Tali's disappearance, but that's what happened to me."

I nod. "Well, it's definitely suspicious."

"Yeah," he says. "Look, I've got to get back to work. I don't know what else I can tell you, but you have my number if you have any more questions."

"OK," I say. "Thanks."

He nods, finishes his coffee, and leaves.

I sit for a while thinking about what he's told me. I'm more convinced than ever that Peregrine had something to do with Tali's disappearance, but Girell's story makes no sense to me. Assuming Girell was right about Carlyle trying to provoke Heller, what could his motive possibly be? Was Heller's lawsuit against Peregrine part of Carlyle's plan, or was it an unintended side effect? What was Carlyle trying to accomplish?

As I leave the coffee shop, I make a mental note to look into Heller's lawsuit against Peregrine. I walk to my car and begin driving home. I'm just walking in the door of my apartment when my phone rings. It's Heller's number.

"Hello?"

"Paul?"

"Yep."

"Have you told anyone about Ananke? Or about what Tali and I have been doing?"

"No." I decide not to tell him about my conversation with Peter Girell. Besides, I didn't tell Girell anything he didn't already know.

"You're certain? This is very important. You've told no one about Tyche, the detectors …"

"No, Dr. Heller. No one. Who would I tell, my ex-wife?" Like she needs another reason to think I'm nuts.

"All right," he says, sounding a bit skeptical.

"Why? What is it?"

"I'm seeing a spike in the data. Lots of cases all of a sudden."

"So?"

"Spikes like this are rare. The PDC numbers tend to average out over time. A sudden increase points to an external cause. To put it bluntly, Ananke doesn't like publicity. If you told someone about what we're doing, it might cause her to … react negatively."

"Well, I didn't tell anyone. Maybe Tali …?"

"No, no," he says. "Tali knows the dangers. She wouldn't say anything."

Not willingly, maybe. But if Tali's being interrogated by the NSA or somebody, there's no telling what she might do. Frankly, I think Heller's jumping to conclusions. I don't see how telling anybody about their little scheme is going to cause a rash of tragedies in the Bay Area.

"What kind of stuff are you seeing?" I ask. "More cases like the fire yesterday?"

"It's an across the board increase in the PDC," he says. "It looks like the level of noise in the network is increasing across the whole detection area. I've never seen anything like it."

"Maybe it's a problem with your equipment."

"What equipment? I've got nearly 300 hundred detectors up, each individually reporting data. Unless they've all decided to suddenly develop exactly the same malfunction, I don't see how it can be the equipment."

"You're the expert," I say. What does he want from me?

"There is one case that stands out," he says. "And it has a crux, in Alameda. Isn't that near you?"

Ah, here we go. "I think I'm done interfering, Dr. Heller. In case you haven't figured it out yet, I'm kind of a basket case lately. I don't think it's good for me to go out of my way to witness horrible tragedies."

"I understand," says Heller. "And I wouldn't ask, except that I'm afraid this spike might have something to do with Tali's disappearance. I don't think she would deliberately tell anyone about Tyche, but there's got to be some sort of connection. Maybe if you go there, you can find some clue about what's happened to Tali."

"That sounds like a stretch," I say. "Even if Tali's disappearance has something to do with this noise in your network, what makes you think she's somehow involved with this particular event?"

"It's a long shot," he admits. "But it's all I've got. I'd go myself, but I can't get there in time. The crux is just over half an hour from now."

"I don't have the randomizer. I wouldn't be able to stop the event."

"You don't need to stop it. You just need to observe it, look for anything out of the ordinary."

"*Observe* it?" I say in disbelief. "You mean you want me to go to the scene of a horrific tragedy and witness a bunch of people dying violently without any chance of stopping it?"

He's silent for a moment. I don't think it occurred to him to think of it that way. Something in Heller's brain is a little off. "OK," he says, uncertainly. "If you want to try to tamper ..."

"I don't want to do anything! I want to be left alone!"

"Then the event will almost certainly occur," he says.

"It's got nothing to do with me," I say. "If you hadn't called, I wouldn't even know about it."

"But you do know about it. So by not attempting to stop it, you're allowing it to happen. You're allowing people to die."

"A moment ago you didn't give a shit about those people," I retort. "And now you want to be the angel on my fucking shoulder? Fuck you, Heller. Anyway, I don't have time to get the randomizer. I couldn't stop it if I wanted to."

"You don't actually need the randomizer," he says. "That is, you don't need it on you."

"What the hell are you talking about? You told me that the randomizer is the only way to tamper with the event. The case, whatever."

"No, I told you that the randomizer is one way to inject true randomness into the situation. There are other ways."

"Whatever. It's not my problem." I hang up.

Jesus Christ, what does any of this have to do with me? I fall for a pretty girl at the BART station and now suddenly it's my job to be the guardian angel of the entire Bay Area? Fuck that. I need to get on with my life. Forget about Tali, try to figure out how to make amends with Martin and Sylvia. Maybe get them some kind of present? Yeah, buy their affection. That always works. Also? You don't have any money. Or a job.

I pace across my tiny apartment for a few minutes, trying to avoid the sad truth: as bad as witnessing the tragic deaths of several people would be, I can't imagine it would be any worse than hanging around this shitty apartment all day. If the weather was decent, I might go to a park and read for a few hours, but it's cold and windy. So I've got nothing to do but sit and think about a tragedy that I might have prevented. Fuck!

I call Heller back. I know he's manipulating me, that he doesn't care about whether those people in Alameda live or die, but it doesn't really matter. I can't just sit here and do nothing.

"Hello?" says Heller's voice.

"What do you mean, I don't need the randomizer?"

"Are you going to do it? Go to the Alameda crux?"

"Yes."

"Are you in your car?"

"Not yet."

"You'd better get going. I'll explain while you're driving."

"All right. Call me back in two minutes."

I get in the car and start toward Alameda. Heller calls me back and I put him on speaker. He tells me the crux is at an intersection downtown, in about ten minutes. When I ask him about the randomizer, he says that the critical part of the randomizer is the part that detects the radioactive decay, because that's the part that actually injects randomness. He says he can hit the button on the device in his shop and text me with the result.

"But I need some way of interfering with the coin toss," I say.

"A push should do it," he says.

"What do you mean, a push?"

"I mean give the target a shove. Right before they toss the coin."

"You're nuts."

"Why?" he asks.

"You mean physically shoving the person."

"Correct. If you time it right, you'll interfere with the toss."

"What do you need the randomizer for, if you could interfere by just shoving people?"

"As I said, the important part of the randomizer is the decay detector. That's what generates randomness. How you translate that randomness into an effect on the macro scale is immaterial. I'll trigger the randomizer here a few seconds before the crux and text you the results. If the randomizer emits a pulse, I'll text you a one, and if it doesn't, I'll text you a zero. You give the target a shove if I text you a one."

"How do I know they will even go through with the toss if I shove them?"

"You don't. The crux may turn out to be a phantom in the data."

"You mean I'll prevent the crux from happening, which means the event will occur as if I hadn't tampered with it."

"Six of one," says Heller. "Counterfactuals …"

"Yeah, yeah," I say. No time for another philosophical quagmire. "How hard do I have to shove them?"

"Not very. A tap on the shoulder might even do it. But a shove is safer. Just make up your mind exactly what you're going to do before you get my text. It has to be decisive, so there's no question about whether you've interfered or not. And make sure you *only* interfere if I text you a one. If you shove the target either way, then you've removed the randomness."

"And Ananke wins."

"Exactly."

"OK, I'm almost there. Text me the exact time, when you get it."

"I will. Thanks, Paul."

Fuck you, Heller, I think. But I hang up without saying it.

Talking to Heller makes me uneasy in a way I can't quite define. Claustrophobia is the closest thing I can think of, like I'm walking down a long hallway that's gradually, almost imperceptibly narrowing. I know that eventually it's going to narrow to the point where I can't even move, and yet somehow it will still keep narrowing until I'm crushed between the walls. And still the walls will narrow until I'm completely obliterated and the hallway itself disappears. But I can't stop walking.

Heller tells me that thinking in counterfactuals will drive me crazy. Maybe that's true, but *not* thinking in counterfactuals may also drive me crazy. That's what freedom is, right? The ability to make choices. If I look back on everything I've done and think, 'I couldn't possibly have done anything differently,' then what's the point in doing *anything*? So thinking that you should have done something differently drives you crazy and thinking that you couldn't have done anything differently also drives you crazy. Maybe the rabbi was right: I'm going to think myself to death.

I find a parking space on a side street down the road a couple blocks from the crux location. Checking my phone, I see that I've got about three minutes. I jog toward the intersection. When I'm about halfway there, I get a text from Heller reading:

9:43:25. 60 ft sw of xing

Presumably that means sixty feet southwest of the intersection. My timing is just about perfect; I see a group of teenagers arguing

good-naturedly about something just past the intersection. If I walk
briskly, I can get to them right around the time of the crux.
Unfortunately, as I near the intersection, the DON'T WALK sign
begins flashing and the light turns yellow. I can't make it in time.
The light turns red as I get to the edge of the curb, and cars begin
to pull forward. It's not a huge intersection, but there's enough
traffic to block my way. I check my phone: ten seconds. The
teenagers are still arguing. One of them, an Asian kid who looks
around seventeen, is poking around in his pockets. He pulls out a
coin.

Cars are still crossing the intersection with just enough speed
and frequency to make it impossible to cross. My phone beeps. I've
gotten a text from Heller. It reads: 1.

Shit. That means I've got to get across the intersection and
shove the kid before he tosses the coin. For a second, I wonder if
just yelling at him will do it. Yelling should be enough to jolt his
nerves a bit, right? But while I'm considering this, there's a
momentary lull in the traffic and without thinking, I dart into the
street. Turns out I've misjudged the speed of an SUV; the guy slams
on his breaks and slides to a halt, knocking me onto the pavement.
I'm stunned, but I hear the kids gasping and shouting. I look up to
see them staring at me – except for the Asian kid, who is watching a
coin fall. It hits the back of his left hand and he slaps his right palm
over it. "Tails!" he exclaims.

The driver of the SUV, a big, red-faced guy, leans out his
window. "Hey, you OK?" he says. "Why'd you run out in front of
me?"

I wave at him, brushing gravel off my pants. "I'm fine," I say,
not feeling it. No point in shoving the kid now (although I kind of
want to), so I continue onto the sidewalk and walk past the group
of kids. As I'm walking down the sidewalk, I get a one-word text
from Heller:

YES

Heller and I hadn't settled on a formal signal for success, but
that can only mean the tampering worked: I prevented whatever
was going to happen, simply by running out in front of traffic. I

guess I must have given the kid enough of a jolt to alter the result of the toss.

I turn around and see the kids getting into a little old Volkswagen parked near where they were standing. Thankfully, they've lost interest in me. The car pulls away, and I jog after it a little ways. The event location – that is, the location of the event that will no longer happen, is at the intersection, a hundred or so yards away. The light turns red as the Volkswagen approaches, so I have plenty of time to catch up. I check my phone and see that the event time has come and gone. Nothing has happened. And there's no way to know what *might* have happened. People are just going about their business. No accolades for me today. How *does* Tali do this? If you fail, you get to see a bunch of people get killed, and if you succeed, nothing happens. I resist the urge to holler "You're welcome!" to nobody in particular.

I'm about to turn around and head back to my car when something catches my eye. No, not something, *someone*. A pretty brunette in a black coat standing on the sidewalk kitty-corner from me, observing the intersection. Next to her stands a tall, blond man in a dark suit and an overcoat. He says something to her and she replies. Then she walks to a Cadillac parked alongside the street and gets in the backseat. He follows.

I try to yell to her, but I'm still hoarse from yesterday and my rasping call is lost in the noise of traffic. I can't tell if she saw me or not. The Cadillac makes a U-turn and pulls away. Tali is gone.

Part Six: A Ram in the Thicket

Once back at the apartment, I try to make sense of what I've just seen. Why would Tali be at the Alameda site? Who was the man she was with? Did Heller know she would be there? Is there something he's not telling me?

There's definitely something about Heller I don't trust. To the extent that I understand him, his actions seem rational, but there's something wrong with a man who wouldn't lift a finger to prevent a tragedy that was going to kill several people. He would have been perfectly happy to let those people die. It was only my insistence on intervening that saved them. *I* did that, I think. I saved lives today.

On the other hand, yesterday I caused a fire that killed several other people. That's the fair way to look at it, isn't it? I can't take credit for saving lives today if I don't take the blame for yesterday's deaths. If I hadn't interfered at the apartment building in Hayward, the event wouldn't have happened. Tina wouldn't have been distracted from her cooking and there would have been no fire. Would have, could have, should have. Counterfactuals. They're coming to take me away, haha!

I'm also suspicious about the way Heller clams up whenever I mention Tali. There's definitely something he's not telling me. Did he know what Tali was up to? If he knew Tali was going to be in Alameda and he didn't want me to see her, why did he send me there? And if Tali and he were somehow conspiring against me, he would have warned her I would be there. I don't really see Tali as the conspiring type anyway; maybe I'm deluded to think that I understand her, but I still don't believe she intended to stand me

up. Something outside of her control prevented her from meeting
me at Garibaldi's. Something involving the man I saw getting into
the Cadillac with her. Was she being blackmailed somehow?

I wonder if I should tell Heller about seeing Tali. What if he has
something to do with her disappearance? That seems unlikely; I
don't think he's faking his concern for her. And yet, there's clearly
something he's not telling me. Maybe Tali disappeared to get away
from him. That makes some sense: maybe she realized that he's off
his rocker, and she didn't want to work for him anymore. But was
she really so afraid of him that she would disappear without
warning? And why would she make a date – OK, *appointment* – with
me if she knew she wasn't going to make it? What could she have
suddenly found out that made her want to vanish?

But the real question is: who was the man with her in Alameda?
Whoever he was, he's the key to Tali's disappearance. Either he had
taken her against her will or they were conspiring together. It didn't
look like she was being coerced physically, but maybe he had some
other sort of leverage against her. There just isn't any way to know.

I spend the next several hours obsessing over the events of the
past few days, trying to consider some angle I've missed.
Intermittently I turn to Heller's book for clues about his behavior
and what might have driven Tali away. I'm struck by a passage on
free will. This part gets a little abstract, so I won't blame you if you
want to skim it.

Free will is the name we give to the phenomenon of consciousness
causing changes in the physical world around us, and as such it can
only be understood insofar as consciousness itself is understood.
But consciousness (alternately referred to as "awareness") seems to
be one of those things that although we know it when we see it, it's
impossible to define.

One thing we know about consciousness is that it exists only in
the present. Although we can talk about being aware of events that
are going to happen or of events that have happened, we cannot be
aware of the past or future in the same sense that we are aware of
the present. In fact, our awareness of both the past and future are
necessarily filtered through that elusive medium known as the
present. To put it another way, we can be aware *of* the past or
future, but we cannot be aware *in* the past or future.

We can only understand free will in terms of consciousness, and we can only understand consciousness in terms of the present. So what is the present? We tend to think of the present as one of three possible divisions of time: past, present, and future. Oddly, however, the laws of physics have very little to say about these divisions. It's true that entropy moves in one direction, with disorder increasing as we move from the "past" to the "future," but the crucial point is that there is no objective past or future intrinsic in time itself. If we look at time as a line, identifying which part of the line is "past" and which part is "future" is as impossible as determining which part is "left" and which part is "right." It depends on your point of view.

We thus resort to saying that the future is "what hasn't happened yet." But this is merely a restatement of the problem. When we say that something *is happening*, we are saying that some cause is having an effect. But cause and effect are the same in the past, present and future. More precisely, the division between *happened / happening / will happen* is meaningless in terms of the laws of physics. We assume that when a scientist talks about the results of an experiment, she is talking about something that happened in the past, but that is merely a recognition of our limited viewpoint, not an indication of the limitation of the laws of physics. In fact, science assumes that the results of any experiment will be the same as the results of an identical experiment conducted in the past (or future). If this weren't the case – if past results were not indicative of future results – then science would be a pointless pursuit.

As far as the laws of physics are concerned, there is no difference between past and future. So if we are aware of the passage of time but time does not actually pass in any objective sense, then our division of time into past, present and future is an arbitrary artifact of our awareness. Maybe the passage of time is simply the mind's way of making sense of reality. We experience only the present moment because that's all our brains can handle. But in that case, the present is just an arbitrary brain-sized chunk of the universe. Essentially we are creating the present by being aware of it.

This presents us with a strange situation. We've said that consciousness can be understood only in terms of the present, but now we see that the consciousness *creates* the present. So consciousness   somehow   creates   the   medium   in   which consciousness works. This seemingly paradoxical notion is not so strange when we consider consciousness as something that gradually comes into being – which of course it does. An infant's consciousness is rudimentary because he has no sense of the present (conversely, we could say that the infant has no sense of the present because he has only rudimentary consciousness). One might object that in fact the infant knows *only* the present, but that is saying essentially the same thing. The present can only be understood as the dividing line between the past and the future, and the infant has no sense of either. Experiences flow past him in a seemingly arbitrary manner and disappear without being made into memories. Only gradually does the child start to notice patterns amid the experiences, and these patterns are stored as memories. Then, as new experiences pour in, they are compared against memories. This comparison is the basis for the child's understanding of the past and future, from which arises his awareness of the present.

It's interesting that a child's gradually developing awareness of space occurs in much the same manner as his awareness of time. As an embryo, a child is aware of no distinction between the internal and the external, between *I* and *other*. After the child is born, and as it grows, it is bombarded with sensory input that reinforces the distinction between the subjective and the objective, and it is the awareness of these categories that gives rise to the child's awareness of *self*. But as with *present*, the concept of *self* is an artificial construct arising from this arbitrary division of subjective and objective. If you take a scalpel to the self in an attempt to separate it from the rest of the universe, you'll eventually find you've got nothing left. We've each individually created a concept of self as a sort of survival mechanism, but in a sense there is no such thing as the self.

But if no self exists, then how can a person be said to have free will? How can someone devoid of a self even be considered a person? My intuition is that the typical understanding of free will has the matter backwards: it isn't the self that has free will; it's the will that creates the self.

An embryo has no sense of time or space and therefore has no consciousness. What an embryo *does* have, however, is a will. Like all living things, from a dandelion to a blue whale, an embryo has a desire to live. The will of a three-week old human embryo or a dandelion is weaker and certainly much less well defined than that of a typical adult human, but the will is unmistakably present. For that matter, it's hard to observe millions of spermatozoa desperately trying to reach an egg and fail to see a rudimentary will at work. Life cannot exist without will, and over time (given a sufficiently complex vessel and suitable environment), will gives rise to consciousness – that is, to the self.

Is the self then just an observer, a sort of passive figurehead created by the will? Not exactly. It is clear that once consciousness arises, it can then affect the will in some way. Consider the young athlete who becomes conscious of the value of winning a triathlon and whose will responds with the determination to do just that. So there develops a sort of feedback loop in which the will creates the consciousness and awareness then strengthens (or possibly weakens) the will.

It may be helpful to think of the will as a sort of vitality or "life force" which can, under the right circumstances, give rise to consciousness. Consciousness can then mold the will, for good or ill. So consciousness is not entirely passive, but it is secondary to the will. Consciousness needs the will, but will does not need consciousness. What then of our choices? Is it not the self that is choosing to have a second helping of lasagna rather than a salad? No, it is the will. Although the self can mold the will to an extent, it is always the will that decides. This explains my experience of wanting to choose the salad but being unable to: the self is aware of the consequences of the choice, but it cannot overrule the will. When it comes down to actually making a choice, the self is reduced to an observer. After the choice is made, of course, I will insist that "I" made it, but that is a fiction borne of the fact that I am unable to understand myself as two competing entities in a single mind. It is not I who chooses, but the will.

This part creeps me out a little. I think maybe it's because whenever I hear somebody talking about the "will," I start thinking about Nietzsche and Hitler. It's not just me, right? I mean, basically what he's saying is that there's this sort of primal life force that drives everything we do and that exists before consciousness, rationality, ethics, morality – all the stuff that makes us human. Maybe I'm misrepresenting him, but I picture this life force as existing in a sort of platonic realm somewhere, like a cosmic storeroom. I remember reading about the Jewish myth of the "treasury of souls," which stores souls until the angel Gabriel is ready to stuff one into an embryo. Something like that, anyway. Except that a soul is a complete thing in itself – it's really the person's identity, his personality – or at least the basis of a personality. There's an implication that God created each soul as a unique thing with its own purpose. The way I picture Heller's storeroom, it's more like one of those machines that spits out a glob of plastic or cookie dough or whatever onto an assembly line. The "will" is just an amorphous blob of goo until it gets shaped into something by the machinery of the factory.

The blob of goo has no personality, no rationality, and no sense of right or wrong. Not only that, but it seems like it lacks the capability of *developing* a sense of right or wrong. Heller calls it a "life force," which is a little weird, considering that he deliberately *doesn't* call determinism a force. He personifies the universe and then reduces free will to some kind of abstract force, like gravity or electromagnetism. If the will really is a "force," in this sense, then it's completely unthinking and unfeeling. All it does, all it *can* do, is exert itself in a purely mechanistic way against the rest of the universe. Sure, it can be limited and molded by consciousness and experience, but it seems to me what Heller calls "molding" is really just behavioral conditioning. The will tries to grab a cookie and it gets slapped, so it learns not to grab the cookie. But it doesn't suddenly develop a sense of morality. It's still the same blob of goo, but now it's been squeezed into a different shape. So it can learn to act morally, but it doesn't become moral. There's a word for people who learn to act morally without actually possessing any morality. It's *sociopath*.

The phone rings. Heller.

"Hello?"

"Paul?"

"Yes, Dr. Heller. What is it?"

"I ... Paul, I think you should come here."

"What's wrong, Dr. Heller?"

"I don't want to say any more on the phone. Can you please come back here as soon as possible? It has to do with Tali."

"OK. I'll be there as fast as I can."

When I get there, he tells me Tali has been kidnapped. We're sitting in the living room and he's obviously shaken. I think he'd probably been trying to convince himself that Tali was OK, that she'd taken off for a few days with a girlfriend or something, but now he is coming to grips that something horrible has happened. On the coffee table between us sits a hard-sided leather briefcase.

"What's that?" I ask.

"Ransom," he says.

"How much do they want?"

"Um? Oh, fifty thousand dollars."

"Do you have that much?"

He gestures vaguely toward the case. Apparently he does.

"Do you know who took her?"

He shakes his head. "Supposed to bring the money to Fairway Mall at five p.m." I notice he left the pronoun off the front of that sentence.

"Are you going to do it?" Notice that I don't define *it.*

"No choice. I can't let them kill Tali."

"Is that what they said? They're going to kill her?"

"That was the implication."

"Who did you talk to? How do you even know they have her?"

"Some man whose voice I didn't recognize. They let me talk to her briefly. She's OK. Scared, but OK."

"Do you know anyone who would want to kidnap her?"

He shakes his head. "No. I did notice something strange this morning, though. Tali's been accessing the Tyche data."

Of course she has, I think. That's how she knew about the Alameda case. "Can you tell what she was doing? Why she was looking at Tyche?"

"No. I can only assume that somebody got wind of what we've been doing and thinks it's some sort of money-making operation. Maybe Tali was trying to show them what Tyche actually does in an effort to get them to realize we're not doing this for the money. That's the only hypothesis I've got. Anyway, I've shut off her access. We can't risk the data falling into the wrong hands."

"Even if it costs Tali her life?"

"If the knowledge of Tyche becomes widespread, we'll have bigger problems," he says cryptically.

I decide not to pursue the matter. "What about the police?"

He shakes his head. "No time. And they'll start asking questions. A lot of what Tali and I do ... it's difficult to explain. We keep it secret because people would tend to get the wrong idea."

Yeah, I think. Knowing about mass murders in advance does tend to make you an object of suspicion. I regard the briefcase. "Five o'clock," I say.

He nods. "At the fountain in the center of the mall." It's after four now.

We sit there for a good minute, not speaking. I know what he's thinking: He's a famous scientist who has figured out a way to predict mass murders, and I'm just some loser who tried to throw himself in front of a train two days ago. Plus, he's probably figured out by now that I've got a bit of a thing for Tali. If one of us is going to risk his life for Tali, it should be me. He's not going to *say* any of that, of course. He's waiting for me to volunteer, the crafty old bastard.

"I'll do it," I say. What choice do I have? Tali's the only thing in my life worth living for anyway.

We waste another minute with him pretending to try to talk me out of it and me assuring him that it only makes sense that I be the one to deliver the ransom. I do get in one jab, suggesting that if things get dicey, there might be running involved, and it would be a shame if he broke a hip or something. He gets a little mad at that and stops talking.

I put the briefcase in the trunk and drive to the mall. I'm tempted to open it up and make sure the money is really inside, but he's told me it's locked. The combination is Tali's birthday, which of course I don't know. To my credit, I never seriously consider taking off with the money, although the possibility occurs to me. I could get that lock open with a hammer and a chisel in about thirty seconds. I no longer have a job and only have enough money in the bank to make my next two rent payments. Fifty thousand dollars would set me up for quite a while.

I park and enter the mall through Sears, feeling acutely self-conscious carrying the briefcase. My heart beats rapidly and my palms are sweating. I force myself to take deep breaths. Some part of my subconscious (my quantum brain?) is telling me something's not right here — beyond the fact that I'm walking through Sears to deliver a fifty thousand dollar ransom for a kidnapped girl I barely know. I'm beginning to realize that this scenario doesn't make any sense. Heller looked like he was reasonably well off, but he hardly seemed like the ideal victim of a ransom scheme. Hell, there are probably software executives in Heller's own neighborhood worth tens of millions. Why pick on a retired physics professor? And Tali is just Heller's assistant, not his daughter. How do they even know he'd be willing to pay the ransom to spare her?

By this point I'm halfway down the mall concourse. The fountain is just up ahead. It's Saturday afternoon, so the mall is packed. I check my phone: it's four fifty-eight. I hesitate for a moment, trying to make sense of the situation. If I had more time, I'm certain I could figure it out. My instincts tell me to take the briefcase and run, but if I do, I know I'll never see Tali again. I keep walking.

I'm at the fountain. Phone says 4:59. I'm looking around, but all I see are teenage girls loitering and parents pushing kids in strollers. Nobody who looks like a kidnapper.

Then I hear it: the same voice that gave me pause at the BART station, coming from somewhere up above: "Paul, don't! It's a —"

I look up, along with several of the shoppers, who are trying to figure out who is screaming. I see her on the second level of the mall, leaning over the railing. A man has clamped his hand over her mouth and pulls her backwards, away from the edge. I'm not sure, but I think he's the same man I saw with Tali in Alameda. They disappear from view.

I run to the escalator, dodging shoppers left and right. The briefcase makes it hard; it weighs at least twenty pounds and keeps me from moving very nimbly. I'm taking three steps at a time, jostling people and occasionally whacking someone on the elbow or knee with the briefcase. They curse and yell as I pass, but eventually I make it to the top. I turn to see, on the other side of the atrium, a woman Tali's size being escorted away by two large men in heavy coats and baseball caps. I run after them, rounding the corner of the atrium and skirting the railing. They are walking briskly and I'm running, so I gain on them. Then one of them stops and turns. I realize he's holding a gun and I instinctively hold the briefcase in front of me. Several loud cracks echo through the mall and I realize a viscous liquid is running down my left arm. Blood?

Not blood. The stuff is charcoal-colored, and it's all over the briefcase, which has three holes punched in it. What the hell?

People are screaming and ducking for cover now. The shooter has rejoined Tali and the other man, and they've put some distance between us, because I'm standing there like a dumbass, holding a ransom that seems to be made of some sort of petroleum byproduct. Not really thinking, I hurl the case over the railing toward the fountain and start running again. I don't get very far.

The blast knocks me to the floor. For a moment I'm dazed, not sure what's happening. Shoppers lying around me on the floor, holding their ears, the three figures retreating toward the Kohl's sign in the distance. I stagger to my feet. My ears are ringing and I see a rainbow.

I blink but it's still there. Not stars, a rainbow. The air is filled with a fine mist, refracting the sunlight streaming through the skylights above into its constituent wavelengths. I stumble through it to the railing, breaking the spell. Down below, carnage. The fountain is wrecked, and bodies are strewn about it, bloody and broken. I nearly puke but force myself to look away. I run after the three figures in the distance.

A bomb. The briefcase hadn't held money; it had held a bomb. Why? What good could possibly come from that? It occurs to me that maybe Heller isn't all that interested in good.

I pursue the trio down the concourse but it's too late; they've disappeared. I'm aware of people shouting and pointing my direction. I make for the nearest exit, find my car, and get the hell out of there.

I drive away as fast as I dare, passing police cars and emergency vehicles heading the other way, sirens blaring. I watch in the rearview as each police car passes, half-expecting one of them to turn around and begin pursuit. Not one of them does. I wonder how long it will take for an APB to be sent out. I'm sure I was caught on the mall security cameras. By five after eleven tonight I'll be famous: the Fairway Mall Bomber. The kidnappers would be on video too, but I'm guessing it will be hard to identify them, since they were wearing caps. The search will center on me. Someone will see me on TV, recognize me as that quiet guy who used to teach high school English in San Leandro. The phrase "history of mental illness" will be used. If they play up that aspect enough, maybe it'll save me from lethal injection.

I drive aimlessly into the foothills. When I reach a sufficiently secluded spot, I pull over, get out and vomit into a ravine. I sink to the ground, leaning my back against the front tire of the Focus. My hands are shaking and I'm on the verge of tears again.

OK, pull yourself together. You can explain this. I go over the story in my head and realize that no, I can't explain it. I don't understand what happened, and the parts that I do strain credulity. Before I talk to the cops, I need to figure out what's going on. I probably still won't be able to offer a credible legal defense, but at least I'll have a better idea how I ended up on death row.

Why did Heller send me to the mall with a bomb? To kill the kidnappers? It seemed a sloppy way to do it. Besides the fact that it wasn't by any means a foolproof way of killing them, there would inevitably be collateral damage. My mind is overwhelmed by images of bodies lying scattered on the mall floor, a concentric tide washing blood into the surrounding shops like some suburban Normandy. I push the images away. Even if Heller didn't care about innocent bystanders being killed, didn't even care about Tali possibly being killed, bombs leave too much forensic evidence behind: timers, detonators, chemical charges – these things can be traced. It made no sense. It was, in fact, the epitome of a senseless crime, just like Ski Mask opening fire on the pier: no motive, no finesse, no thought of self-preservation. Just chaos for the sake of chaos.

So Heller had sent me to the mall to cause chaos. Why? It was a pointless question, at least from an ethical perspective. Chaos was its own reason. But from another angle, a purely causal perspective, the question did have an answer: he sent me to the mall because Tali and her kidnappers were going to be there. Even if the ransom was fake, the kidnapping was clearly real – or was it? Perhaps the whole thing, even Tali crying out to me, was play-acting. This thought, too, I rejected: no, I still couldn't believe Tali had anything to do with it. Either the kidnapping was real or she was the best liar I'd ever known. I was going to work on the assumption that Tali was a victim in this. The alternative was that Tali had saved my life in order to execute some absurdly complex ruse involving her own kidnapping. Besides being highly unlikely, that would mean that my life really was as hopeless as it had seemed that day – only three days ago! – I had nearly stepped in front of a train. If that was the case, well, I'd probably find out soon enough – and there wasn't any harm in allowing myself to remain deluded a bit longer.

So the kidnapping was real. Was the ransom demand? Heller said he had received a call from a man whose voice he didn't recognize. He also said that he had talked to Tali, and that she was scared but unharmed. He said that he had gotten the impression they were going to kill her if he didn't pay.

I don't buy it, for the reasons I mentioned earlier. Heller just wasn't a very good target. Why kidnap the assistant of a retired physics professor? And if they had demanded money, the sensible thing to do would be to either pay the ransom or go to the police. Heller hadn't wanted to go to the police, supposedly because he didn't want them looking too hard into what it was that he and Tali did. But the more I think about it, the less sense that rationale makes. What concern would Heller's work be to the police, unless it was somehow linked to the reason for Tali's abduction?

Ah. Now we're getting somewhere. Tali had been abducted not for money, but for some other reason. And Heller's response was to send me with a bomb to the Fairway Mall, where the kidnappers were watching, along with Tali. Maybe, it occurred to me, Heller wasn't sending a bomb *instead* of the ransom: maybe the bomb *was* the ransom. Maybe the kidnappers had demanded that Heller blow up a bomb in the middle of Fairway Mall as the price of Tali's freedom. It makes sense, in a twisted way. That is, detonating a bomb in a mall still seems pointless, but while this theory doesn't provide a motive for the bombing, it does adequately explain Heller's actions. And while I can't see someone demanding that Heller hand over $50,000, I *can* see someone demanding that he make a bomb. A chemistry teacher might be a more sensible choice, but on the other hand, anyone who had seen Heller's shop would know he was capable of making a bomb. He could probably build an atom smasher with all that crap.

I'm still missing something, I know, but I'm starting to think that I'm going to have to pry the missing pieces out of Heller. I stand up and steady myself against the car. I'm still shaking a little, but as long as I keep shoving images of the dead and maimed at the mall out of my mind, I can manage all right. I get back in the Focus and head toward Heller's house. I wonder if the cops have identified me yet. Probably not, but it won't take them long. If they aren't looking at the security footage yet, they soon will be. They'll follow me out of the mall to my car and get my license plate number. Once they have that, I'm pretty much fucked. But hopefully I have an hour or two.

I stop at a McDonald's and get a Big Mac and a chocolate shake. I'm starving, and I figure there's a good chance it may be the last chocolate shake I'll have for a while. Once I have some food in my stomach, I take a few swigs from the bottle I keep under the front seat of the Focus. My hands are almost steady. I drive the rest of the way to Heller's place and park down the street a bit. It's getting dark now, which is good. I don't want him to see me coming.

I avoid the driveway, making my way through the woods adjacent to his property. I circle around the back of the barn and wait there at the corner, where I can keep an eye on the path between the house and the shop. Lights are on in both places; Heller's got to be in one of them. I figure eventually he'll walk from the shop to the house or vice versa. I'll sneak up behind him and get him in a headlock. I'm about six one, almost two hundred pounds; I don't see a little old guy like Heller giving me much trouble.

Anyway, that's what I'm thinking when something whacks me in the back of my head, knocking me unconscious.

I come to a few minutes later – if my internal clock is to be trusted – lying on my back on a cot in Heller's shop. Something cold is pressing against the back of my head. I try to sit up, am overcome with vertigo, and lie down again. Heller is standing about twenty feet away, bent over his workbench.

"You son of a bitch," I groan, feeling the back of my head. I've got a bad bump, and my hair is matted with sticky blood. My head is resting on a bloody towel on top of a bag of ice.

"Sorry about that," says Heller, not looking my way. "But I didn't think you'd give me a chance to explain myself if I didn't subdue you first." I notice a revolver resting on the bench, maybe six inches from his right hand.

"Explain yourself? You sent me into a crowded mall with a bomb!" It hurts when I yell.

He nods, turning to face me. "I'm sorry about that too. It couldn't be helped."

I'm starting to think Dr. Heller is the first truly evil person that I've ever met. He shows no remorse for what he's done. He's elevated this deterministic force, this thing he calls Ananke, to the point where it completely supplants his own sense of right and wrong. He truly believes that what's going to happen is going to happen, and that there's no moral difference between an earthquake and a mall bombing. Either way, it's just cause-and-effect at work; whether he is somehow part of the chain of events – say, by building a bomb and sending me to a crowded mall – is irrelevant. Shit happens.

On the other hand, I still don't quite believe that bombing the mall was his idea. Even in a completely deterministic world where free will plays no part, an action still requires a cause, and there was simply no reason for him to want to kill a bunch of random strangers in a mall. It's too random, too senseless even for a sociopath like Heller. After all, even someone like Ted Kaczynski, the Unibomber, didn't kill people for no reason. His reasons might seem crazy to a normal person, but his motivations possessed a sort of internal logic: they made sense to *him*. I just can't see how the mall bombing made sense to Heller, unless he had done it under duress. I decide to test my theory that the bombing had been a kind of ransom paid to Tali's kidnappers.

"You could have killed her, you know. Tali."

He shakes his head again. "I knew they'd keep her out of the probable range of the event."

"So you do care about her," I say.

"Of course," he says, turning to face me. "Although my personal feelings are no more relevant than those of the friends and families of the people killed by that bomb."

That bomb. Not *the bomb I built and conned an innocent man into bringing to a crowded mall.* Just *that bomb.* I wonder if Heller's mind exists in a sort of permanent dissociative state, watching himself commit horrific, unforgiveable crimes as if he were watching the villain in a movie.

"You're a fucking sociopath," I say, managing to sit up slowly. "And if you don't tell the cops that you lied to me about the ransom, I'm going to do everything I can to make sure you go to jail too."

He laughs. "Of course you will, Paul. Everything you do is completely predictable. It's what makes you such an effective dupe."

"I may be a dupe," I say, "but I'm not a murderer. I didn't know what was in that briefcase. Those deaths at the mall were *your* doing. You used me."

"I used you," he agreed, "and Ananke used me. Round and round we go."

"Fuck Ananke!" I yell. "Ananke didn't do this, understand? You built a bomb and sent me to the Fairway Mall, knowing that it was going to explode and that people were going to die. That was a *choice you made.*"

He sighs. "I did make a choice once," he said. "It happened over two years ago. Everything that's happened since …" He shakes his head.

"You're denying any responsibility for anything you've done in the past two years? You're not a fucking child, Heller."

"Would you like to hear about the choice I made? It might help clarify things for you."

I shrug. "I'd rather hear you tell me you're going to confess to the police that you lied to me about the briefcase."

"Would a written statement be acceptable?" he says. "I ask because I'm not expecting to live much longer."

I nod dumbly. Could it really be that easy?

"All right, then. I'll do my best to explain. At Stanford I had been working on ideas related to probabilistic futures. I had a colleague, Dr. Emil Jelinek, who had written quite a bit about his hypothesis regarding quantum minds – the idea I mentioned earlier that part of the brain is a kind of quantum computer. We used to go out drinking fairly often, and at one of these sessions, after about six or seven rounds, one of us – I don't remember which – suggested the idea that we try to build a psionic field detector. The little black box I showed you earlier." He points to the workbench.

I nod.

"It was a ridiculous idea; Emil and I both had a lot of theoretical work to do before trying any kind of field test. It was like the Wright brothers trying to build a space shuttle. But it was harmless fun, and it gave us something to do while we were drinking. We set up this workshop to work on it. Over the next several months we spent hundreds of hours working on the thing. We had virtually no data to work with, but we kept tinkering away, running on intuition and wild-assed guesses. And to our utter surprise, we started to see results. Nothing definitive, but we began to see correlations between the disturbances the detectors reported and future events. At this point, we only had a few of them set up, a mile or so apart in Oakland. We knew that violent deaths were the events most likely to cause quantum fluctuations, so Oakland seemed like a logical choice."

I can't disagree with that.

"We continued to fine-tune the detectors and we got them to the point where the correlations almost *had* to be the result of seemingly unpredictable future events. We assembled all the data and wrote up our results in a paper that we planned to submit to an academic journal. We knew there would be a lot of resistance in the physics community, so we went over everything a dozen times to make sure our data was good and that we weren't making any unwarranted assumptions. Everything checked out. We were on the verge of making history.

"We finished our final rounds of edits on the paper, and we were having a drink to celebrate. Emil was sitting right where you are now. You see those tanks over there? They hold gases like Argon and Helium. They're under pressure, up to 230 PSI, so when they're in the tank they're actually in their liquid state. These are inert elements, completely harmless except for the fact that they're under pressure. About as dangerous as a car tire sitting on the floor of your garage. Anyway, as we're sitting here celebrating, the valve breaks off one of those tanks over there, shoots across the room and embeds itself three inches into Emil's skull. He falls over dead. I could hardly believe it. I've worked with tanks like that for years and never heard of anything like that happening. The worst that's ever happened is a valve that won't shut all the way, and then you just open the windows and go for a walk. It was an absolutely freak occurrence.

"I called the police and they came out and investigated. They agreed that it was a one in a million thing. They'd never heard of anything like it. I'm pretty sure that I was under suspicion for a while, but they couldn't find any evidence the tank had been tampered with. Somehow it corroded just enough, in just the right way, that it happened to give way right when Emil was sitting in its path. Bizarre.

"Obviously I couldn't publish the paper under the circumstances. Besides the fact that it was supposed to be a shared triumph, there was the very real possibility that people would think I killed Emil so I wouldn't have to share the credit. The whole thing was so depressing that I shoved the paper in a drawer and tried not to think about it.

"A few months later I finally forced myself to come back out here and look at the paper. I figured I might as well go over the data one more time to make sure I hadn't missed anything. I logged into the server and out of habit I checked the latest data. I noticed there was a weird spike in the PDCs the day that Emil died. That is, it started to spike about an hour before he died, peaked with his death, and then fell off again. The disturbance was recorded by only one detector – one that was sitting right here on this bench. I was stunned. It was the strongest correlation I had ever seen. That one data point was better evidence than all the rest of the data we had collected combined. I decided to rewrite the paper to include the incident of Emil's death. It would strengthen our case and in a weird way it would be a tribute to Emil. His own death had demonstrated our theory.

"Then the server crashed, catastrophically. I couldn't recover any of the data. I have backups, of course, but the backups were wiped too. Somehow, despite the fact that I use the same antivirus software used by the Defense Department, a virus got onto my network and wiped *everything*. I'd been meaning to upload the data to an offsite storage service, but I kept forgetting. Fortunately, I had most of the data on an optical disc. Always good to keep a copy of your data on non-magnetic media, in case of a major electromagnetic disturbance. I got the network up and running, made sure I cleared all traces of the virus, and put the disc in the drive. The damn thing wouldn't read. Kept saying there was no disc in the drive. I was pretty furious at this point. I got in my car, determined to go to the electronics store and buy another disc reader. As soon as I got on the road, it started to rain like crazy. I was frustrated, not thinking clearly, and driving too fast. I lost control of the car and went into a ditch about two miles from here. Had to walk all the way back here. I got back inside the shop and realized that the disc, which I had slipped into my pocket, had broken in half. The seat belt must have hit it. In my other pocket was the only copy of the paper Emil and I had written. It had gotten soaked in the rain and the ink smeared. It was almost entirely illegible.

"I could hardly believe my bad luck. At that point, that's all I thought it was. Bad luck. I mean, what else could it be? Some supernatural being reaching down from the heavens to prevent me from publishing the paper? Well, I wasn't going to let a string of bad luck stop me. I spent another six months assembling enough data that I could reconstruct the paper. I no longer had the data on Emil's death, which was unfortunate, but I was confident I had enough proof to convince skeptics that Tyche worked. This time around, I kept a close eye on the data for the local receptors, so I wouldn't be blindsided by another accident. I mean, I was fairly certain Emil's death and my subsequent mishaps were accidents, but I didn't want to take any chances. Nothing showed up in the data, so I assumed I was safe. I reconstructed the paper and was going to go over it one more time before I sent it to the *Journal of Theoretical Physics*. Guess what happened then?"

"Wild jackals stole the paper," I deadpan.

"Close," he says. "A fluke electrical fire broke out, melting the server. The sprinklers went on, so it didn't get very far, but the fire managed to destroy all my digital copies of the data and the paper, as well as the hard copies I had printed out. I had several offsite copies – I had learned my lesson with the previous run of bad luck

– but by this point I was genuinely disturbed by everything that had happened. I am far from a superstitious person, but I couldn't help thinking *someone is trying to keep this paper from being published*. You should have seen the look on the face of the insurance adjustor when I explained to him what happened. I think they were suspicious because of the accident with Emil. The adjustor kept asking if anything I was working on in my shop was 'inherently dangerous.' I told him, 'not unless you believe in a malevolent deity who supernaturally interferes with the scientific method to avoid discovery.' I don't think he found it amusing. There's no box on the form for 'act of a goddess.'" He smiles at me.

"Tali was a graduate student of mine at the time, and with Emil gone I needed some help, so I hired her as my assistant. Tali was fascinated with the project, and she took over most of the day-to-day work. I was probably pretty useless at the time; I couldn't shake the idea that someone had interfered with our efforts to get published. Emil and I had discussed the idea of what we called active deterministic interference – essentially the deterministic universe actively working against efforts to change the future. It's an idea that crops up in science fiction a lot: somebody finds a way to predict the future and attempts to change it, but circumstances conspire to cause events to come out exactly the way they were predicted. Usually the hero of the story inadvertently becomes central to the chain of events leading up to the event he was trying to prevent. For example, there's a Philip Dick story where the reign of an oppressive future regime is threatened by the rise of a popular religious sect. The regime sends a man back in time to assassinate the founder of the sect before he can start causing trouble, but of course the agent ends up becoming the sect's founder. That sort of thing. It's a way of dealing with the paradoxes of time travel: how can someone in the future send an agent back to prevent the founding of a religious sect if the founding of the sect is part of the causal chain that leads to the agent being sent back? Or, more succinctly: what happens if you travel back in time and assassinate your own grandfather? The answer you find in a lot of science fiction stories is: *you can't*. Somehow the universe will prevent you from killing your own grandfather in order to resolve the paradox."

I'm confused. "But you're talking about predicting the future, not time travel."

He nods. "True, but the paradox occurs either way. If you can predict an event in the future and use that knowledge to prevent the event, then the event won't happen and can't be predicted. The prevention of the event is dependent on it occurring. Paradox."

My head hurts, and not just from the blow to my skull. "Yeah, OK," I say wearily. "Go ahead."

"As I said, the idea of the space-time continuum actively rejecting paradoxes had occurred to us, but it was only an academic possibility. For one thing, we had never seriously discussed trying to prevent any of the events we were predicting. For another, we were only dealing with *probable* futures, not definite futures. That gave the universe some wiggle room: if we ever did manage to prevent an event from occurring, it might just mean that we had managed to shift the odds a bit. There was no definite paradox involved.

"But the more I thought about it, the more I was convinced that the string of improbable events that prevented me from publishing that paper was an instance of active deterministic interference. Somehow we had forced the hand of determinism into revealing itself. And that notion prompts some interesting questions. First, why did the universe act so decisively to prevent publication of that paper? Second, if it didn't want the paper published, why had it let us get as far as we did? That is, why not kill Emil and me in a car wreck a year earlier?

"While pondering these questions, I came to a couple of troubling realizations: I was now thinking of 'the universe' as something that had motives and intentions. Not long before, if someone had come to me with the question 'why did the universe do *x*?', I would have laughed in their face. There is no *why* with the universe; there are just the brute facts of matter, energy and the physical laws that determine the interaction thereof. If someone asks, 'why did the apple hit Newton on the head,' science can answer 'Because of gravity,' and it can explain with some precision how gravity acts. But science can't answer the question 'why did the universe want Newton to get hit on the head?' Science deals with causes, not goals or intentions. You can trace the reasons for the apple hitting Newton on the head back to the Big Bang and you can trace the consequences to the end of the universe, and you're still not going to get an answer to the question 'what was the purpose of Newton getting hit on the head with an apple?' Science doesn't deal with purpose, with teleology. It can answer 'why' questions, but only in a causal sense.

"So I realized that it was foolish to keep asking questions like 'why didn't the universe want our paper to be published?' But I was convinced that it was equally foolish to deny that there was something out there, some force or being, that was somehow acting purposefully to prevent the publication of the paper. My understanding of this thing was far from complete and I wanted to avoid, as much as possible, using any terms that would bias my own thinking and methodologies. What I needed was a metaphor, something that I could use to represent the thing in my thinking. I knew it was more than some impersonal force, like gravity or electromagnetism, but I also knew it wasn't a human being. It occurred to me to use a name from mythology, perhaps the Egyptian god of destiny, Shai. But I resisted personifying the thing.

"Eventually I came to another troubling realization: if this thing, whatever it was, truly didn't *want* to be discovered, and if it really was the deterministic force underlying the universe, then my attempts to define it using scientific methods were doomed to fail. Already it had killed my partner, stymied my attempts to communicate our theories to the greater scientific community, and destroyed all my data. If it was actively working to prevent me from pinning it down, then my efforts to do so were as doomed to fail as if I were trying to determine the position and momentum of an electron simultaneously. There was a sort of impenetrable cloud of indeterminacy about the thing.

"As a physicist, I'm used to dealing with indeterminacy, but generally the practical results of quantum indeterminacy are negligible. There aren't a lot of direct, real-world consequences to not being able to pinpoint the location of an electron, you know? Indeterminacy doesn't usually run you off the road and melt your server.

"It occurred to me that perhaps I was going crazy; that Emil's death had caused something to snap in my brain, that I was thinking irrationally. I decided what I needed was a second opinion.

Now scientists are a skeptical lot as a rule, so there weren't many people I knew who would both hear me out and who were qualified to weigh in on the matter. Finally I decided to send an email to an Australian physicist I had met in Bern a few years earlier, a Dr. Bentley. Bentley was a brilliant man who had done some important work on quantum entanglement. And I knew that he was a man of faith, an Episcopalian if I remember correctly. I thought, 'here is a guy who believes in a purposive entity behind the creation of the universe who doesn't let that belief interfere with his ability to do serious theoretical physics. If anyone can give me an unbiased answer regarding my suspicions about this thing, it's him.' So I sent him an email telling him the whole story, just as I've told you, and asking him whether I'm completely crazy to be a bit nervous about continuing this line of research. Three days later, I get an email from a secretary in his department informing me that Bentley had died in a windsurfing accident two weeks earlier. That's when I started to really get worried."

I have to stop Heller at this point. "Hang on," I say. "If you're trying to convince me that this force or whatever it is killed Bentley to keep him from learning about your research, I'm not buying it. You said yourself that he died before you sent him the email. How could Ananke or whatever we're calling it reach into the past and kill him?"

He smiles painedly. "You can think of it as Ananke reaching into the past to kill him, or you can think of it as Ananke leading me to send an email to a man who is already dead. What's the difference? Either way, Ananke prevents the promulgation of information about her existence. Anyway, I confessed my fears to Tali, who is a pretty smart cookie herself. I had resisted telling her before because I know she's a lapsed Jew, and she has very little tolerance for any sort of mysticism or superstition. She's as atheist as they come. To my surprise, she sympathized with my point of view. In fact, she confessed that she had started to think of this deterministic force in personal terms herself. The data she was seeing was too weird to account for in any other way.

"As I said, she was pretty much running the show at this point, as I was lost in my own worries and philosophical ruminations. Every day she would spend an hour or so going over local news reports, attempting to make correlations between the psionic field disturbances the detectors were reporting and the fires, shootings and car accidents reported in the news. We had agreed at the outset that we would never attempt to witness any of the events in person, partly because it was too dangerous and partly because we weren't sure how observation would affect the data. At one point, though, the psionic disruption coefficients inexplicably started to drop, and she confessed to me that her curiosity got the better of her and she decided to visit a few of the sites and observe from a distance. At the first two events she noticed nothing out of the ordinary. The third was a pileup on I-680. While she was waiting for the event to occur, she noticed a car stalled on the shoulder and wondered if that was the cause. She took her eyes off the road long enough that she didn't see the brake lights come on in front of her. By the time she saw it, it was too late to stop and she swerved to avoid the car. Predictably, this caused a chain reaction that brought about the twenty-car pileup she had gone there to observe. She was pretty banged up and spent three days in the hospital. When she came back, she found that the oscillations had returned to their previous intensity – in fact, the intensity was inexplicably slightly higher during her time in the hospital. The only conclusion she could come to was that *she* was the reason for the variations. The presence of someone who had foreknowledge of the event near the space-time coordinates of the event decreased the probability of the event occurring. She found herself unable to think of this thing she was studying as some kind of impersonal force any longer: it had not only anticipated what she was going to do; it had *used* her to make one of the events happen. She started calling it Ananke, after the Greek goddess of destiny. At least that was the formal name she gave it. More frequently she simply thought of it as 'the bitch.'"

"OK, stop!" I say. "You're contradicting yourself again. How could Tali's presence at the accident on 680 have reduced the probability of the event occurring, when her presence was the cause of the event?"

Heller sighs. "That question is impossible to answer. Maybe it didn't reduce the probability. We can't know what the probability of the event occurring would have been if she hadn't known about it, because she *did* know about it, and that's the only data point we have. All we can say is that the intensity of the impression of the event is consistent with a lower-than-typical probability, when compared to the other data points. Another way to say it is that Ananke is capable of using agents who are aware of the event to cause the event, but that the odds of Ananke succeeding are intrinsically lower because of that awareness."

I'm honestly not sure whether he has answered my question or not. I decide to let it go. I still think Heller is a sociopath, but I'm starting to see *why* he's a sociopath. He really has bought into the idea that everything he does has already been anticipated by some mysterious being – possibly even *dictated* by that being. Once you start thinking in those terms, madness can't be far behind. You can either question everything you do, paralyzed by anxiety, or you can stop questioning anything. I guess Heller picked door number two.

"At some point are you going to tell me who kidnapped Tali, and why you sent me to the mall with a bomb in a briefcase?"

"I'm getting to that," he says. "It's important that you understand the background. Otherwise none of the rest will make sense."

I'm pretty sure that it's not going to make sense regardless, but I shrug and let him continue.

"So Tali and I were in agreement that if we wanted to stay alive and continue our research, we should think about Ananke not as an impersonal force, but rather as a being who was acting in an intelligent, premeditated way to attempt to keep us from thwarting her plans, whatever those plans were. So we were back to my original questions: why didn't Ananke want us to publish, and why hadn't she stopped us earlier? We were pretty sure that Ananke was trying to prevent widespread knowledge of her existence in the scientific community, because that would lead to more experimentation, the construction of more and better psionic field detectors, and a corresponding decrease in Ananke's range of action. The more people out there with foreknowledge of probable events, the lower the probability of those events occurring. If you think of the most probable events as the ones that Ananke most wants to occur, then you can see why she is loath to allow their probability to decrease. But again, if that's what Ananke wants to prevent, why hadn't she prevented it earlier? Why not kill me and

Emil in a car crash before we ever came up with the idea for the psionic field detector? For that matter, why allow us to be born in the first place? Why not kill us in utero? Or kill our grandparents before they had a chance to reproduce, just to be extra sure?

"The only possible answer is that there are some events that Ananke can't predict or control. And since Ananke *is* determinism, that means there are some events that are, in some sense, non-deterministic. It might be a stretch to say that such events are 'uncaused,' but if they have a cause, they are outside Ananke's bailiwick. The possibility of nondeterministic events occurring is, of course, not news to a quantum physicist. We've known for decades that in theory some events are completely random and therefore unpredictable and uncontrollable. But we also know that above a subatomic level, such events are so rare that they are generally negligible. Still, over a large enough scope of timespace, there is enough randomness that Ananke must in some cases cede a bit of power to it.

"But was that all there was to it? Had some random event, occurring on the quantum scale, somehow resulted in Emil and me building the first psionic field detector? It seemed highly improbable. It's not like we had flipped a coin and said, 'Heads, we build a psionic field detector, tails we build a model of the Queen Mary out of toothpicks.' And even if we had, coin tosses are more than ninety-nine percent deterministic. It was hard to see how any event on the quantum scale could have had any effect on whether we built the psionic field detector or not. And the other thing to keep in mind is that if it were a simple matter of it being a binary choice between building that detector and not building the detector, Ananke might not have known the outcome of the random event, but she would have known the possibilities. That is, she would have foreseen that the invention of the detector was a probable outcome. And if she could have foreseen that, she would have prevented it."

I shake my head. "You've lost me again."

"Think of it this way: there's a hall with three doors in it: one door lets you into the hall from outside. The other two doors each open into a bedroom. There is a bed in each room, and under the mattress of one bed there is a thousand dollar bill. If you don't find the bill, I get to keep it, so it's in my interest to keep you from getting into the room that has the money. I have a lock that I can put on one door to keep you out, but I don't know which room the bill is in and I'm not allowed to look under the mattress. Which door do I put the lock on?"

"The door from the outside, obviously," I say. "The one that lets me into the hall."

"Exactly. So if building the psionic field detector was simply the result of a binary choice, even if the outcome of the choice was completely random, Ananke would have foreseen it and prevented the choice from being made. She would have locked the door to the hall, so there'd be no possibility of me picking the right door. In other words, she could have killed me and Emil on the way to the bar where we first came up with the idea, or done any number of other things to prevent that decision from ever being made. So why didn't she?"

I shake my head. I hear the faint sound of sirens in the distance. I get to my feet and go to the window.

"What is it?" asks Heller. Then he hears it. "Damn! I thought we had more time. I had hoped to explain it all to you, to make you understand. But Ananke, as usual, has other plans." He goes back to the workbench and starts writing something on a pad of paper.

I see flashing blue and red lights through the trees. Should I run? It seems pointless. Where would I go? Maybe it's Heller's fatalism talking, but everything seems so hopeless. Is Heller writing his confession? Giving me absolution? I wonder if it will matter.

"Why do you care?" I ask, watching as a man with bolt cutters severs the chain holding the gate shut. He swings the gate open and police cars pour in. "Why is it so important that I understand?"

"You might still be able to save Tali," he says.

"Save her from what?"

But the only answer is the sound of a gunshot from behind me. I turn to see him fall to the floor. There's a dime-sized hole in his temple. His eyes are open, staring blankly. A pool of blood is spreading out from beneath his head. The revolver, its barrel still smoking, is clutched in his hand.

The door to the shop crashes open and men in SWAT gear rush inside. I've already raised my hands, dropping the ice pack to the floor, and I'm trying to look as harmless as possible. They hit me anyway.

Part Seven: Active Interference

Heller never had a chance to tell me his theory about why Ananke let him come up with the idea for the psionic field detector, but I have plenty of time to think about it in jail. They're holding me in the Santa Clara county jail in San Jose. Not surprisingly, the police aren't convinced by Heller's hand-written suicide note absolving me of responsibility for the bombing. They think he's covering for me so that I can continue his "work" after his death. I gather, from the sorts of questions they ask me, that he and Tali are suspects in several unsolved crimes that have occurred in the Bay Area over the past few months. And now I'm suspected of being involved as well. More than suspected: they have me dead to rights on security video from the mall. Not only that, they have a 911 recording made from my phone regarding an apartment fire in Hayward. I don't even try to explain the whole quantum physics/determinism angle. I figure my best bet is to play dumb; maybe they'll buy that I was just an emotionally troubled man who had been duped into bringing a bomb into a mall. I'm sadly convincing in this role: my recent separation, attempted suicide and stalker-like pursuit of a woman I barely know weigh heavily in my favor. Turns out being a basket case has its benefits. My lawyer says my odds of getting the death penalty are fifty/fifty. Hilarious. Maybe I should flip a coin.

I have my mother to thank for the lawyer. He's nothing special, just somebody she found in the phone book, I think. Better than a public defender, I guess. My mother heard about my arrest on the news and visited me the next day. I think she expected me to tell her the arrest was all some big mix-up; obviously I wouldn't have been involved in a mall bombing. Her exact words were "you never even go to the mall," which gave me a pretty good laugh. When I was noncommittal about my involvement in the bombing, she became very quiet and excused herself shortly thereafter. That may have been the first time I'd ever seen my mother at a loss for words. I think that up to that point my mother had always thought of me as a sort of non-entity, someone who for better or worse was going to coast through life without leaving any kind of mark behind. In a perverse way, I'm a little bit happy to have proven her wrong.

I tell my lawyer the whole story, as best as I can. His eyes glaze over when I get to the quantum physics stuff. I tell him he should really reader Heller's book to get a better understanding of what's going on, but he makes it clear that if my defense rests on some quasi-mystical theory involving mythical Greek goddesses, I might as well come to court with my sleeves rolled up because I'm going to get the needle. Despairing of getting him to appreciate the abstract nuances of my case, I decide to put him to work on something more concrete: I ask him to find out whatever he can about David Carlyle and Heller's lawsuit against Peregrine. He says he doesn't see how that's going to help my case, but he agrees to do it.

I spend the next couple of days reading the rest of *Fate and Consciousness* (my lawyer did get them to give me back my Kindle, so at least he's not completely useless). The book makes more sense now that I know what Heller is tap-dancing around: he's trying not to reveal anything specific about Ananke — anything that another physicist might take as a starting point for his own research on the matter. No wonder his physics colleagues hate this book: it *is* pseudoscience. As soon as he gets close to anything like a quantifiable empirical observation or verifiable hypothesis, he retreats into abstractions — digressions about Greek mythology, Stoicism, karma, quantum computing, or any of a dozen other areas tangentially related to the matter at hand. "Get to the point!" one of the reviewers had written, but getting to the point is the one thing Heller couldn't do. He admits as much in the foreword:

This book is necessarily incomplete because its subject resists description. By this I don't mean merely that it's vaguely defined or elusive, but rather that the subject *actively resists description*. It (or she, as I will refer to her) does not want to be described, because the act of description entails setting limits and the setting of limits entails a reduction in the range of possible action. The more specifically I describe her, the more likely it is that I will fail to do so.

I hadn't known what to make of that the first time I read it; I took it as a scientist somewhat awkwardly trying to employ poetic license. I know something about bad metaphors and I assumed that "the subject actively resists description" was one of these. How could the subject of a book actively resist description? Even if the subject were a person, the only way she could actively resist description would be to physically prevent the description from being written, to literally pull the pen out of his hand – which is a little wacky, even for Heller. And yet, given what Heller had told me, I now realize that's exactly what he meant: if he was too specific about how Ananke worked, Ananke would stop the book from being published – or worse. In fact, now that I think about, maybe it was Ananke that had prevented Heller from finishing his explanation to me. She might have directed the police to Heller's place, causing him to kill himself rather than be sent to prison. It makes a weird sort of sense. Any transmission of specific information about Ananke would increase the probability that someone else would duplicate or build upon Heller's work, and that meant an encroachment on Ananke's territory. She killed him to keep that from happening. On the other hand, I'm an unemployed English teacher well on his way to death row. What could I possibly do with that information? Something tells me I'm not at the top of Ananke's hit list.

In any case, I think I have an idea where Heller was going. A bell goes off when I get to a chapter about the philosophy of Immanuel Kant. Heller is taken with Kant's idea of genius:

Genius, Kant says, is "the exemplary originality of the natural endowments of an individual in the free employment of his cognitive faculties." Genius is a natural human ability; it is not measurable or traceable, and the vagaries of language cannot adequately articulate it. Genius cannot define itself. Genius must, nonetheless, inspire imitation, so that the concept of the product of that genius may be derivatively articulated. Genius must inspire concept, but it cannot conceptualize.

In other words, genius is a *non-deterministic quality of consciousness*. As it can neither be taught nor specifically defined, it must be considered, in a strict sense, to arise outside the realm of cause and effect. It is also, therefore, completely unpredictable.

Kant believes that genius applies only to artistic endeavors; to his way of thinking, the scientific mind can never be radically original. There is no such thing as a new idea in science, because the value of a scientific theory obtains from its ability to accurately describe existing natural phenomena. Thus Einstein can be thought of as *discovering* relativity but not *inventing* relativity. Relativity is an attribute of spacetime; it was "out there" waiting to be discovered. Further, the notion of relativity can be taught, whereas no one can be taught to compose like Mozart or paint like Picasso.

This strikes me as a confused understanding of the situation, however. The proper analog of the ability to compose like Mozart is not the theory of relativity itself, but the *ability to intuit the existence of special relativity*. One can no more be taught how to intuit new ways of looking at spacetime than one can be taught how to compose like Mozart. Certainly, once one is aware that special relativity exists, one can define and communicate it, but so can one transcribe Mozart's *Requiem in D Minor*. Doing so requires some intelligence and skill, but no genius. Was Einstein less a genius than Mozart? Was his grasp of concepts that eluded his peers any less inexplicable than Mozart's ability to make a fool of Salieri?

Noting that scientific genius results in theories that correspond to the natural world seems as impertinent to me as pointing out that Shakespeare was incapable of painting a self-portrait. What we are concerned with is not the *output* of genius, but its inner workings – and those inner workings are just as mysterious in the case of an Einstein as they are in the case of a Mozart or Shakespeare.

I think this is Heller's roundabout way of saying that the idea for the psionic field detector was the work of genius. That is, it was completely original and unpredictable. Even Ananke, who knew that Heller was working on a theory of probable futures and that Emil Jelinek was working on a theory of quantum minds, could not have predicted that when they met in that bar – when Heller got his chocolate in Jelinek's peanut butter, so to speak – they would hit upon the idea of the psionic field detector. As far as Ananke knew, these two guys were just shooting the shit over beer. Maybe, toiling away at Stanford, one or the other of them would make some infinitesimal progress toward increasing the collective understanding of spacetime, but it was no concern to her; they were like June bugs bouncing against a screen door. But then suddenly there were Heller and Jelinik standing in her living room, deciding how they were going to rearrange her furniture. No wonder Ananke went ballistic.

I wonder if the psionic field detector was Heller's idea or Jelinek's, or if it was somehow both. I remember what Heller had said about part of the human brain being a quantum computer. If it were true, then it would be possible for the human brain to try out many solutions to a given problem simultaneously. Did the capacity of the quantum brain vary by person? Did people like Heller and Jelinek have the ability to try out a million solutions simultaneously rather than, say, a thousand? Was genius just a matter of having a bigger quantum brain? No, it had to be more complicated than that. For one thing, the genius of Einstein was completely different than that of Mozart. And Tali had talked about the quantum brain as a computer that was assigned to solve problems. But what was the "problem" here? Heller and Jelinek hadn't been trying to solve any particular problem, at least not consciously. Or did their quantum brains take any input they were given as a problem to be solved?

However it happened, that night Heller and Jelinek came up with an idea with huge potential consequences; an idea that originated from outside the flow of cause and effect, like a boulder falling into a mountain stream. The water rushed around the boulder, trying to compensate for the new obstacle, but the flow of the stream was irrevocably changed. Heller and Jelinek had survived in the wake of the boulder for some time but they were both doomed to eventually be swept downstream. The stream could be diverted momentarily, could even have its flow disrupted into an uncontrollable, chaotic, roiling ferment; but eventually the stream would reassert itself, and a mile downstream the effect of the boulder would be lost amid the inexorable flow.

It's a depressing thought. Heller and Jelinek somehow managed to break out of Ananke's deterministic death grip for a moment and she reacted by crushing them both under her heel. Heller shot himself, but Ananke had already defeated him at that point. The cops showed up at his house as quickly as they did because he was already under suspicion for several other crimes. If he didn't kill himself, he was going to go to prison eventually. Either way, his encroachment on Ananke's turf would end, and that was all she cared about.

If Heller is to be believed, the world is essentially a machine and we are just cogs. Hell, we probably don't even amount to being cogs. I'm probably not even a ball bearing. Every once in a while an eccentric gear may jump out of place and muck up the machine's operation for a few minutes, but the machine has repair mechanisms and multiple redundant systems that prevent the malfunction from amounting to anything. The machine rumbles on as it always has.

I wonder, though, if there's any other way to muck up the machine's workings – or even to exert some level of control over it. Heller identified two weaknesses: quantum randomness and moments of unpredictable genius. What if there are other weaknesses he hasn't found yet, because he hasn't been looking in the right place?

Two days after my arrest I get another visitor: Rabbi Freedman. He asks me how I'm holding up.

"I'm OK," I say. "Better than those people at the mall."

He nods. "That was a horrible thing."

For some reason, his remark makes me angry. He sounds like Heller, acting as if the bombing was something that just happened, an "act of God" as the insurance companies say.

"You understand that I walked into a crowded mall with a bomb," I say.

"That's what I hear," says Freedman.

"And all you have to say is 'that was a horrible thing'?"

"What would you have me say?"

"Call me a murderer. Tell me I'm going to hell. Acknowledge that a crime was committed."

"I don't know what you did," says Freedman. "You say you carried a bomb into the mall, and I believe you. Presumably you had your reasons."

"Had my reasons!" I exclaim. "What reason could I possibly have for carrying a bomb into a mall?"

"Did you know it was a bomb?"

"No, but I should have."

"So your crime wasn't murder; it was being a little dim. And that's probably not entirely your fault. You may have been born a little dim."

I can't help laughing. "I'm having that engraved on my tombstone," I say. "Paul Bayes, 1976 to 2013. He was born a little dim."

He smiles. "Is there anything I can do for you, Paul?"

"Do for me?" I ask. "No offense, but why are you even here, Rabbi? Why don't you go visit the families of the people I killed?"

"It's not my place to intrude on their lives. I pray for them, and that's about all I can do. You, on the other hand, I feel some responsibility for. I thought you could use a friend."

I want to keep arguing with him, tell him he's a fool for giving a shit about me when I'm at best a complete schmuck and at worst a mass murderer. But I find myself unable to muster the strength. I'm on the verge of tears. Finally I manage to sputter, "Thanks, Rabbi."

We talk a bit more, first about Tali and Heller and then Deb and the kids. He tells me he's done a little poking around but hasn't been able to find out anything about where Tali is. He asks me if there's anything that he can do for Deb or the kids, but I tell him no. The fact is that they're probably better off without me. Rabbi Freedman leaves after about an hour with a promise to visit me again when he can.

I sit for a while pondering his words and trying to understand why he bothered to visit me at all. On a surface level, it makes no sense. A normal, rational person would conclude that if I had anything to do with the mall bombing, I deserve nothing but anger and scorn. If someone does something wrong, the appropriate response is to demand justice. For every crime, there's an equal and opposite reaction. But that isn't the way Rabbi Freedman thinks. He seems to have transcended the knee-jerk push-pull physics of human interaction.

My mind keeps going back to something he said the night I met him: the true God is a God of love. Does that mean that love is a fundamental aspect of reality? That it underlies everything, at an even more basic level than the quantum phenomena Heller studies, possibly a level more basic than reason itself? Heller would laugh at the idea, I'm sure — but then Heller was a sociopath. He was completely rational and batshit crazy. Because for all his genius, he was missing something — call it empathy or inner peace or self-awareness or whatever you like. In his obsessive search for truth, he lost some vital quality of *humanness*.

The funny thing is, as I read his book I get the sense that Heller was pretty close to understanding this, at least on an intellectual level. The section on consciousness creating the present reality reminded me of something, and when I read the part about Kant, I realize what it is: Heller's notion of consciousness coming into being as the result of the concepts of time and space becoming impressed on a child's mind is just a slightly muddled adaptation of an argument from Kant's *Critique of Pure Reason*. I took a class on Kant in college, and amazingly some of it actually stuck with me.

Before Kant, it was assumed that time and space were real things existing in the universe outside of the observer, and that the principle of cause and effect could be deduced through empirical observation. But Kant (relying on the philosopher David Hume) argued that this is nonsense: you can't observe cause and effect; you can only observe one event habitually occurring after another. If you observe enough objects falling from the Tower of Pisa, for example, you might hypothesize that objects dropped from a height will always fall toward the ground at a particular rate. You might go on to call this hypothesis the "law of gravity," and then you can confidently explain that objects dropped from a height fall "because of gravity." But all you've really said is that objects can be expected to fall because objects have always fallen in the past. How do you know that objects in the future will act the same way as they did in the past? You have no experience of the future, so the best you can do is assume that they will. Where does this assumption come from?

Kant argued that our minds are essentially hardwired with the concepts of time, space, and causation. We don't come to understand time and space by observing them; time and space are categories that we apply to our observations. This is more or less what Heller is saying when he says that consciousness creates the present. The present isn't something that exists independently of us; it's the direct result of our application of *a priori* categories to our encounter with the universe (*a priori* is a fancy philosophical term meaning "prior to experience"). This is a trippy idea if you think about it, because in a very real sense it means we are creating the universe we experience. In fact, if you pursue this line of reasoning far enough, you realize that it isn't at all clear that there's a universe out there to be observed. After all, I have no direct access to the universe; all I have access to is my observations of it. And if those observations are at least partly created by my own *a priori* intuitions, why not just go all the way and assume that the whole universe is in my head? In fact, that's what a lot of philosophers after Kant claimed. The most extreme version of this point of view leads to solipsism, the belief that only I exist.

I'm not sure Kant ever satisfactorily addressed the question of how we can know that an objective universe exists. But the neat thing about his philosophical schema is that it allows him to smuggle in certain intuitions that are *a priori* and *pre-rational*. He doesn't have to give a rational explanation for causation because causation is just an arbitrary concept that exists in the mind. But once you successfully smuggle in one pre-rational *a priori* concept, it's tempting to smuggle in a few more. For example, Kant suggests that human morality is grounded on *a priori* principles. Kant doesn't think that you can develop a sense of morality simply by observing the world around you; at least the basic principles have to be hardwired in your brain. And if the principles of morality can be hardwired into one's brain, why not the concept of love? Or the idea of God Himself?

Heller seemed to be in agreement with Kant about the nature of space and time, but he doesn't mention morality, love or God. Did Heller think about these things? Did he agree with Kant that morality was *a priori*? Or did he think that morality could somehow result from the application of reason to experience? Did he even believe in morality, or in good and evil? Whatever Heller's concept of morality was, it failed him. For that matter, so did mine.

I still don't understand why Heller sent me to the mall with a bomb. I'm certain that he had been pressured to do it by Tali's kidnapping, but I don't know why someone would want him to do that. It made sense from Ananke's perspective: the bombing brought the police to Heller's door, prompting him to kill himself. It took me out of play too, for that matter, and it almost killed Tali. If she had been a little closer to the bomb, if I had dropped the case on the floor instead of tossing it into the fountain, she and I would both likely be dead. But then close only counts in horseshoes and hand grenades, as they say. Tali doesn't deal in *almost*s.

This realization prompts another unsettling line of thought: Ananke could have killed Tali, but she didn't. Why? I don't flatter myself that I'm important enough for Ananke to worry about; I imagine she doesn't particularly care whether I'm a free man or rotting in prison. But Tali … Tali is an actual threat to Ananke's plans. In fact, if anything she's a greater threat than Heller was. Heller was content to keep his studies academic; it was Tali who insisted on acting on the psionic field detector data to change the future. So why had Ananke killed Heller but not Tali?

It occurs to me that I don't actually know that Tali is still alive. Maybe her kidnappers killed her after the bombing. For some reason I don't think so. Maybe I just want to believe that she's alive, the way that I wanted to believe that she hadn't intentionally stood me up. I don't know what I'll do if Tali is dead. Actually, I do know what I'll do: nothing. I'm in prison, on suicide watch. I don't have a lot of options. Still, it's better for what's left of my sanity if I imagine she's still alive. And she *had* been alive the last time I had seen her; if the kidnappers had wanted to kill her, why didn't they do it in the midst of the chaos after the bomb went off? They hadn't been shy about sending a few bullets *my* way.

So, assuming that Tali isn't dead – why not? Did something happen to negate her as a threat to Ananke? Or was Ananke planning on using her somehow, the way she had used me? I laugh ruefully as I realize I'm giving Heller a pass. By putting the moral onus on Ananke, I had reduced Heller's own role in the bombing to that of a tool in her hands. Maybe Heller's at the Pearly Gates right now with a blood-spattered note from Ananke absolving him of any responsibility. I wonder if he's having more success with Saint Peter than I'm having with the California justice system.

Back on the subject: it could be that Tali is alive because Ananke simply hasn't had the opportunity to kill her yet. Clearly there are some limits on what Ananke can do in the wake of an unplanned event. Jelinek's death had occurred six months after his and Heller's "genius moment," and Heller didn't succumb for another two years after that. I think about the mountain stream again. On the leeward side of the boulder, there's a dead zone where one can rest, free of the inexorable pull of the stream. Jelinek and Heller had bobbed about for a while in the relative calm provided by the boulder but eventually they were caught up in an eddy that carried them back into the stream. So is that it? Is Tali just bobbing about in the eddies behind the boulder, waiting to be carried downstream? To mix a metaphor, is Ananke just waiting for the opportunity to strike?

I may be full of shit, but I don't think so. Tali had been courting death nearly from the moment I met her. We could easily have been killed in a wreck on the way to Embarcadero that day. A spray of errant buckshot could have killed her at the pier. She might have been accidentally shot during her abduction, or hit by a piece of debris during the bombing. Somehow she had survived, and that makes me wonder if Ananke still has plans for her.

My lawyer returns a few days later with some information about Heller's lawsuit. Apparently he had filed a two million dollar suit against Peregrine, claiming that they had unfairly denied his claim. The suit rested on the document claiming that Heller's work was a fraud. A week after the suit was filed, the matter was settled out of court. My lawyer has dug up another interesting piece of information too: Heller apparently filed papers of incorporation a few days after the suit was dropped. The description of his business on the paperwork is "Actuarial Consulting Services." Did Heller go into business with Peregrine?

My lawyer also gives me some information on Peter Girell's old boss, David Carlyle. Up until about a year ago he was the Claims Director for the Western region. Then he was promoted to the head of a new division, called Predictive Analytics. His promotion occurred three days after Heller filed his papers of corporation. Interesting. Included with the biographical information is a picture of Carlyle: it's the man I saw get into the Cadillac with Tali.

I get a preliminary hearing a week after my arrest. I'm hauled into a courtroom in the Hall of Justice in downtown San Jose and sit there like a dumbass for twenty minutes waiting for something to happen. Eventually it becomes clear that the prosecution is having trouble producing a key witness. The mall's head of security, who was supposed to verify the authenticity of the recording, hasn't shown up and he isn't answering his phone. They send a deputy to his house and he is found unconscious in his bathtub, apparently having slipped in the shower. He is rushed to the hospital. The prognosis is good, but he's not going to be making a court appearance anytime soon. My lawyer informs me that the prosecution will have to re-file charges and that until they do, I'm free to go. I tell him that's a pretty shitty joke, and he assures me he's not joking. This stuff happens occasionally: if a key witness is unavailable, the suspect has to be released until charges can be re-filed. The judge tells me not to leave the state and confirms that for now at least, I'm a free man. I can hardly believe it. Is this Ananke at work again? Or just dumb luck?

I'm transported back to the jail, where I change back into street clothes. I walk outside and flag down a cab. Half an hour later I'm home. As I get out of the cab, I notice an unmarked police car pulling up to the curb half a block down from my building. I may be a free man, but the police are keeping me on a short leash. I should have asked them to give me a ride.

The apartment seems positively welcoming after three days in the San Jose County Jail. I take a shower, make myself a TV dinner, and go to bed. It's barely dark outside, but I'm exhausted. I sleep well, for the first time in three days. When I wake up, it's still dark. I go to the window and see that the car – or another one just like it – is still there. I wonder if it's the only one. Am I important enough to warrant more than a single police car? Probably. I'm kind of a big deal now. But it's hard to see how they'd watch the whole apartment complex. My apartment has a pitiful little patio that backs up against a central courtyard flanked by three other buildings. Unless they've got somebody camped out in that courtyard, it would be pretty easy to slip out unnoticed. And if they catch me sneaking out, it's not like they can do anything but follow me. I'm a free man, for now.

I know what I need to do. I may be headed to death row, but I'm not going until I've confronted David Carlyle. I'm going to find out where Tali is and what the hell Peregrine is up to.

I put on jeans and a black sweatshirt and hoist myself over the wall into the courtyard. A dull glow behind the building on the east side of the complex tells me the sun is about to rise; the dim light and morning fog makes it impossible to see if there's anyone in the courtyard. My shoes crunch on the frozen grass as I make my way toward the neighboring building. The building next to mine is set back from the road fifty yards or so; if I exit the courtyard on the far side of it and cut across the lawn to the road, it's unlikely I'll be seen by the occupants of the car. I skirt the edge of the building, open the metal gate and make my way to the road, sparing a glance for the car. Its lights are off and I see no movement in the car. I duck down a side street toward a strip mall. The sun is coming up, but I'm still freezing. I walk to a McDonald's, get an Egg McMuffin and a coffee and take a seat. Peregrine's offices won't even open for another hour; I might as well sit and warm up a bit. After half an hour, I call for a cab.

I tell the driver to take me to the Peregrine building in the city. It's rush hour so traffic is terrible, but an hour and a half later he lets me out on a circular drive in front of a high rise in the financial district. The ride costs me $93. I put it on my credit card. Why not? I'm probably not going to live to pay the bill.

I go inside and walk across the marbled lobby to the reception desk. "I'm here to see David Carlyle," I say.

"And your name?" asks a pretty young receptionist.

"Paul Bayes," I say. It doesn't seem to register with her. I guess she doesn't watch the news.

"Do you have an appointment, Mr. Bayes?"

"Nope," I say. "But he knows who I am."

"OK, hold on a moment."

She makes a quick call, speaking in hushed tones into the phone. "Fortieth floor," she says to me with a smile. "Go on up."

I smile back, nodding at her. "Thank you," I say. I walk through a metal detector staffed by a bored-looking security guard to the elevator and punch 40. The elevator shoots up, depositing me on the 40th floor. A stocky man with an earpiece meets me as I get off the elevator. He seems familiar to me, and after a moment I realize why: he's the second man I saw with Tali at the mall. Carlyle's right-hand thug. He goes over my body with a hand-held metal detector and gives me a thorough pat-down, then gestures toward a big wooden door with a metal plaque reading *David Carlyle, Vice President of Predictive Analytics*. I walk down the hall and open the door.

Carlyle, wearing a precisely tailored dark blue suit, is staring out the floor-to ceiling window. It's a breathtaking view: to the right is the Bay Bridge, connecting the peninsula to Oakland and the rest of the East Bay; to the left is the Golden Gate, leading toward Sausalito and the great redwood forests on the Northern California coast. In the middle of the Bay is a small island with a cluster of buildings, a lighthouse and a water tower: Alcatraz. Clowns to the left of me, jokers to the right … The office is tastefully, though sparsely decorated: On the built-in bookshelf behind me I notice books by Nietzsche, Machiavelli and Ayn Rand. Never a good sign. Next to *Atlas Shrugged* is a small marble figurine of a falcon.

He turns, smiling. Not the vapid smile of the receptionist, though; more like the smile of a man watching a cat batting at a moth on the other side of a window pane. He's of medium height, thin and compactly built, with closely cropped blond-silver hair. His movements are precise; he projects an air of certainty. He's definitely the man who was with Tali in Alameda.

"Mr. Bayes," he says. "Good to meet you. My name is David Carlyle. You may call me David, if you like. Do you mind if I call you Paul?"

I shrug. "I just want to know where Tali is."

"Have a seat, please," he says. I remain standing. "Would you like something to drink? Water, Coke, scotch …"

"Scotch," I say. The hell with it. I sit down in the plush leather chair facing his desk. He pours two drinks and hands me one, taking a seat across from me. I notice a little black doodad on the desk.

"Tali is fine," he says. "And I can offer you proof of that. But before I do, I'd like to ask you a question. Does that sound fair, Paul?"

I shrug again and take a gulp of the scotch. It tickles my throat.

"Why did you do it?" he asks.

"Do what?" I reply.

"Come on, Paul. Why did you walk into Fairway Mall with a bomb?"

"What does it matter to you?" I ask. "Is the mall one of your clients?"

He laughs. "Fair question. Answer mine first, and I'll tell you everything you want to know."

"My lawyer ..." I start.

"Your lawyer," Carlyle says, "is an overpaid ambulance chaser who has already thrown in the towel on your case. Do you know how rarely insanity pleas work? But that's neither here nor there. Peregrine has hundreds of lawyers on retainer, including several excellent criminal lawyers. If you tell me what happened, I can offer you an actual defense. No guarantees, of course – the evidence against you is pretty strong. But you'll at least have a shot at avoiding death row. Maybe even an acquittal."

I realize he could be lying. He might use whatever I say against me. But what would his angle be? Anyway, how much worse could anything I tell him hurt me? My conviction is already a near-certainty. And maybe he really can answer some of my questions. Maybe he knows what happened to Tali.

"Heller told me it was a ransom. Fifty thousand dollars."

He claps his hands together. "Of course! For the return of Miss Stern. I should have thought of that."

"So you do know something about Tali's disappearance."

He laughs. "Well, of course I know. I was the one behind it."

"You son of a bitch!" I yell, getting to my feet. "You're the reason I was arrested!" By the time I'm halfway around the desk, Carlyle has pulled a gun from his desk – a nine millimeter semi-automatic.

"Let's keep this civil," says Carlyle, without a hint of irony.

I raise my hands and back away.

"Please, sit," he says. "Allow me to explain."

I sit down. My hands are shaking with anger. I throw the rest of the scotch down my throat and cough a few times. "Is she all right?"

"As I already said, she's perfectly fine," says Carlyle, dropping the gun to his lap.

"Why did you kidnap her? What do you want?"

"I didn't kidnap her," he says. "And what I wanted is exactly what I got."

"Mass murder?"

He shakes his head. "No. Not killing for its own sake; the bombing was important because of what it represented."

"Which is?"

"Proof. Proof that Heller could predict future events."

"He already had proof. They've known for over a year."

He nods. "Yes, but *I* didn't know. I can't run this division on theories. I need actual information."

"So that's all this is to you?" I snarl. "Mass murder is just business to you?"

"Look," says Carlyle. "I didn't make those people die. I didn't *want* them to die. And if Heller is to be believed, what I did or didn't want doesn't particularly matter anyway."

"Heller was a fucking sociopath."

"Maybe," he says. "Or maybe he just had the sort of clarity that comes with an expanded perspective. Think of it this way, Paul. Do you believe in God?"

"I don't know," I say. "I suppose. What does that have to do with anything?"

"Well," replies Heller, "if there is a God, and He's really omnipotent, then apparently he allowed you to walk into that mall with a bomb and kill all those people. God intentionally let those people die. So is God a sociopath? Or does God see a big picture that we can't?"

"Yeah, I get it. But Heller isn't God."

"Of course not. But you have to admit that predicting the future put him solidly on God's turf. In the end, it was too much for him to take."

"And that doesn't send a shiver up your spine? The guy who invented the technology put a bullet in his brain, and that doesn't make you wonder whether you should rethink your business plan?"

Carlyle shrugs. "Heller was trying to reconcile his notions of morality with his knowledge of the future. He was trying to figure out what it all *means*. I'm not. I don't give a shit what it *means*. To me, Tyche is just a tool."

"A moneymaking tool, you mean."

"Sure, and why not? If these events are going to happen anyway, why not make money off them?"

"So how does it work? You find out a building is going to burn down and cancel their policy the day before the fire?"

He smiles. "The idea would be to fine-tune the system a bit so that we don't have to be so obvious about it, but yes, that's the general idea. I mean, imagine the possibilities, Paul. What if we could charge our clients for information on future plane crashes? What if we could stop selling homeowner's insurance policies a month before a massive earthquake? We're talking *billions* of dollars here. Maybe *trillions*. The opportunities are almost unimaginable."

"And this all started because of an accident in Heller's shop?"

He looks surprised for a moment.

"I had a conversation with one of your ex-employees. A guy named Peter Girell."

"Ah," he says, nodding. "I should have known. Yes, that's how it started. I sent Girell to investigate the accident but the poor guy wouldn't know a quark from a Cuisinart. It seemed like it would be a straightforward case, so I decided I'd look into it myself. After interviewing Heller I realized the problem: his work revolved around what appeared to be a patently absurd hypothesis. Two of them, actually: first, that it was possible to predict violent events occurring in the near future; and second, that the future actively resisted being changed. If I rejected those hypotheses, I'd have to conclude that Heller was a harmless eccentric puttering around with a soldering iron, which meant that I'd have to pay his claim. If, on the other hand, I accepted that it was possible that Heller could predict the future and that the future resisted being changed, I could classify his experiments as 'inherently dangerous.' Heller was completely up front about everything; partly I think he was still in shock about the accident, but I also think he saw the dilemma I faced and was somewhat amused by it. I asked him to give me a list of colleagues who could give an expert opinion on his hypotheses, and he refused, saying that he didn't know of anyone who was qualified, and if he did, he wouldn't give me their names because it was 'too dangerous.' I asked him what he meant by that, and he told me that talking to anyone in the scientific community about his work would put their lives at risk. I thanked him for his time and denied the claim.

"All in a day's work, but that case haunted me for weeks. I couldn't put my finger on it. It wasn't an ethical issue: the matter really could have gone either way, and it's not like Heller went bankrupt as a result of the claim being denied. In any case, as you may have surmised, I'm not exactly a fountain of empathy. I've seen children die because our company – because *I* denied an experimental treatment. It's part of the business. So what was the problem?

"I realized that what I couldn't get out of my mind was the possibility that Heller was right. What if he *could* predict future tragedies? Can you imagine how much that knowledge would be worth to a company like Peregrine?

"I sent Girell back to Heller's house with some dummied up documents for him to sign. The documents basically said that Peregrine would be canceling his policy based on the fact that we believed, as a result of our investigation, that his work was a fraud. Heller's no dummy, of course; he realized that the document stating that his work was a fraud directly contradicted our own stated reason for denying his claim. His work couldn't be both completely bogus *and* inherently dangerous. A week later I was notified that Heller was suing us for two million dollars. I fired Girell and denied knowing anything about the documents. Then I went to Peregrine's board of directors and informed them of the problem. I suggested that we could buy Heller off by paying him a million dollars to produce proof that he could predict violent future events. If he succeeded, the results would be worth billions. If he failed, we'd be out a million dollars. If we went to trial, the court costs alone could easily exceed that. They agreed. I lobbied to be made the director of a new division, Predictive Analytics, which would manage Heller and act on any information he gave us. That was a tougher sell, but they went along with it. I think close to half of the board members saw it as a chance to give me enough rope to hang myself. If Heller failed, the division would be shut down and I'd be fired. I was willing to take the risk because I really did think Heller was on to something.

"Heller accepted the deal. He dropped the lawsuit, quit his job at Stanford and started working on the project full-time. He hired Miss Stern to help him. Every time I stopped by, they were hard at work, but ten months later they still hadn't produced any hard evidence. I was getting pressure from the board. I gave Heller a hard deadline: I wanted firm evidence of foreknowledge of a significant event within the next week. The week passed and he still hadn't given me anything. He pleaded with me, saying that he couldn't *force* an event to occur. I pointed out to him that there had been a fire in Oakland two days earlier that had killed eight people. He made some excuse about the detectors in that area not working properly. I gave him another week. When that week passed and still he had given me nothing, I decided that Heller needed to be convinced of the seriousness of the matter. I had Miss Stern disappear and told Heller that he had one more week. If he didn't give me proof by the end of the week, I'd have Miss Stern killed. Lo and behold, this time he came through with a prediction: he was sixty percent certain that on Saturday at five p.m., between five and nine people would be killed at the Fairway Mall, near the fountain in the atrium. I told him good, he'd better not be lying, because I was going to be at the mall at five p.m. and if nothing happened, I was going to shoot Tali in the head.

"I have to tell you it was quite a relief to me when you showed up with that briefcase. Sorry for shooting at you, by the way. I couldn't afford to be caught. I could hardly wait to tell the board the next morning that Heller had given me proof. But then I heard on the news that Heller was dead and the bomber had been apprehended at his house. No wonder Heller was able to predict the bombing, I thought: he caused it! I didn't know at that point how he had conned you into bringing the bomb to the mall, but I knew that he was somehow responsible. There was no other explanation for why you'd be at his house.

"But then it occurred to me that just because Heller was responsible for the bomb, that didn't mean he didn't have foreknowledge of it. That is, maybe Heller *did* know about the bombing in advance, but he wasn't willing to risk that forty percent chance that he was wrong. Maybe he cared enough about Tali that he was willing to be the guy who built the bomb if that's what it took to save her life. He couldn't go to the mall himself, of course. Besides the fact that the bomb would likely kill him, a bombing that he personally committed wouldn't be adequate proof. So he suckered you into doing it, figuring I wouldn't make the connection.

"It's a little maddening when you think about it. I mean, let's assume that Heller was telling the truth: that the psionic field detectors showed a sixty percent chance of a mass killing at the mall. Heller probably told himself that there was a sixty percent chance that somebody was going to set off a bomb at the mall whether he did it or not, so he really wasn't responsible for killing those eight people. On the other hand, it was the lack of certainty that caused him to act: sixty percent wasn't high enough for him. He wanted to be personally responsible for the bombing to increase the odds. But of course he knew beforehand that increasing the odds was impossible, because anything he was going to do would already have been factored into the odds. So should he have sat back and waited for someone else to bomb the mall? Or should he have tried to warn the people at the mall? If he had, would he get karmic brownie points for trying to do the 'right thing,' even though he couldn't possible have changed the outcome? For that matter, should Heller be considered a murderer, even though those people were most likely going to die whether or not he killed them?" Carlyle seems amused by the whole situation, as if it were a brain teaser on the back of a cereal box.

"He should have tried to stop it," I say. "Maybe that forty percent chance was the possibility he wouldn't send me to the mall with the bomb."

Carlyle shakes his head. Somehow I know what he's going to say before he says it. "It doesn't work like that. Virtually everything you do, every choice you make, is deterministic. In a sense, it's meaningless to talk about what Heller should have done. There is no *should*; there is only what was going to happen and what did happen. And those two things are really the same thing, separated into arbitrary categories of past and future. I think maybe this is why Heller's hypotheses resonated with me: I've always felt like morality was sort of like window dressing. It doesn't have any effect on the underlying reality. There is no *ought*; there is only what *is*."

"So what's the point?" I ask. "If there's no free will, no morality. What are you trying to accomplish?"

"There's no *trying*," says Carlyle. "There is only what is going to happen. And what is going to happen is that I'm going to become the CEO of the most powerful company in the world. And then I'm going to have some fun." He smiles and finishes his drink.

"Good luck running your little division without Heller," I say.

He laughs. "I don't need Heller. I've got his data and his equipment. Not to mention the actual brains behind the operation."

"You're still holding Tali?" I demand, eyeing the gun in his lap.

He laughs again. "Holding? No." He presses a button on his phone. "Miss Stern, could you come in here a minute. I think Paul Bayes would like to see you."

A moment later Tali walks in the office, looking tired but unhurt. She's wearing a very professional looking skirt and jacket. Her curly brown hair is pulled back in a ponytail. "Hello, Paul," she says.

"What is this, Tali?" I ask. "Do you work for these guys?"

She nods. "I've been helping them get up to speed on Heller's system. We've moved the Tyche server here to the Peregrine building." I open my mouth to object, but she holds up her hand. "It's not as bad as it sounds, Paul. Dr. Heller and I had reached an impasse with his work. We couldn't make any progress from a strictly scientific standpoint, because Ananke kept stonewalling us. The problem with science is that it's a collaborative activity, and the more people who know about Ananke, the harder she fights against discovery. But in business, secrecy has value. Peregrine isn't about to tell its competitors about Ananke, and as long as we keep the Predictive Analytics division small and swear all of our employees to secrecy, we may have a chance to do some actual good."

I can't believe what I'm hearing. "Actual good? Tali, this guy just got done telling me how he's going to revoke fire insurance policies before fires break out. How is that good? Who is that helping, besides Carlyle and Peregrine's stockholders?"

She shakes her head. "It's more complicated than that. I mean, you're right, Carlyle is a manipulative, amoral asshole. But he's also a genius." Carlyle shrugs and goes to get another drink. I see that he's put the gun back in the drawer.

"A genius!" I yell. "Tali, he had you kidnapped! He's responsible for Heller's suicide, for all those people dying in the mall! He's a sociopath! How can you not see this?"

"I *do* see it, Paul," Tali snaps. "I'm not a child. I've seen more people die than I care to remember. Do you realize that when I let you live that day at the BART station, I was taking dozens of lives in my hands? There was no guarantee I would make it to the second crux in time, and even if I did, there was a fifty percent chance that cop would *still* go to the wrong restaurant for lunch. Even as things turned out, an old man was killed and a teenage girl will probably never walk again. And that was a *good* day, Paul. Half the time I fail completely. Do you understand that? I've gone to the sites of twenty-three tragic mass killings in order to prevent them, and I've failed thirteen times. That's forty-six deaths I've been a part of. So don't lecture me about my choice of business partners. I'm in insurance. That's always what I've been doing, just playing the odds. It's a lousy business filled with lousy people. And let me add that I appreciate the irony of you lecturing me on responsibility, Mr. leaves-his-life-up-to-a-coin-toss."

She's right, and it hurts. A lot. What do I know about any of this, about what she's been going through since she realized the sort of power Heller had unleashed? I've got no right to say anything. And yet, something still bugs me. Something doesn't fit. "I'm sorry, Tali. I just don't get it. This guy kidnaps you and now you're working for him? Just like that?"

"As Tali says, it's a little more complicated than that, Paul," says Carlyle. "For one thing, saying I kidnapped her is being a little overdramatic. I met Tali at her car that night, just after the Pier 39 shooting, which I understand you witnessed. I expressed to her my frustration at Heller's apparent lack of progress with the Tyche system and I suggested that Peregrine might have to resort to legal recourse to force Heller to turn over his data. I know that Tali and Heller are paranoid about anyone finding out about Tyche ..."

"Not paranoid," says Tali. "The more people who know specific information about the system, the less reliable it is. If you'd have dragged us into court, there'd have been lawyers, expert witnesses ... who knows what Ananke would do? She'd probably have killed us all before we ever got to trial."

"Like I said," says Carlyle, grinning, "paranoid. Not without reason, actually. I had one of our investigators tailing Tali. He followed her to the BART station and observed her meeting with you. He had a hard time figuring out what that was about. Tali watched you flip a coin and then called out to you when it looked like you were going to step in front of the train. Eventually we pieced together that it had something to do with trying to prevent the Pier 39 incident. I have to admit, as much as I thought about the potential of being able to predict future events, it never occurred to me to try to *stop* them. I wouldn't have thought it was possible.

"Anyway, my investigator followed the cab you two got into for a few miles, but he lost you before you got on the bridge. I don't know what you told that driver, but I don't think the devil himself could have kept a tail on him. The investigator returned to the BART station and waited near Tali's car. When she returned, he convinced her that it was in her interest to meet with me.

"I told Tali I wanted a demonstration of what Tyche could do. I suspected that she could somehow remotely tap into the Tyche data, so I figured I'd hold onto her until she could demonstrate foreknowledge of an event."

"Hold onto her?" I ask. "How is this not kidnapping?"

"She was free to leave. I put her in an empty office down the hall and kept her under watch. I even let her keep her phone, since I suspected that was how she tapped into the Tyche system. But I told her that if she left or attempted to contact Heller, I would pursue legal action against them. I suppose you could call that blackmail, but it wasn't kidnapping."

"Why didn't you want her to contact Heller?"

He laughs. "Are you seriously asking me that? Heller convinced you to carry a bomb into a crowded shopping mall. The reason I approached Tali rather than Heller is that I think Tali is basically pragmatic and reasonable. Heller was not. Heller was a true believer. He really believes in all this Ananke bullshit."

"He's not wrong," says Tali.

"Oh, I know," says Carlyle, with a wave of his hand. "I mean, I believe in Ananke too, I suppose, the same way I believe in Mother Nature or Lady Luck. It's a sort of mental crutch. But Heller literally thinks there's some mysterious, nearly omnipotent and omniscient being out there who is conspiring against him. The point is, there was no telling what he would do, or what he would convince Tali to do. No, I needed Tali isolated from Heller, so she could think rationally about what she was doing, what she was trying to protect. As she says, she and Heller were at a dead-end. I can do so much more with the system than they could. And it's my system! I paid for it! Legally, ethically, practically, any way you want to look at it, she was obligated to give me that data.

"At first, she tried to stonewall me, insisting, as Heller had, that she couldn't *make* events happen. I told her, fine, we'll just wait until one comes up. I've got time. I think she thought she could out-wait me." He smiles at Tali. She stares coldly back at him. "But then a fire broke out in an apartment building in Hayward. Eleven people died. It was exactly the sort of event that Tyche was supposed to be able to predict, but Tali had given me no warning of it. She insisted that nothing had showed up in the data, and even showed me the Tyche app on her phone. But of course I didn't know what I was looking at; I was completely dependent on Tali to explain the readings to me. And for all I knew, she had rigged the app to give false readings. It was meaningless. So I told her I was giving her one more chance. She either gives me warning of the next event or I cut her loose and file suit against her and Heller. Then, for her next trick —"

"God damn it, Carlyle," Tali snaps. "It wasn't a trick. I don't know what happened. The data clearly indicated a high probability of an event in Alameda. If I could have thought of a way to keep leading you on, I would have, but I knew I was screwed at that point. I had to give you something. But somehow, somebody must have tampered with the outcome. There was a crux, so it's possible that Heller somehow …"

"It wasn't Heller," I say. "I was there. I stopped the Alameda event. Whatever it was, it didn't happen because of me."

"You?" asks Tali, confused. "Why would you …?"

I shrug. "I thought it was what you would want. I didn't realize you needed the event to happen. I also interfered with the apartment fire in Hayward. That is, I guess I caused the fire. So that was my fault too."

"Aha!" says Carlyle. "I shouldn't have doubted you, Tali. It hadn't occurred to me that Heller had enlisted Paul as his errand boy before the bombing."

"I wasn't his errand boy," I growl. "It was my idea. He just wanted me to observe …"

"And did you observe?" asks Carlyle, that smug grin flashing across his face again.

I get his point, and I can feel the blood rushing into my cheeks. I *had* been Heller's errand boy.

"At the time," Carlyle continues, "I thought Tali was playing me for a fool. I tried to get her to admit that she had fabricated the Alameda event to make me think the Tyche system was unreliable, but she insisted – truthfully, as it turns out – that she had given me an accurate reading of the data. Not only that, but she then informed me that her access to Tyche had been cut off. She said she thought Heller must have suspected that she was being forced to use the data, so he revoked her access. I didn't believe her about that either."

"It's true," I say. "Heller saw that she had been accessing the system and he cut her off."

"Well, then I have to apologize about that as well," says Carlyle, glancing at Tali. Tali nods almost imperceptibly.

"At that point, I didn't have a lot of options," Carlyle continues. "I thought Tali was lying about being cut off, so I decided to call her bluff. I called Heller and told him I was going to kill Tali if he didn't produce evidence of foreknowledge of an event. I never intended to go through with it, and I certainly didn't expect Heller to respond by sending someone with a bomb into a crowded mall. Maybe I should have; the guy was obviously insane. But he gave me what I wanted: a prediction of a major event at the mall. You know the rest. I never held Tali against her will; she came along to the mall as a gesture of goodwill. I think by that time she had realized that protecting Heller was doing her no good, and that it was in everybody's interest to force Heller to give up Tyche."

"When you showed up at the mall," Tali says, turning to me, "I knew what must have happened. Carlyle had scared Dr. Heller so badly that he didn't dare leave matters up to chance. He was determined to make something bad happen at the mall, because he was convinced that if it didn't, I would be killed. I knew what had to be in that briefcase. But Paul, you have to understand that there's no way that you could have known. What happened at the mall, it wasn't your fault. It wasn't anybody's fault. It just happened."

"Bullshit," I say. "I know it's not *my* fault. I mean, I'll take the blame for being a complete dupe and a dumbass, and for thinking you were an innocent victim in all this, Tali. But I'm no murderer. And this didn't 'just happen.' Jesus Christ, Tali. You sound like Heller. Heller made the bomb, and this son of a bitch provoked him into doing it. If there's any justice in the universe, both of them will rot in hell for it."

"I'm sorry, Paul," says Tali. "I don't particularly like the way things turned out either, but you have to understand that they couldn't have happened any other way. You see that, don't you?"

I shake my head. More of Heller's fatalistic bullshit. I wish I'd never met this girl.

She continues, "And maybe you don't care, but part of my deal with Peregrine was that they pay for your defense. It's a tough case, but they have very good lawyers. If there's anyone who can win it, it's them. Or at least save you from death row."

I laugh humorlessly. "Saving me from certain death, that's kind of your thing, huh, Tali? What happens to me after you swoop in and save me, that's not really your concern. And hey, fuck all those people who are going to die in fires and car crashes that you could be preventing, right?"

Tali says nothing. Her expression is unreadable.

"Well, Paul," says Carlyle, unfazed by my outburst, "I appreciate you taking the time to come down here and answer my questions. I've got nothing further for you, so if you're satisfied that Tali is all right, I'll let you be on your way."

Nice. Let me be on my way. Where am I going to go? Maybe I'll have a cab take me to the Golden Gate Bridge. They've made it pretty hard to jump from these days, but where there's a will, there's a way.

Part Eight: Tali the Destroyer

I stand up and head for the door. As I do, there's a knock from the other side.

"Come in," says Carlyle. "We're finished in here."

The security guard who'd frisked me earlier walks in, holding a manila folder in his left hand. His right hand is inside his jacket. "Mr. Carlyle, I need you to come downstairs." I step out of his way, keeping my hands in sight.

"What for?" Carlyle says, frowning.

The man glances at Tali. "Sir, the security audit is complete and your suspicions were correct."

For a moment no one says anything. Carlyle is studying the security guard, as if trying to probe him telepathically. His eyes fall to the folder in the man's hand.

"Get them both out of here," says Carlyle. Tali takes a step back. She has a guarded look on her face, but she doesn't really seem surprised.

"Yes, sir," says the guard. "But first, I really need to get you downstairs. It isn't safe here."

Carlyle is losing his temper. "Mike, the only threats to my security are the two people standing in front of you. So I repeat: *get them out of here.*"

The man bites his lip. "Sir, I don't think that's a good idea."

"Jesus Christ, Mike. Are we playing charades? What's in the fucking folder?"

"Preliminary results of the security audit," says Mike, glancing at Tali again. "We've found evidence that someone has been masking the results of the Tyche program."

"Someone?" asks Carlyle. "She's standing right next to you, Mike. It's not a secret. We knew she was probably spoofing the results. That's why we did the audit."

Tali suddenly looks scared.

"Yes, sir," says Mike, uncertainly, but doesn't make a move.

Carlyle's face is turning red. He speaks slowly, through gritted teeth. "Mike. Could you please draw your gun and escort these two individuals out of my office?"

"Sir, it's just that ... we were able to remove the mask she implemented and get a look at the actual data. It shows a high probability of a violent death occurring near detector number 21482 in the next –" He glances at his watch. " – fifty-five seconds."

Carlyle's eyes fall to the little black doodad on his desk. He reaches out and picks it up, looking at the label on its back side. I can tell by the way the color drains from his face what number is on it.

"Mike," he says slowly. "Please take this thing and escort these two out of my office as quickly as possible."

Mike doesn't move.

"Mike," says Carlyle again. "Pick that goddamn thing up and get it out of here or I will shoot you in the face."

Mike moves toward the desk, but as he does so, Tali strikes him on the back of the head with something. The marble falcon falls from her fingers to the carpet. Mike pulls a nine millimeter pistol from a shoulder holster but then stumbles, dazed from the blow. The gun falls from his hand and he slumps to the floor.

I manage to catch the gun and point it at Carlyle just as he retrieves his own gun from the desk. Mike is moaning on the floor, holding his head. Blood pours between his fingers.

"Get out of here," I say to Tali. "If somebody's going to die here, it's not going to be you."

She hesitates. "Paul, I want you to know ..."

"I do," I say. "It's OK. Heller was right. I'm still alive so that I can save you. I don't know why exactly, but I know he was right. Don't make a liar out of him. You owe him that much."

She nods dumbly and backs out of the room.

OK, Carlyle, me and you. You've got a lot more to lose than I do, brother.

"I'm not going to shoot you," I say. "I don't care what the goddamned machine says. I'm not a murderer. I didn't kill those people at the mall, and I'm not going to kill you. Now I'm going to back out of this room, and you're going to let me. We're all going to live to fight another day."

He smiles and shakes his head slightly, not letting his eyes off me. His hand is steady on the gun. "It doesn't work like that," he says.

"You know," I say, "I'm getting really fucking tired of hearing that. It works however you want it to work. I don't shoot you, you don't shoot me. Nobody dies. The machine is wrong this time."

"If you believe that," he says, "take the detector with you."

I look at the little black box sitting innocently on the desk. It's just an antenna, I tell myself. All it does is collect data. It can't *do* anything. But somehow I know that's wrong. That little box knows that someone is going to die near it in the very near future, and if I pick it up, that someone is going to be me. But if I don't?

"Time's almost up," he says.

If I pick it up, I know he won't shoot me until I'm out of the room, because the farther the detector gets from him, the more likely he is to live. And the more likely I am to die. Fantastic.

I pick it up and stuff it in my jacket pocket, holding the gun on him the whole time. I back slowly toward the still-open door. I'm only two feet from the doorway when Mike's hand clutches my ankle, pulling me toward him. I lose my balance and fall to the floor. Mike gets on top of me and draws his hand back. I can see that he's got the marble falcon in his hand. His shirt is soaked with blood.

"Let him go!" Carlyle yells. "Mike, for Christ's sake, let him go!"

Mike swings at my head with the statue, but I manage to get my arm up in time to block it. I see he's got a crazy look in his eyes, like he isn't all there. A head injury will do that.

"Mike!" Carlyle yells again. He's backed all the way against the window, like he's worried about getting the plague or something, waving the gun toward us. "Get off him! You have to let him go!"

Mike raises his hand to take another swing. Carlyle fires his gun, hitting Mike in the shoulder and causing him to drop the falcon. He loses his balance and falls on top of me. Insanely, Mike is still grabbing at me, clutching at my face, my hair, my clothes. He gets a firm grip on my jacket but I twist out of it. I push him away and scramble out the door, slamming it behind me. I'm shaking bad from the adrenaline, but I manage to run down the hall. Tali is waiting in the elevator, holding the door open for me. "Come on!" she yells.

As I near the elevator, I hear a noise behind me and turn to face it. Carlyle is pointing his gun in my direction. I fall to the ground as the gun goes off, firing wildly in Carlyle's direction. I'm aware of a cacophony of gunfire echoing through the halls, but it's like I'm observing it from outside. I have no idea which shots are his and which are mine. Finally the noise stops, and Carlyle and I face each other down the hall. Not knowing whether I've been shot, I look down at my chest. Something is wrong: I'm not wearing my jacket. It had gotten torn off during my struggle with Mike. And the psionic field detector is still in the pocket.

A spot of blood has appeared in the center of Carlyle's shirt and spread rapidly across his chest. He falls to the floor, still. On the floor just behind him is my jacket.

I stumble onto the elevator and we go down. The guard in the lobby doesn't give us any trouble; I'm waving Mike's gun around like a man with nothing to lose.

We find Tali's car in the parking lot and peel away. Tali seems to be driving aimlessly, taking the path of least resistance to put as much space between us and Peregrine as possible. Whenever there's a green light, she takes it.

My hands are still shaking, but I'm starting to calm down a little. I keep expecting to see a splotch of blood appear on my chest the way it did on Carlyle. I can hardly believe none of his shots hit me. And now he's dead.

It's too bad in a way that both Heller and Carlyle are dead. If there were any justice, Heller would have lived to see what Carlyle had become: the perfect expression of Heller's "life force," striving to conquer, to overcome, to exert his will over the entire planet. Peregrine *über alles!* That's what you get when you combine genius, will and reason and leave out morality, Heller, you motherfucker. Human beings reduced to numbers on a corporate spreadsheet.

Tali pulls over and starts doing something with her phone.

"What now?" I ask.

"Shut up," she says. A worried look has come over her. "Jesus," she mumbles. "Jesus."

"What? What is it?"

"I was afraid of this," she says. "Ananke is fed up."

"What does that mean? Fed up with what?"

"We need to get out of the city."

"And go where?"

"Doesn't matter. We just have to get out."

We head toward 101 to get on the Golden Gate Bridge, but traffic is backed up. "Shit, shit, shit," Tali is muttering.

"What? What's going to happen?"

"Take a look," she says, handing me her phone. It takes me a few seconds to realize what I'm looking at: it's a map of the Bay Area, but most of it is covered with red blotches.

"What is all that stuff?"

"Take a guess," she says, making a U-turn.

I'm not really in the mood for riddles, but it's not like I have anything better to do. I study the map while she maneuvers down side streets, trying to find an alternate route to the bridge. After a few minutes, I see it.

"Fault lines," I say.

She nods.

"Holy shit," I say, staring at the map. I've figured out that I can zoom out by pinching my fingers together on the screen. The red just keeps going, covering almost the entire Bay Area, from Monterrey to Santa Rose. Even Sacramento is half red. "My God," I say. "How big ...?"

"Nine point oh, maybe nine point five."

"Jesus Christ." The 1989 Loma Prieta quake that wrecked the Bay Bridge was a six point nine. An eight point nine would be a *hundred times* as powerful.

She's given up on the main roads and is attempting a shortcut through the Presidio. Finally she gives up on roads altogether, driving across long stretches of grass in a beeline toward the bridge.

"How long do we have?"

"Until one forty-three," she says. That's eight minutes from now.

"Why didn't you check this earlier? You could have been out of town by now!"

"I couldn't!" she snaps. "I was doing everything I could to keep Peregrine from getting the real data."

"Why?"

"Jesus, Paul, if you haven't figured it out by now …"

I hear sirens behind us, but I know there's no way in hell we're pulling over. I look behind us and see flashing lights several cars back. Tali cuts across another lawn.

"I thought you said if Peregrine kept the data secret …"

She shakes her head. "That was bullshit. Peregrine can't use the data any more than we can. If they start making decisions with major consequences based on the Tyche data, Ananke is going to stop them. I tried to tell Carlyle, but he wouldn't listen. I had to pretend to come over to his side, to act like I thought Peregrine could use the data."

"But why hasn't she stopped them already then? Why did she let things get this far?"

"You remember what I said about Carlyle being a genius? That part was true."

Shit. I'm starting to understand now. Carlyle's epiphany about using Heller's data to remake the insurance industry had been just that: a stroke of genius, uncaused, unpredictable. Ananke never saw it coming. Sure, why not? If there are such things as artistic genius and scientific genius, why not business genius? And Carlyle's plans weren't subtle, like Heller's had been. Carlyle was planning on taking over the world by taking advantage of the Tyche data. And now Ananke was going to put him in his place – if she had to destroy the whole Bay Area to do it.

We fly through the toll gate and get on the bridge. The phone says we have six minutes. The sirens are loud now; the cops are on the shoulder, gaining fast.

"What's she trying to do?" I ask.

"Dunno," says Tali, swerving wildly around a Miata. "Take out the Peregrine building, for sure. Wipe out as many detectors as she can. Destroy the data. Bankrupt the company. Probably all of the above."

"Jesus." I have to warn Deb and the kids. There isn't time for them to get out of the Bay Area, but maybe they're far enough away from the epicenter that they'll be OK if they can get outside. I call Deb first, figuring that if something happens to me, she can warn the kids. If she answers, that is. I haven't talked to her since my arrest. She probably thinks I've gone completely nuts. The phone rings three times and it seems like an eternity. Finally she answers.

"What do you want, Paul? I'm at work."

"I know," I say. "You need to get outside, out of the bank. There's going to be an earthquake. A big one."

"Paul, God damn it. I don't know what you're trying to do, but I'm not falling for it. You've lost it, Paul. I knew you were on the edge when you stopped by that night, but … Jesus. How are you even calling me? Aren't you in prison?"

"I was released," I say. "Deb, please. I don't have time to explain. Just get outside, away from any buildings. Then call the school and tell them there's been a family emergency. Tell them …" But I'm talking to myself. Deb has hung up. Shit!

We're halfway across the bridge now. Tali is on the shoulder, topping out the Lexus. I'm afraid to look how fast we're going. The cops are actually falling behind. They probably figure this is the sort of thing they have helicopters for.

Suddenly I realize what I have to do. It's like an epiphany, beamed into my brain directly from heaven. Maybe this is my one moment of genius. Or maybe Ananke sees it coming and doesn't really care. She's got bigger things on her mind. I guess it doesn't really matter.

I dial the kids' school. My heart is pounding is so loudly I wonder if they'll be able to hear it through the phone. The school secretary answers. "Mark Twain Elementary School, Janet speaking. How may I help you?"

"Hi, Janet," I say. "My name is Paul Bayes. Do you recognize my name?"

Silence.

"I'm going to assume that you do. Janet, I've planted a bomb somewhere in the school. It's set to go off in exactly five minutes. If you can get the kids out of the school in five minutes, they will live. Do you understand?"

After a moment, she says, in a hoarse whisper, "Yes."

"Good luck, Janet," I say, and end the call.

I don't think Tali heard me, which is just as well. She's too focused on keeping us on the road. Well, if there was any reasonable doubt about me being a cold-blooded mass-murderer, I've erased it. Not even Peregrine's lawyers could save me from lethal injection now. The important thing is that the kids are safe. They do fire drills all the time; they have to be able to get everybody out in five minutes, don't they?

I'm distracted from my thoughts by the sight of Alcatraz out my window, bobbing up and down in the water. No, that's not right; islands don't bob. Shit, that means *we're* bobbing. It's hard to tell how much, being on the bridge, but I estimate that we're swaying a good thirty feet from side to side. Funny, if it weren't for the horizon moving up and down like that, you wouldn't even know. I turn around and immediately wish I hadn't: the cops have fallen well behind, but that isn't what bothers me: I'm watching the gigantic suspension tower behind us twist and sway crazily, like one of those inflatable balloon guys that car dealerships put up to attract customers. It makes me queasy and I turn to face front.

The view that direction isn't much better: Tali is still careening through traffic and the tower in front of us is starting to squirm too. I can feel the movement, now, side-to-side and up-and-down. Occasionally the road warps enough beneath us that I can feel the tires momentarily leave the asphalt. I want to scream at Tali to slow down, but I know we're dead if we do. We keep going.

Soon the second tower is behind us as well. Solid ground is just up ahead. I wonder if it will be an improvement. I hear something like an explosion behind us and turn to see the base of the first tower has sheared almost completely in half. It's falling to my right as I'm facing it, toward the ocean and away from the Bay. It's pulling the second tower with it. Tali slows and pulls the wheel to the right as suddenly we're driving on the side of a hill that's getting steeper by the second. The driver of a pickup in front of us panics and brakes. The pickup's wheels lock and it spins into the lane to the left, slamming into a Schwann's truck. Tali swerves to the right,

taking advantage of a gap between two Priuses barely big enough
for the Lexus and then swerves back to the left. The asphalt is
broken ahead of us; the bridge is separating from the land, pulling
up and away from the weight of the falling tower. The Lexus leaps a
three-foot the gap with aplomb, and suddenly we're back on solid
ground.

Except it's not solid. Not by a long shot. I've driven through
earthquakes before and not even known it at the time. One of them
was a four point three. Between the cushioning of the tires and the
motion of the car, you don't even notice the ground move a few
inches. But this one I feel. It's like we're riding ocean swells. And in
addition to the sickening up-and-down movement, there's a sort of
sideways twisting motion that makes it hard for Tali to keep the car
on the road. The engine roars wildly at random intervals as the
ground slips back and forth underneath us, alternately increasing
and decreasing the friction on the tires. At the first opportunity, she
pulls over. After a moment's deliberation, we decide we're safer
outside of the car and off the road. The fewer big heavy things that
can fall on us, the better. It's like running through the waves on the
beach; our knees buckle and occasionally we're knocked flat on the
ground, but we keep moving away from the road and the wildly
swerving cars. We make our way to a grassy hillside and fall to the
ground. The bridge is completely gone, and huge waves are crashing
over the rock shore below us. It's hard to see from here, but I think
the Bay Bridge is down too. In the distance I see the city on fire.
There are plumes of black smoke rising to the north and east as
well.

The quake is over. At least the first one is. Usually there are
aftershocks for a while after these things. Still, I figure the greater
risk is staying here. Tali evidently agrees. "We've got to get away
from here," she says. "A quake like this … it's going to be bad."

I nod. Disasters bring out the best and the worst in people, and
I don't think either of us particularly feels like playing the odds. We
get back in the car and head north. The highway is blocked in
several places, but we manage to make slow progress by exiting and
taking surface streets a couple of times. Fortunately, it's the middle
of the afternoon so the evening rush hadn't yet started by the time
of the quake. At first I'm surprised that there aren't more

emergency vehicles passing us going the opposite direction, but then I remember that there's no longer any way to get to San Francisco from here. Probably all four bridges are out, which means that the city is only accessible from the south – or by air. And the highways from the south are probably hopelessly blocked too. There won't be any help anytime soon for people on the peninsula. The city is going to burn for days. The East Bay probably isn't in much better shape. Deb is most likely dead, unless she happened to be in the bank's vault at the time of the quake. Those vaults can take quite a bit. The kids should be fine, assuming they got outside in time. I resist the urge to call the school again. Even if I got through, they probably wouldn't tell me anything. I try calling Deb a few times but there's no answer. Then I try her parents' house in Modesto. No answer there either. I turn off my phone.

We spend the next six hours fighting traffic on 101 North; we're not the only ones who are getting the hell out of Dodge. There are a few aftershocks, but the worst seems to be over. At nine p.m. we finally stop for gas and food near Santa Rosa. The little corner store is out of just about everything: bottled water, ice, beer, sandwiches … pretty much anything you might want under the circumstances. They're rationing gas; we're allotted four gallons. Dinner is black licorice, Wheat Thins and diet raspberry iced tea. Better than nothing, but not by much. While Tali is waiting for the bathroom, I call Deb's parents again. This time her mom answers.

"Hello?" she says.

"Hi, Mom," I say. I don't know what else to call her. "It's Paul."

"Paul, my God, where are you? Were you in the quake?"

Something isn't right. Deb's mom never liked me even before I was the prime suspect in a mass murder, but now she sounds genuinely concerned. Concerned about my whereabouts, if nothing else.

"I'm fine," I say. "Do you have the kids?"

There's a pause. "Yes, Paul. The kids are here."

"And they're OK?"

"They're fine, Paul. I think they would like to see you."

"Have you heard from Deb?"

After another pause, she says, "She's not answering her phone. The bank doesn't answer either." I can tell she's crying.

I don't know what to say. I find myself blubbering, "I'm sorry, I tried to warn her …"

She cuts me off. "You tried to warn her about an earthquake?" she snaps. "Jesus Christ, Paul. What is wrong with you?"

It's an excellent question. What *is* wrong with me? Why am I trying to prove to Deb's mom that I'm really an OK guy? That ship has *sailed*, pal.

"I'm sorry," I bluster again. "I just meant that I wish there was something I could have done."

There's a rustling sound and then a man's voice: Deb's father. "Paul," he says. "Martin and Sylvia are here. Where are you? Can you get here?"

"I'd like to talk to them," I say. "Can you put Martin on the phone?"

More silence. "I don't think that's a good idea, Paul."

"Why not?" I ask.

"They've already been through a lot," he says.

"I'm their *father*," I snap. "Now put them on the goddamn phone."

"I'm not going to do that, Paul," he says. "They deserve better than you."

It hits me like a punch in the gut. I want to scream at him, tell him to go fuck himself, but the fact is he's right. I was never much of a father and now I'm a wanted fugitive. I'm guessing their house is filled with cops right now scaring the shit out of Martin and Sylvia, all because of me.

I take a deep breath. "OK," I say. "But I want you to do something for me. Tell them I love them both. And tell them I'm sorry."

Silence.

"Please," I say, swallowing a lump in my throat. "Can you please just tell them? I won't bother you again."

After a pause, he says, "I'll tell them."

"Thank you," I say. "You can tell the police to go home. I won't be stopping by tonight."

"You know they'll find you, Paul," he says. "Do the right thing and turn yourself in."

I hang up. By the time Tali returns from the bathroom I've managed to mostly compose myself.

"Any news?"

"Kids are OK," I say. "Wife is still missing. Cops are at my in-laws' house. How long does it take to trace a cell phone call?"

"Not long, I think," she says. "But all they can do is pinpoint what tower you're using."

"They'll know what road I'm on."

"But not which direction you're going."

I almost laugh at that. "You're a real glass-half-full kind of person, aren't you? What kind of lunatic would be driving south right now?"

She shrugs. "The kind of lunatic that would call in a bomb threat to save his kids from an earthquake?"

I cringe. "You heard that, huh? I thought you were distracted."

"I heard enough."

"Was I convincing?"

"As a homicidal maniac? Absolutely."

"Good. I'm going to put that on my resume."

"Hey, it worked, didn't it?"

"I guess so," I say. "The kids are OK. That's the important thing. They're going to hate me, but there's nothing I can do about that."

"I'm sorry, Paul."

I shrug. "You should get out of here. The cops will probably be here soon."

"What are you going to do, turn yourself in?"

"I don't know. I'll figure something out."

She laughs. "What are you going to figure out? You need to decide right now whether you want to survive or not. If you sit here and try to 'figure something out,' they're going to put a needle in your arm."

"I'll hitch a ride with someone."

"And then what? If the FBI isn't already looking for you, they will be soon. You think you can escape the feds on foot, with twenty dollars and a handful of black licorice? I'm not leaving you, Paul. We're in this together."

"You don't have to do that, Tali."

"Yes, I do," she says. "Wait, no, you're right. I don't have to. But I'm going to."

"Why? You'll go to prison if they catch us."

"They're not going to catch us."

The fuck they aren't. "If you say so."

"I do," she says. "I'm going to get you out of this. I promise."

Yeah, I think. You're going to save me, just like you saved your sister. But I don't have the energy to fight her. "All right," I say. "Hey, they can track my cell phone even when I'm not using it, right?"

"I think so," she says. "You should take the battery out."

"I've got a better idea," I say. I walk across the parking lot to a pickup that had been following us since Petaluma. The driver, a young man in a black t-shirt and jeans, is waiting at the register with his own nutritionally challenged dinner. The truck's bed is loaded with boxes and camping supplies. I shove my cell phone between two of the boxes and walk back to the car.

"Good thinking," Tali says.

"Thanks. I still think we're fucked, but it's worth a shot. We'll have a better chance if we get off the highway. If they stop that guy, it's not going to take them long to figure out they've been had. And if we're three cars ahead of him …"

"Got it. We'll go east at our first opportunity. There's a bunch of winding roads through the foothills. If we keep heading that direction we'll eventually hit the interstate. It'll be a hell of a drive, but they won't be expecting it."

"And then what?"

She smiles. "We'll figure something out."

Great.

We get back on the road and take the first exit off 101 leading east, wending our way into the foothills to the east of Santa Rosa. I find myself staring at Tali. I still don't really understand why she is doing this. She's a smart girl with a bright future. She hasn't done anything illegal – not anything she could reasonably be prosecuted for, anyway. Why would she go out of her way to aid a fugitive wanted for mass murder? Is it just because that's who she is? Is she driven to help other people even at the expense of her own life? Or am I not giving her enough credit? Is she actually choosing to help me of her own free will? I wonder what difference it really makes in the end.

"I want you to know I'm sorry," I say.

"What for?"

"For accusing you of not caring. About me, and about all those people. I know you were doing the best you could. It's not your fault I fucked everything up."

"Paul," she says, gently but sternly, "you didn't fuck anything up. I meant it when I said the bomb wasn't your fault. You couldn't have known what Heller was up to. He was insane. I know that now. I guess I've known for a while."

"But if I hadn't believed him, if I had just thought to ..."

"You weren't thinking clearly. You were worried about me."

"Yes," I say. "I was. But so was Heller. Heller thought he was saving your life by sending me there with a bomb."

"And he also knew he'd be killing lots of other people in the process. I'd rather not be saved, if that's the price."

"But in Heller's mind ..."

"Jesus, Paul. Get out of Heller's mind, for God's sake. I'm serious. The man was brilliant, but he was like ... I don't know, Icarus, flying too close to the sun. Or Medusa, turned to stone by her own reflection. I mean, we grab these names from Greek mythology, Ananke and Tyche, thinking we're being so clever, like if we name something, we've figured it out. Like somehow we've managed to get the upper hand. But the more I think about it, the more I'm convinced that we've missed the point. Maybe the Greeks understood something that Heller and I didn't. Have you ever noticed how many characters in Greek mythology think they have something figured out and then it bites them in the ass, precisely because they think they've figured it out? It's called *hubris*. I mean, there's Daedalus, who gets his ass trapped in his own labyrinth; Oedipus, who marries his own mother; Narcissus, who falls in love with his reflection ... Narcissus is a great one, because it's his own self-reflection that dooms him. Sound familiar?"

I'm pretty sure she's talking about Heller's obsession with his own ideas of free will and determinism, but she could just as well be talking about me. Relentless introspection is what almost made me throw myself in front of a train. I guess I'm more like Medusa than Narcissus: I don't like what I see.

"Heller said that if you look too closely at free will, it disappears," I say.

"He's right," she says. "He should have listened to himself."

We both laugh at that. One thing Heller didn't need to do was to spend more time listening to himself.

"He should have found a hobby," I muse. "Golf, maybe. Or fishing."

"I think you're completely right about that," says Tali. "Heller needed to get out of his head. Toward the end, he wasn't the man I studied under at Stanford. He had changed into something else. A sort of mystic, almost."

"An oracle, maybe. Weren't they all insane too?"

"Yeah," she says. "From the volcanic gases they inhaled. Foreknowledge drove them nuts. Appropriate. You know who one of the biggest heroes in Greek mythology is? Odysseus. The guy who tied himself to the mast of his ship so that he wouldn't be tempted by the song of the Sirens. The Sirens were evil creatures who tried to lure passing ships into the rocks. Odysseus had his sailors plug their ears with beeswax. So he could hear the song, but wasn't free to take any action, and the sailors were free to act but couldn't hear the song. You can hear or you can act. But if you try to do both, you're doomed. Heller didn't possess the wisdom of Odysseus."

I'm thinking about Odysseus' crew trying to clean the beeswax out of their ears when I fall asleep. I awake just before morning, as the last of a series of winding mountain roads spits us out into a suburb west of Sacramento. I ask Tali if she wants me to drive for a while. She's reluctant, but I can see she's exhausted. I finally convince her that she's going to feel pretty dumb if her big escape plan ends with us crashing head-on into an eighteen wheeler.

We stop for gas, coffee and breakfast burritos. Tali's been paying for everything in cash; evidently she had been somewhat prepared to make a run for it. After discussing our options briefly, we decide to continue east to Interstate 5 and then head south toward Mexico. I don't have my passport, but it's not like it would do me any good anyway. I'll have to hide in the trunk while Tali bats her eyelashes at the border guards. The eventual goal would be to get to a country with no extradition treaty with the U.S. – maybe the Cayman Islands. Tali seems to have looked into the matter somewhat. I defer to her expertise.

I get behind the wheel and start driving south. Tali falls asleep and doesn't wake up until Bakersfield. Soon we're approaching the foreboding slope of highway north of Los Angeles known as the Grapevine. I ask Tali if she thinks Peregrine is finished.

"Who knows," she replies. "But Carlyle is dead, and even if the Tyche system survives the earthquake, they'll never get anything useful out of it without me or Heller. Anyway, Peregrine is almost certainly going to go bankrupt trying to pay out all the claims in the Bay Area. And once it's under bankruptcy protection, there's no way it's going to get away with trying to maintain an experimental program that's never made them a dime. So Peregrine may survive in some form, but Tyche is done for. Ananke made sure of that. Nobody is going to trespass on her turf for a long time."

"So Ananke wins."

"Ananke is Ananke."

"What's that supposed to mean?"

"It means there's no fighting Ananke. There never was any real chance we'd succeed. If you make life into a battle between free will and determinism, you're going to lose. Conflict belongs to Ananke. The key is not to get into the fight in the first place."

"So you just give in to fate?"

"No. You do your thing and let Ananke do her thing."

"And how do you do that, exactly?"

She looks over at me and smiles. "I don't have any fucking idea."

After a moment, I say, "I went to see your sister, Beth."

"You did? When?"

"The day before the mall fiasco. I was trying to figure out what happened to you. Why you disappeared, I mean."

"How did she look?"

"Peaceful. There was a rabbi there, named Freedman."

"That son of a bitch just won't give up."

"He seemed like a nice guy."

"He is. But he's also a son of a bitch."

"If you say so."

"I'm sorry, I shouldn't talk about him like that. He means well. I just ... All that religious crap, I don't buy it. I guess it works for him, but it never did anything for me. I mean, where was God on the pier that day, when that girl got shot? And if I hadn't been there, it would have been a whole lot worse. That wasn't God that stopped that shooter, it was me."

"And Dave," I say.

"Who?"

"The off-duty cop. His name is Dave."

"Yeah," she says. "Me and Dave. We saved those people, not God. If God gave a shit, he wouldn't have left the matter up to a coin toss."

I don't have anything to say to that. I don't know where God was, or is. Does Ananke work for God? Or do they share sovereignty over the universe? Maybe God is just Heller's life force. Maybe we're all little globs of God that were injected into embryos once upon a time, and now we're stuck in a battle to the death with Ananke. A battle we're going to lose.

Neither of us mention it, but we know that Beth is dead. Probably Rabbi Freedman as well. I'm mostly glad about Beth; it isn't right for someone to be suspended like that between life and death. I can only hope that she's truly at rest somewhere. And hopefully her father is roasting in some special level of hell.

Oddly, I find myself profoundly saddened by the thought that Rabbi Freedman is gone. I barely knew the man. What was it about him? I've never been a particularly religious guy, but somehow you have to admire a man that shows up at the bedside of a comatose girl to read psalms to her. I mean, talk about a job with no sense of gratification! Nobody even knew he was there. He had no way of even knowing whether she heard him or not. I guess that's what people mean by faith. You show up and do your thankless job, not knowing if anybody knows or cares.

The thing is, though, it didn't seem like he thought of it as a thankless job. I think he actually liked sitting there with Beth, reading to her and praying over her. How do you explain that? Faith again, I suppose. Some people would say Freedman was deluded, wasting his time. I wonder, though. With all my running around the

Bay Area, desperately trying to alter the outcome of events, what did I actually accomplish? I saved some lives in Alameda and I cost some in Hayward. And then I set off a bomb in the Fairway Mall. On balance, I've got a lot of red in my ledger.

And what about Tali? She certainly meant well, but look at what she wrought with all her good intentions. The whole Bay Area is in ruins! Maybe that's not entirely her fault, but Ananke was clearly reacting against the idea of the expansion of the Tyche program. If Tali hadn't started tampering with events, maybe none of that would have happened. Jesus, am I really riding in a car with a woman who almost singlehandedly caused a catastrophic earthquake? And I'm relying on her to save me. What does that make me?

We stop for sandwiches in a suburb south of San Diego. It's our last stop before crossing the border. I wonder what our chances are of making it across. If the cops have figured out that Tali and I are together, they aren't good. Otherwise we might actually make it. Even with recently tightened border security, they don't search most cars heading from California to Mexico. But then what? It's a long way to the Cayman Islands from Tijuana. I guess we'll "figure something out."

We sit on a picnic table behind the shop eating our lunch. The place is pretty much deserted. It's just after noon now, and the weather is surprisingly warm. You can't beat southern California in February. Too bad we can't stay.

I finish eating and use the bathroom. When I come back the trunk of the Lexus is open. Tali is walking toward me, holding something in her hand.

"It's that time, huh?" I say, motioning to the open trunk.

"You're not claustrophobic, are you?" Tali asks.

"Just don't leave me in there longer than you have to."

"I'll let you out as soon as we're across the border. Promise."

"Thanks. Good luck."

I glance around. Satisfied that no one is watching me, I climb into the trunk.

"Here," she says, holding out her hand. She's holding the gun. "We might as well have all our contraband in one place. And if they search the car, I can say you held me at gunpoint."

I'm not sure how I could threaten her at gunpoint from the trunk, but it's better than anything I can come up with. And let me tell you, when your best option is hiding in the trunk to sneak across the border into Mexico, somewhere along the line you've made a horrible fucking mistake.

She closes the trunk and everything goes black. After a moment, the car begins to move. There's a short stretch of highway and then we gradually come to a halt. It's stop and go for the next half hour. I try to stay still, but the trunk is hot, cramped and uncomfortable, and I find myself constantly shifting to avoid losing sensation in my limbs. I stop moving and hold my breath as I hear Tali talking to someone. The whole exchange probably only lasts thirty seconds, but it seems like an hour. My heart is beating so loud I'm convinced somebody putting his ear to the trunk could hear it. My hands are sweating so bad I can barely hold onto the gun, so I set it down as gently as I can on the trunk floor. Probably just as well if I'm not holding onto it; a border guard who pops the trunk and sees me holding a gun will shoot first and ask questions later. This is what happens when you start fucking around with Schrödinger's Cat: if you're not careful, you end up the one in the box.

Finally the car starts moving again, gradually speeding up to what feels like a decent highway cruising speed. Ten minutes later the car slows to a halt. The trunk pops open. Against the blinding sunlight a figure is silhouetted: Tali.

"Rise and shine," she says.

"Did we make it?"

"We made it."

"Thank God," I say. I climb out of the trunk, still holding the gun. We're in the parking lot of a gas station in what looks to be a pretty sketchy area of Tijuana – which could be pretty much anywhere in Tijuana. There are a couple of customers getting gas, but nobody seems to be paying much attention to us. People getting in and out of trunks is probably a pretty common sight around here. It's a relief to be out of the trunk, but the sunshine that had seemed pleasant in San Diego now feels oppressive. I'm not sure if it's actually gotten hotter or if the effect is purely in my mind. I've crossed a lot of lines over the past few days, but somehow crossing into Mexico has hammered the point home: there's no going home again.

"We should get going," Tali says.

I shake my head. One thing about being locked in a trunk for half an hour: it gives you some time to think about where you went wrong. "We were lucky to make it this far. You need to get out of here, Tali. I'll take my chances on my own."

"No way," she says. "I told you. We're in this together."

"But we're not," I insist. "You aren't wanted for murder. Carlyle is dead. Peregrine is out of the prediction business. You could go back to work, get a fresh start."

"My home is gone," she says. "Heller is dead. Beth is probably dead, and even if she isn't, she's never going to wake up again. My parents are probably dead, and if they're not, well … fuck 'em. You're all I've got, Paul."

"And you're all I've got," I say. "But you deserve better than me. You deserve better than this."

"Goddammit, Paul. Stop that. Stop playing the martyr."

I laugh humorlessly. "Playing the martyr? Jesus Christ, Tali. I'm not *playing* the martyr. I am literally facing a death sentence. You think the mall bombing didn't make the news down here? Crossing the border may have bought me a couple days, that's all."

"Not if I'm here to help you. You can stay out of sight, and I can—"

"You can't save me, Tali! Get that through your head. You tell me I spend too much time reflecting on my faults, but you know what? You should fucking try it sometime. You might notice a pattern affecting the people you try to save. Most of them aren't doing so well right about now."

She seems taken aback. "That's not fair," she stammers. "I had no way of knowing …"

"Maybe not at first," I say. "But the earthquake you caused should have given you a pretty big hint."

"You're blaming *me* for the earthquake?"

"You and Heller, sure. Who else would I blame? Carlyle? Carlyle might be more directly to blame, but you and Heller are the ones who went into business with him."

She shakes her head. "I know what you're doing, Paul," she says, jabbing her finger at me. "You think I've got some kind of messiah complex, that I can't help myself from trying to save you. But I already told you, that's not it. I know what I'm doing, and I'm choosing to do it. I got you into this, and I'm going to do whatever I have to do to help you."

"I don't believe you," I say. "I don't think you're thinking clearly. You've lost your sister and your purpose in life, and you're latching onto me as your next project. And you know what? I'd let you do it if you weren't going to end up in a federal penitentiary as a result. I'm a lost cause, Tali. You need to let me go. Find something else to live for. Get on with your life."

"You're a condescending asshole," she says.

"Now you're getting it."

"And you're wrong. I can save you."

"I'll settle for whatever cash you have on you."

She eyes the gun. "You going to shoot me?"

"If I have to."

"Bullshit," she says. But she gets her purse from the car and hands me a thick wad of hundred dollar bills. "Five thousand dollars," she says, handing it to me.

"Thanks," I say, stuffing the money into my pocket. I stuff the gun back in my waistband.

"So this is it, then," she says. "You're just going to ride off into the sunset without me."

"You make it sound pretty fucking romantic. I'll be lucky to live through the week."

"Jesus, Paul. Don't say that. If you're going to do this, you have to believe you're going to make it. Don't give up."

"I'll try," I say.

"You've got to do better than try. I'm going to expect a postcard from the Cayman Islands in a few weeks."

"I'll send you a letter," I say. "It won't say where I am, but it will tell you how fast I'm going."

"Ha-ha," she says. "Quantum physics humor. I've heard them all."

"Did you hear the one about the guy in a trunk of a Lexus who's dead and alive at the same time?"

This time she actually laughs. "No. How does it end?"

"I'll let you know," I say.

"I'm sorry things turned out this way, Paul," she says.

"Me too," I reply. "Goodbye, Tali." I turn and walk away. After a moment, I hear the Lexus squeal out of the parking lot behind me. I watch as Tali gets on the highway, headed back toward California. I cross the street toward a little dive bar with a flickering neon margarita glass on its roof. I figure I'll have a drink and try to find a way to get to the bus station. From there I can try to work out a route to Mexico City, a thousand or so miles to the southeast.

The bar is dank and smoky. A couple of old guys who look like regulars are slouched over the bar. A dour-looking bartender nods at me as I walk in.

"*Baño?*" I say. It's stupid; every bartender in Tijuana knows the English word for bathroom. But I guess I might as well start using Spanish as much as possible.

He points to his left.

"*Gracias.*"

I walk to the bathroom and open the door. Inside is a toilet that looks like it hasn't ever been thoroughly cleaned and a sink that's chipped and streaked with rust. Above the sink is a cracked and corroded mirror. In the mirror is a man who looks he made a wrong turn in San Leandro and just kept going.

Jesus Christ, I think to myself. What am I doing? There isn't a chance in hell I'll make it to the Cayman Islands. If I'm lucky, I'll be shot to death by Mexican police. And if that's the best case scenario, why wait? I pull the gun from my waistband and hold it in front of me. I feel a little bad about making the bartender clean my brains off the ceiling of his bathroom, but then I remember I've got $5,000 in my pocket. I put it on the back of the toilet. If I had a pen and paper, I'd leave a suicide note that read:

Now you can renovate your fucking bathroom

But I suppose the message is implied. Unlike my father, I know to shut the fuck up when I have nothing to say.

Something falls from beneath the wad of bills, striking the tile floor with a loud *ping!* I crouch down to see my 50p coin. I must have slipped it in my pocket before I snuck out of my apartment yesterday morning.

Fate – or Ananke – seems to be telling me something, and I've decided I'm done fighting it. I pick up the coin, take a deep breath, and flip it into the air. Heads, I live; tails, I die. It comes up tails. Without ceremony, I pick up the gun, push the barrel against my temple and squeeze the trigger.

Click.

I squeeze it again.

Click.

I look at the gun, puzzled. Removing the magazine, I notice that it feels light. It's completely empty. Tali, I think. She didn't trust me with a loaded gun. And with good reason, it turns out. I can't help but smile.

I put the gun back in my waistband and the money back in my pocket. I open the door and walk to the bar. *"Una cerveza, por favor,"* I say. The bartender nods. To myself I whisper, *"Hoy vivo."*

Today, I live.

Afterword

At the risk of belaboring the obvious: this book is a work of fiction. Although I share some characteristics with Paul Bayes, I am not he. So if you want to correct Paul's understanding of physics (or anything else, for that matter), you'll have to email him. The email address I have for him is paulmbayes@gmail.com, but of course I can't guarantee he'll respond. The same principle applies if you'd like to take him to task for his excessive use of profanity or any of his other foibles: there's no sense in complaining to *me* about it.

For the record, I'm well aware that Paul's understanding of physics (both classical and quantum) is a little fuzzy. For example, he uses the old Bohr model of electrons "whizzing around the nucleus" of an atom, which has been pretty well discredited, and he doesn't really understand the relationship between quantum mechanics and classical mechanics. He himself admits that he's no expert and that he's gotten a lot of his information from Wikipedia. What do you expect?

That said, obviously I believe Paul to be a generally reliable witness or I wouldn't have chosen him to tell this story. Tali, who has a background in physics, is more reliable on technical matters than Paul, but of course her statements are being filtered through Paul and it's possible that he's gotten some of the details wrong. The same goes for Dr. Heller – except for the excerpts from *Fate and Consciousness*, which are verbatim. Although Heller was clearly mad and *Fate and Consciousness* shows signs of that madness, I'm hard-pressed to find any factual errors in his book. While Heller arrives at some outlandish conclusions, his grasp of physics is first-rate, as one would expect, given his background. You should, however, take his philosophical and theological ramblings with a grain of salt.

I've done my best in this book to obey Samuel Delaney's dictum that science fiction must not contradict "what is known to be known." It could well be that a year from now, some real-world Tali toiling away in a university lab will make a discovery that shows the events in this book to be impossible, but that's the risk one runs when writing about unknowns that are in the process of becoming known. All I can say is that as of *right now*, I don't know of anything in this book that's impossible, either physically or logically. Extremely unlikely, yes, but not impossible.

That said, when you write a novel based largely on hard science, certain readers will pore over the text in an effort to find errors. I know because I'm one of those readers. So as a preemptive strike, allow me to point out a few "cheats" in *Schrödinger's Gat* that I included as a concession to storytelling. If you'd rather find the cheats yourself (or if you'd like your opinion of this book to remain unsullied), feel free not to read the next few paragraphs.

First, although the idea of the human brain taking advantage of quantum phenomena has gotten some serious attention recently (see, for example, Jeffrey Satinover's fascinating book *The Quantum Brain*), the notion of the "quantum brain" as a sort of separate computing module is pure fantasy. That isn't to say it's necessarily wrong, but if the brain does take advantage of quantum phenomena (as I suspect it does), it probably does so in a much more subtle and interesting way. Similarly, it's doubtful that there's any such thing as a "psionic energy field." Physicists have spent no small amount of time looking for some peculiar sort of energy associated with human consciousness and have come up with nothing. Again, this doesn't necessarily mean that no such energy exists, but if it does, it's exceedingly difficult to detect.

The biggest cheat in *Schrödinger's Gat*, though, is the manipulation of coin tosses to alter the course of the future. Surprisingly, the problem isn't that a coin toss can create alternate universes, but the fact that so many other events can. The "many worlds" interpretation of quantum theory holds that anything that can happen *does* happen. The quantum wave function never collapses to one possibility or another; both occur, even though I experience only one of them. As Heller puts it:

> We only experience one timeline, but that doesn't mean that only one of them is real. To put it more precisely, when you say that something 'happened,' you're saying that an event occurred that you experienced in some way. That is to say, it occurred on your timeline, in your history. But if there are alternate futures, then who's to say that for people on those alternate timelines, completely different events haven't happened?

This idea is perfect fodder for science fiction, of course, but it presents a couple of practical problems. First, the number of universes created every nanosecond is so large that it may as well be infinite. A coin toss is just one type of event among hundreds of trillions of other types of events that cause universe-splitting. So to say that Universe A^1 and A^2 were created as a result of a coin toss in Universe A is to arbitrarily pick out two universes from many trillions of other universes. In other words, there's nothing special about a coin toss, and therefore no reason to think that a coin toss would leave a greater "psionic impression" than any other event. So how is it possible for Heller to pick out coin toss events in the data?

One possible explanation is that the coin toss bifurcation results in two very large sets of universes that are dissimilar to each other. That is, a coin toss results in a stark break in the continuity of possible universes, and it is this break in continuity that can be detected. This seems to be what Heller is hinting at when he talks about coin tosses having "a very distinct probability signature that shows up in our data."

This leads us to another problem, though: the whole point of the many worlds interpretation is that the alternate universes split off from each other, each becoming a completely independent and self-contained universe. In other words, after these universes are created, they go their separate ways and never again meet. If that's true, however, then there's no way a person in one universe could ever detect evidence of something occurring in another universe. So how can Tyche possibly detect a break in the continuity of other universes?

The answer is that until the universes split, all possible futures obtain for the universe in question. It isn't necessary for Tyche to gather data from *parallel* universes; it only has to gather data for universes that will split off from the current universe. Some future paths are much more probable than others, where "probability" is simply a measurement of the number of futures that meet specified criteria. For example, there may have been x number of possible futures where the Allies won World War II, y number of possible futures where the Axis won, and z number of futures where Martian invaders defeated both the Allies and the Axis. There are presumably far fewer futures where z happens than where x or y happens, making it far less probable than an individual in 1939 will find himself on the z path. To predict the likely outcome of the war, the individual in 1939 doesn't need to know anything about universes that have already split from his own; he simply needs to know the rough distribution of x and y (assuming z is negligible). Of course, the ability to know this distribution implies that the possible futures somehow communicate backwards in time with the present, which is dubious but not, as far as I know, at odds with many-worlds. In any case, there are so many different interpretations of quantum theory (as well as sub-interpretations of many-worlds) that it isn't difficult to find a reputable physicist who will back up whatever nutty ideas you have, within certain parameters.

These "cheats," however, are somewhat tangential to the main themes of *Schrödinger's Gat*, and in fact I employed them primarily to highlight the underlying weirdness about quantum theory and what it implies about the universe we inhabit. The remarkable thing about writing this book was how *few* liberties I actually had to take. With the exception of the cheats I just pointed out, Heller's statements are entirely consistent with quantum theory. In fact, his observations about the double slit experiment and box pair experiment are *quantum theory-independent*, meaning that you don't have to accept quantum theory to appreciate the utter weirdness of the results. Light really does act differently depending on whether you observe it or not, and the causal relationship between observation and phenomenon does appear to be able to occur backwards through time. In case you don't believe me, here's an excerpt from *Quantum Enigma: Physics Encounters Consciousness*, written by two scientists with PhDs in physics:

This "which-box?" experiment, or "look-in-the-box" experiment, establishes that each atom was concentrated in a *single box of its pair, that it was not spread out over both boxes.*

But before you looked, you could have done an interference experiment establishing that something of each atom had been in *both* boxes. You therefore could choose to prove either that each atom had been wholly in single box, or you could choose to prove that each atom had not been *wholly* in a single box. You can choose to prove either of two contradictory situations ....

A theory leading to a logical contradiction is necessarily an incorrect theory. Does the ability to demonstrate either of two contradictory things about atoms (and other objects) invalidate quantum theory? No. You did not demonstrate the contradiction with *exactly* the same things. You did two experiments with different atoms .... Did your free choice determine the external physical situation? Or did the external physical situation predetermine your choice? Either way, it doesn't make sense. It's the unresolved quantum enigma.

Important point: We experience an enigma because we believe that we *could have* done other than what we actually did. A denial of this freedom of choice requires our behavior to be programmed to correlate with the world external to our bodies. The quantum enigma arises from our *conscious perception* of free will [italics in original].

Further:

The creation of past history is even more counterintuitive than the creation of a present situation. Nevertheless, that's what the box-pairs experiment, or any other version of the two-slit experiment, implies.

The authors later point out:

One can evade the quantum enigma by denying it meaningful to even consider experiments that were not in fact done, and claim that the conscious perception that we could have done them is meaningless. Such denial of free will goes beyond the notion that what we choose to do is determined by the electrochemistry of our brain. The required denial implies a completely deterministic and conspiratorial world, one in which our supposedly free choices are programmed to coincide with an external physical situation.

It is, of course, this "completely deterministic and conspiratorial world" that becomes Heller's obsession, and it's not difficult to see why. If he doesn't deny the reality of free will, he is forced to admit that there are basic truths about the universe that are ultimately unknowable, that to an extent the universe hides its fundamental nature from scientists. Rather than accept the limitations of science, he accepts that the universe is deterministic – and then tries desperately to find loopholes in that determinism.

I should note that one way to preserve free will is to define it to mean something like "the ability to make choices in accordance with one's desires." By this definition, a person can have free will even if all of her actions are determined. In other words, one can be said to have acted freely in a given situation even if one could not possibly have acted differently. By this definition a person in a locked room is free as long as she doesn't try to open the door. This is a position that many philosophers take, but it's not, in my opinion, a very satisfying one. We can assume that such a definition of free will offered little consolation to Heller, and that it is his attempts to reconcile a more robust sort of freedom with determinism that leads to his plight.

We can certainly sympathize with Heller. Although *Schrödinger's Gat* is a work of fiction, the world in which it takes place is real, and it is a very, very strange place.

Acknowledgments

Writing a book like this is impossible without a lot of help.

I'm indebted to Bruce Rosenblum and Fred Kuttner for their description of the "box pairs" experiment in *Quantum Enigma: Physics Encounters Consciousness*, which I adapted for use in Dr. Heller's book, *Fate and Consciousness*, and for allowing me to use an excerpt from the book in the afterword. *Quantum Enigma* also includes the most straightforward explanation of the weirdness of quantum mechanics and quantum theory that I've encountered. I highly recommend it as an introduction to quantum mechanics and its implications.

Ransom Stephens helped me work through a lot of the quantum physics stuff and made numerous helpful suggestions to improve *Schrödinger's Gat*. If you managed to get through this book, you will totally dig his novel *The God Patent*.

Chris Lubbers did his best to make sure I didn't completely mangle any philosophical concepts or play too fast and loose with Heller's thoughts about free will and determinism.

Other valuable feedback was provided by Robb Bajema, Jeff Kirvin, Joel Bezaire, Calli Shell, Jeff Ellis, Nicklaus Louis, Alice Stuart, Kristin Crocker, Mark Fitzgerald and Colleen Diamond.

The Philip K. Dick story about time travel that Heller mentions is "The Skull." It's a good illustration of the idea that spacetime rejects paradoxes.

Much of Heller's philosophy of the will coheres to some extent with the writings of the German philosopher Arthur Schopenhauer. I had never read Schopenhauer and noticed the similarity only after writing most of it. I have read Nietzsche, though, and may have been unconsciously influenced by Schopenhauer through him.

Thanks also to everybody who supported the *Schrödinger's Gat* Kickstarter, particularly Christopher Turner, Shannon Cogan, Jeremy Kerr, Agnes Kroese (AKA "Mom"), Brian and Donna Hekman, Scott Semester, Elisa Lorello, Sheila Redling, Suzy Cilbrith, Sean Simpson, Daniel McCann, Neva Cheatwood (AKA "Crazy Aunt Bea"), Tracey S. Bowen, W. Jason Duncan,

Christopher Finlan, and Paul Reinhardt. I am humbled and gratified by your faith in me.

Bibliography

"Ananke (mythology)." Wikipedia. Wikimedia Foundation, 22 Oct. 2012. Web. 01 Nov. 2012.

"Arthur Schopenhauer." (Stanford Encyclopedia of Philosophy). Stanford University, n.d. Web. 01 Nov. 2012.

Capra, Frijof. The Tao of Physics. HarperCollins. 1991.

Dick, Philip K. "The Skull." N.p.: Public Domain, n.d. Kindle ed.

Feynman, Richard P. Six Easy Pieces: The Fundamentals of Physics Explained. London: Basic, 2011. Kindle ed.

"Free Will." (Stanford Encyclopedia of Philosophy). Stanford University, n.d. Web. 01 Nov. 2012.

"Genius in the Twentieth Century." JRank. Net Industries LLC, n.d. Web. 1 Nov. 2012.

"Internet Encyclopedia of Philosophy." Kant: Aesthetics. N.p., n.d. Web. 01 Nov. 2012.

Johnson, George. A Shortcut through Time: The Path to the Quantum Computer. New York: Vintage, 2004. Print.

Kant, Immanuel. The Critique of Pure Reason. Public Domain. Kindle ed.

"Karma in Jainism." Wikipedia. Wikimedia Foundation, 31 Oct. 2012. Web. 01 Nov. 2012.

Mensky, Michael. Quantum Physics of Consciousness. N.p.: Cosmology Science, n.d. Kindle ed.

Rosenblum, Bruce; Kuttner, Fred. Quantum Enigma: Physics Encounters Consciousness. Oxford University Press, USA; 2nd edition. Kindle ed. 01 July, 2011.

Ross, Nancy Wilson. The World of Zen. [S.l.]: Vintage., n.d. Print.

Satinover, Jeffrey. The Quantum Brain: The Search for Freedom and the Next Generation of Man. New York: J. Wiley, 2001. Print.

Stephens, Ransom. The God Patent. Vox Novus. 2009. Kindle ed.

"Schrodinger's Cat." Wikipedia. Wikimedia Foundation, 22 Oct. 2012. Web. 01 Nov. 2012.

"Yin and Yang." Wikipedia. Wikimedia Foundation, 30 Oct. 2012. Web. 01 Nov. 2012.

Zukav, Gary. The Dancing Wu Li Masters: An Overview of the New Physics. Fontana; 1st Edition. 1980.

About the Author

Robert Kroese's sense of irony was honed growing up in Grand Rapids, Michigan - home of the Amway Corporation and the Gerald R. Ford Museum, and the first city in the United States to fluoridate its water supply. In second grade, he wrote his first novel, the saga of Captain Bill and his spaceship *Thee Eagle*. This turned out to be the high point of his academic career. After barely graduating from Calvin College in 1992 with a philosophy degree, he was fired from a variety of jobs before moving to California, where he stumbled into software development. As this job required neither punctuality nor a sense of direction, he excelled at it. In 2009, he called upon his extensive knowledge of useless information and love of explosions to write his first novel, *Mercury Falls*. Since then, he has written two sequels, *Mercury Rises* (2011) and *Mercury Rests* (2012), and a humorous epic fantasy, *Disenchanted*. *Schrödinger's Gat* is the closest he's come to writing a "serious novel." Oh, and it's pronounced *KROO-zee*. Seriously.

I love to hear from readers! Email me at rob@robertkroese.com or connect with me on the Internet:

Website: robertkroese.com
Facebook: facebook.com/robertkroeseauthor
Twitter: twitter.com/robkroese

If you enjoyed *Schrödinger's Gat*, I would also greatly appreciate a review on your favorite book retailing website. Thanks!

38827927R00115

Made in the USA
Middletown, DE
28 December 2016